What readers are saying about DANCING WITH ICE

Compelling and driven. But what I didn't expect was the sensitivity. It was like reading Callahan's heart.

Superb. I laughed. I cried. I couldn't put it down. I must read it again.

Thornton Edwards wrote the words; the characters told the story.

This is not a book about a cop. It is the story of an incredible person who happened to be a cop.

VISIT OUR WEBSITE

Learn more about Thornton Edwards at
www.thorntonedwards.com.

- Read the author's autobiography online.

- Learn about his twenty years as a Tucson
  Police Officer.

- Discover what he is doing with his life
  today.

- Find out what books he has in the works.

- Order copies of DANCING WITH ICE
  online.

- View upcoming opportunities to meet the
  author.

- Contact the author regarding your
  questions or responses.

DANCING WITH ICE

Thornton Edwards

For Dorothy,
Enjoy the journey!

Thornton

Arizona House of Graphix
Arizona

First Paperback Edition

The characters, dialogue, events, and plot in this book are all products of the author's imagination or are used fictitiously. Any similarities to real persons, living or dead, are purely coincidental and not intended by the author.

Library of Congress Control Number: 2002092258
ISBN 0-9721852-1-6

Printed in the United States of America

ACKNOWLEDGMENTS

Just about everybody who's written a book has experienced lonely moments when words to write would not appear. These moments I would smile and dream. Dreams of when my book was published and what I would say to thank the people that made it possible. Each person has a name, and each person had a purpose, much like angels do.

I knew for many years that I had a story, but I didn't know if I had the ability to relate it properly. And then one evening, my personal angel, my wife, set a box of sharpened pencils and several legal pads in front of me and said, "Tell your story, the world needs to hear it." I will begin by thanking her, because she brought to the process talents that I don't think she was even aware she had. She was not only an editor she was an unbelievable coach.

I would also like to thank Karen Salvador who was always at my door with what I needed, even before I knew I needed it. She pushed me when I stalled, shoved me when I deserved it, and pulled me when I needed the strength. Special thanks to Anne Cavanagh for steering us in the right direction and encouraging us to continue. And to my friend Robert Mahoney, who waited his turn to help us through the final stages of editing.

Inside my heart, I will always have a special place for my friends and clients who suffered through my mood swings and massaged away my doubts with their spirit.

For Victoria,

because without her, my words would have remained

frozen in ice. And because of her,

I have learned to dance.

And for my stepdaughter, Carina, who stood by my side

to make me smile, when I wanted to cry.

And for my children, Tammy Allison and Tom Thornton,

who lived this with me and loved me in spite of it. Thank

you for giving me my grandchildren,

Taylor, Kaitlin, and Austin.

A little while and
I will be gone from among you,
whither I cannot tell.
From nowhere we came;
into nowhere we go.

What is life?
It is a flash of a firefly
in the night
It is the breath of a buffalo
in the winter time.
It is the shadow
that runs across the grass
and loses itself in the sunset.

~Crowfoot's dying words

CHAPTER ONE

JUNE, 1978

"'I COULD SHOOT YOU right now, you know?' he said. I jerked my head back and froze. It was too late for me to react. I focused on the handgun, just a few inches from my face. The voice said something else, but the words didn't register. I stared at the hole in the end of the barrel. This was a new fear for me. I had nothing to compare it to."

Michael Callahan continued to drive. His passenger, Matthew Jordan, sat quietly, staring through the windshield in front of him.

"'So do it,' I said, 'shoot me.' I felt this huge lump in my throat as I tried to swallow. My heart was pounding so loud that I could hear it. I held my breath. I couldn't take my eyes off the gun."

Their car came to a stop at the red light. Callahan tightened his two-handed grip on the steering wheel and then relaxed, repeating the motion several times. "It was a family fight call. You'll learn to hate them, Jordan," Callahan grimaced. "It's the worst of the worst. Everybody is pissed off at each other and when you get there, it's you they become pissed at."

"What did you do? How did you get out?" Jordan was a police recruit, currently attending the eighteen-week Tucson Police Department Training Academy. The recruits spent five working shifts with training officers that were hand-picked by command personnel. This was his second shift with Officer Callahan, a six-year veteran of the Tucson streets.

"I watched Monday Night Football with him." Callahan turned the white Dodge police unit onto South 6th Avenue and headed south. "It actually turned out to be a pretty good ballgame."

"The guy stuck a gun in your face and you watched a football game with him?" Jordan wanted to believe him, after all Callahan was his training officer. "That's a little hard to swallow, Callahan. Are you messin' with me?"

"Sorry, even I can't make this shit up. That's the way it went down."

"What led up to it? How did you go from having a gun in your face to being like buddies?" Jordan knew that Michael Callahan was not a conventional cop. Many of his exploits had made their way to the Academy as examples, some good, some excellent, and some 'please don't ever try this'.

"A lot happened in just a short time," Callahan answered. "Some I would like to forget."

Officer Michael Callahan's actions were precise but easy. At 33, he had maintained his solid build of 6'2" and 205 pounds from his days as a college basketball player. The police officer heritage ran in his Irish family. Two uncles had been cops in Detroit, both killed in the line of duty. He knew life was tough; he wanted to be tougher. His friends often referred to him as "Thumper," a name that stuck from his teenage years when he was active in Golden Gloves boxing. Being physical was his life. His childhood had taught him that and his tour in Vietnam had reaffirmed it. He couldn't imagine being any other way. It was 1975, six years since his discharge from the Air Force and in some ways it seemed like yesterday.

Jordan waited. He wanted to hear everything that happened on that call. Every detail. "Do you feel like talking about it?" Damn it, Jordan said to himself. Why in the hell did I say that? He instantly knew he was in trouble.

Callahan glared. "Just how much will this session cost me, Dr. Jordan? What a lovely set of ink blots you have, Doctor."

"I'm sorry, Callahan, I didn't . . . " Jordan stopped talking and shook his head.

"Sorry! What in the hell do you have to be sorry about? This is the real world out here. Cops and bad guys, pieces of shit and assholes, and sometimes it's hard to tell the difference. I'll tell you what happened, every goddamn detail. Maybe, just maybe you can learn a little bit about survival. And also, learn about how you can get your ass in trouble.

"All right, all right," Callahan took a deep breath. "You didn't say anything wrong. Let's go on from here."

Jordan nodded and smiled.

"I pulled to the curb and stopped," Callahan continued. "The neighborhood was nice, better than most in this area. Three and four bedroom homes, probably four to five years old with well maintained grass lawns or gravel yards. I drove slowly, next to the curb, until I found the house number 1625. I stopped three houses away, to listen, maybe get a clue as to what was going on. On some family fight calls, you can hear hollering and screaming from a block away. I didn't hear anything out of the ordinary this time."

"Did you know that a gun was involved?" Jordan asked.

Callahan stared at the recruit, but didn't speak. His look said it all.

"Out of the corner of my eye, I see two women walk slowly to the sidewalk, across the street and before the 1625 address. One heavy, middle-aged woman, wearing an apron over a cotton dress, appeared as nervous as a cat. She put her hand to her mouth, shaking her head back and forth like she was watching something. The other woman, much taller, thinner, and in her twenties, saw my police car and motioned me to drive forward. The younger woman, wearing skin-tight jeans and a tank top stepped to the passenger's side door and leaned down. Her top covered what looked like two Boy Scouts fighting in a wet pup tent."

Jordan caught his laugh and turned it into a cough as he looked away.

"She told me that the kids were next door, but the wife, Andreanna was still inside with her husband, Chapo. Isn't that a great name, Jordan? Andreanna."

"Yeah, sure," Jordan answered, wanting Callahan to get on with it. "Don't they dispatch two units on a 10-31? Where was your backup?"

"I was beginning to wonder the same thing," Callahan agreed. "I eased a bit closer, less than one house away. Two little girls darted from the residence and ran behind the red pickup in the driveway. The woman on the curb had been wrong; the children were not in the house next door. I turned my engine off. And listened. I moved a little closer and then I heard a male voice hollering and a female voice telling him to calm down. And then there was this 'thud' from inside the house, like something hitting a wall. One of the girls, about five or so, ran from behind the truck screaming 'Mommy' and she went back into the house.

"I grabbed the radio and asked for the ETA of my backup. The unit came back and said three to four minutes. I knew I couldn't wait that long, I had to go in. I ran to the house and found the little girl crying, just inside the front door. I grabbed her and pulled her outside, sending her to the neighbor's house."

"Could you see his wife?" Jordan asked. During his two previous field weeks he had been on three family fights, none of any consequence.

"Yeah, she was in the living room when I pulled the little girl outside. She was a small woman, about thirty years old. She had her hair in a ponytail that made her look even younger. She didn't appear to be physically assaulted, but sometimes you can't tell. She saw me and put her hands to her mouth and said, 'This is so embarrassing.' I asked her if she had been assaulted and she said no. I asked her if Chapo had a weapon and she again said, 'No, that's not like him.' She looked back over her shoulder and yelled, 'See what you've caused, Chapo?' I told her it was all right, not to worry about it."

"Did you ask her why they were fighting?"

"She said she didn't know. He had been real moody lately, not acting himself. She said he had only had a couple of beers, so alcohol wasn't the cause."

"Did you get a feeling that something was going to happen, Callahan?" Jordan watched as Callahan turned the overhead emergency lights on and followed the car in front of them to the curb.

"No, just the opposite," Callahan answered, placing the car in park. "I figured that with no apparent violence, the situation was pretty much over. All I needed to do was get her out of the house for a while, a cooling off period."

"What are you doing?" Jordan asked, his mouth remaining open. "Why are we stopping this guy?"

"He ran a red light. He really shouldn't pound the steering wheel like that," Callahan laughed. "He could hurt himself. C'mon with me. I'll let you write the warning."

"Warning?"

"Yeah, poor bastard. He's already taking care of his punishment," Callahan chuckled as they walked up to the car.

"What makes you decide which to write, a citation or a warning?" Jordan watched the appreciative driver wave as he pulled from the curb.

"You did a good job with this," Callahan said, handing the written warning back to Jordan. "Now log it on our activity sheet. Now to answer your question, warning or ticket? It's your judgement. Have you ever heard, spirit of the law or letter of the law? Let's just say, right then, the spirit moved me."

"I never saw that guy run that light, Callahan. How do you train yourself to pick up on those kinds of things?" Jordan's eyes were trying to catch everything as Callahan pulled back into traffic.

"Ask a woman, especially a mother."

"What in the hell are you talking about?"

"Multitasking, doing more than one thing at a time. A room full of kids, laundry, making dinner, taking care of their husband. Same thing applies out here. Get what I'm saying?"

"Yeah, I do," Jordan smiled, one of those, I really hope I do smiles.

"He told me to get my ass out."

"Who did?" Jordan shook his head, fearing that he had missed something.

"Chapo. I still hadn't seen him, but I knew that he was somewhere in the hallway."

His brain never stops, Jordan thought, and he has the incredible ability to pick up exactly where he left off. What did he call it, multitasking?

"Andreanna told him to shut up and it pissed him off. He called her a name that even I don't like to use. 'Quit acting like this,' she screamed, and before I knew it, she was across the room and down the hall. I was right behind her, begging her to stop. She didn't until she found him in the hallway. Chapo was not a big man, but was built like an athlete. His hands were empty, no weapons of any kind. And then she grabbed his arm, telling him to quit acting stupid. With his forearm he shoved her aside and she fell into the wall. 'Now you've got a problem, buddy,' I said, pushing him back down the hall.

"Andreanna pleaded, grabbing my arm with both hands, she said, 'Don't hurt him. I'm okay. He didn't hurt me. I'll leave, and then you can go too, officer.' Chapo just stood there staring at me with his hands at his side. Without taking my eyes off him, I asked her if she had somewhere that she could go. Somewhere she could take the kids for awhile. She said her mother lived about ten minutes away; she could take them there.

"'He's a good person, really,' she added. 'He has never acted this way.' She didn't know what was wrong. He wouldn't talk to her.

"I stood at the front door and watched her gather her children. 'Go on,' I said. 'I'll talk to him.' A few seconds later, the car backed from the carport. Andreanna shook her head as she drove away. I turned around and the television caught my attention. Monday Night Football, Washington versus Dallas. Dallas was ahead. It was still early, I thought. Second quarter. God, I hate the Cowboys. I looked around. The house was immaculate, except for an empty Michelob bottle on the coffee table.

"'You got your wish, Chapo,' I said. 'She's gone. Now maybe you can calm down.' No answer. I heard a door close in the distance. I took a step toward the hall, but turned and watched an incomplete pass on the TV screen. 'Damn,' I said. And then I looked back at the hallway. That's when I found myself staring down the barrel of a .357 Magnum.

"'I could shoot you right now, you know?' Chapo's voice was calm, a notch above a whisper."

"So you told him to go ahead and do it?" Jordan swallowed hard, he felt his palms sweating.

"'Give me your gun,' Chapo said.

"I slowly took a step backwards. I watched his eyes. 'There ain't no way in hell that you're getting my weapon from me. So if you're going to shoot me, do it now.'

Chapo licked his lips and swallowed. His look began to soften. His anger was now fear. He had screwed up, and he knew it. He had committed a crime. 'Let me think about this,' he said. He backed away form me and closed the door. Now I had some distance between us.

"'Stop moving and shut up,' Chapo had ordered.

"'Fine,' I stopped and said, 'But can I have a beer?'

"'What in the hell are you talking about?'

"'If I'm going to die, at least you can let me have a beer. Beer. And football. Not exactly the way I figured that I would die. But, close enough.'

"'You're crazy!' he said.

"'Can I watch the game before you shoot me?' I requested, nodding at the TV screen. Chapo was confused, and I was taking advantage. The handgun was lowered. Not much, just a few inches. 'I suppose that you're a Cowboy fan?'

"'Yeah, so?' Chapo said, glancing at the screen.

"I knew it was time to roll the dice. I started backing away, slowly, making sure that Chapo could see my hands. In my six years on the police department, I had been in similar situations hundreds of times. I had always eluded the use of deadly force in resolving them. But, this time was different. Staring down the barrel of a gun was a first. Keep him talking; keep up the bullshit.

"'Stop,' Chapo ordered.

"'It's tied at half,' I was running out of options. 'I'll take Washington for five bucks.'

"'You're on duty, you can't do this.'

"'I'm not supposed to be held hostage either, but I am. Get me a beer. I'll be over watching the game.' I sat down on the front edge of the couch and loosened the top button of my shirt.

"He said, 'You don't think I'll shoot you, do you?'

"'You would have done it already,' I said."

"Did he get you a beer?" Jordan asked.

"Yeah, and he put it on the end of the coffee table. He didn't want to come near me again. He was being a little careless with the gun and it was scaring the shit out of me."

"Then he said, 'I fucked up, didn't I?'

"'Yep, you sure did,' I said and opened my beer.

"'I'm going to jail. Right?' I noticed Chapo's handgun was now pointing at his feet.

"'Put the goddamn gun down before you shoot yourself. Or me.'

"Chapo said, 'Not yet,' and he began to cry. That scared me even more. Somehow, I had to calm this guy down. I could see he was seriously considering turning the gun on himself. He walked over to a chair across from me. He still held the gun but it was now pointing at the floor."

"I hate to keep asking this," Jordan scowled, "but where was your backup?"

"I didn't know, and I definitely didn't want him showing up then. Here I am sitting on a couch, holding a beer, and some guy has a gun on me. Think of some of the possibilities."

"Or if anybody else would have come in the door," Jordan said, clenching his teeth. "His wife or the kids."

"Yeah, I know. Believe me, all of that went through my mind. And then he started to talk. His real name was Ramon Salazar. He had grown up just a few miles from where he lived now, but the circumstances were much different. His parents were poor and they struggled to raise their family of seven boys. It got even worse when his father was murdered outside a local bar. He learned that honesty and an education were his only means of escape from his environment of crime and drugs. Chapo said he attended the University of Arizona and received a degree in Business Administration. His degree and hard work propelled him upwards within the manufacturing company that he worked for. Two days before, he learned his company was being sold. To remain on, he must assume a lesser role, which involved a considerable pay cut. He was told he would have to start over. He chose not to tell his wife, so instead his stress and fears built up inside."

"How long did you talk to him?"

"About two hours."

"Two hours! You were there that long?" Jordan shook his head.

"Yeah, until the game was over," Callahan answered. "About ten minutes after he started talking he put the handgun on the coffee table and slid it to me. I unloaded it and left it there. We watched the game as he talked, until I saw lights flash through the front window and a car come to a stop in the driveway."

"Your backup or another unit checking up on you?"

"No. Cops don't pull into driveways, fear of being blocked."

Jordan smiled and nodded, filing that one away.

"I walked to the door and opened it without saying a word. Andreanna hurried around the front of her car and asked me, 'Why are you still here?'

"'Monday Night Football. Chapo owes me five dollars,' I told her. I got in my unit and drove down the street. I could have been shot, I thought. My hands began to sweat and my heart raced all over again. I had to pull over and catch my breath. I looked back and thought of all the things that could have happened. Scary."

Jordan started to speak. Callahan stopped him.

"I know what you're going to ask. My backup stopped a drunk driver en route to my call."

"Why didn't the dispatcher check up on you?"

"Well, they're supposed to. She lost me."

"What do you mean she lost you?"

"Each dispatcher maintains a card on the officers, individually, working his or her frequency. I wanted to know why myself so I drove directly to the station and went up to communications. The supervisor is a good friend of mine and I explained the situation to him. I didn't want to get anyone in trouble, but this is serious stuff. It seems my card had fallen off the desk area in front of her and in between the consoles. They had no idea where I was for over two hours. Looking back, it was definitely for the best, wouldn't you say, Jordan?"

"It's amazing that no one got hurt. Hell, no one even went to jail."

"We all learn from our mistakes, I guess. I let my guard down, and it damn near got me shot." Callahan sighed and shook his head when something in the road ahead caught his attention.

"Sometimes you pay a price for learning," Jordan agreed. "When did this happen, in your first year?"

"Three days ago."

Jordan was speechless.

CHAPTER TWO

WHY DID HE LOOK AT me like that? Callahan asked himself as a car approached from the opposite direction. The driver's eyes caused Callahan to hold his stare. Not curious eyes, but eyes that pierced and took control. They were the same eyes that stared at you in that one nightmare you remembered from childhood. Callahan shuddered. His skin began to crawl.

Why am I like this, he thought? Why can't I just drive, listen and go where I'm told? Because I see the eyes in the oncoming lane, and they bother me. That vehicle has to be stopped. There was no definition for gut feeling or police intuition – it was just there. However, *just there* didn't stand up very well in court.

"Day shift sucks," Callahan said. It was approximately 1100 hours on a very uneventful November morning.

"So, nothing much happens during the day, huh, Callahan?" Jordan joked.

"Until now," he answered without moving his eyes.

Callahan made an abrupt U-turn in front of oncoming traffic. Several cars swerved to avoid the police unit. Waving an apology, he pushed the accelerator to the floor. His eyes searched the road ahead.

"Now what did I miss? Why did you turn around?"

Matthew Jordan had just received another lesson in police work, far removed from the classroom. Still rubbing the knot on the side of his head from the impromptu change in direction, Jordan had more questions, many more questions.

Callahan had seen the fear in the driver's eyes. Winding through the midday traffic, he settled his police unit behind the car that had drawn more than his curiosity. Now he could see those same eyes staring at him from the rearview mirror of the car ahead of him.

They were following a car that was large and old, not uncommon for this area of town, but the California plates and very white driver were out of place. This section of the city, south of 22nd Street and east of 4th Avenue, was predominately Mexican, with a smattering of Anglos, and a small neighborhood occupied by Blacks.

"What did he do?" Jordan blurted out. "Why do you want to stop him? What's your probable cause?"

"If you look real close, you'll find our reason to stop him," Callahan blurted out.

"Where?"

"The driver's side taillight lens has a small crack in the bottom corner. When the driver applies the brakes, white light shines through. That's a traffic violation."

"This vehicle needs to be stopped," Callahan continued. Quickly, he pulled the back of his hand over one eye, then the other as he blinked twice. "I don't know what he's up to, but I do know that he saw us and it made him very nervous."

"Let's see what we have, then who we have," the veteran officer remarked in a tone a bit louder than a whisper. Jordan knew if he was to learn, he must be silent. He must listen and watch.

During Jordan's eighteen-weeks at the Tucson Police Department Training Academy, his training, as with most law enforcement training facilities, consisted of academics, physical and firearms training, and on the job, in the field training assignments. Unlike a rookie, non-commissioned recruits were unarmed and possessed no arrest powers other than that of an ordinary citizen. Jordan was seven weeks from a commission, and the realization that law enforcement was not just a job. It was a way of life.

"One-Adam-Seven," the constant chatter on the police radio now became personal. Callahan heard his designator being called, but ignored it. *I need to find out who this guy is.*

"One-Adam-Seven," the radio repeated, as the request went unheeded.

"Callahan, they're calling us," Jordan said, a panic crept into his voice.

"Then answer them," Callahan barked back.

"But I'm not sure where we are, I'm not familiar with this..."

"Make up something, damn it! She doesn't give a shit where we are." The recruit froze.

On the other end of the radio frequency was Barbara Wells, a veteran dispatcher of nine, long, tension-filled years. For two-plus years she had been assigned Frequency One, the officer's communication line from the city's Southside. Each area of assignment within Team I and the officers that patrolled the designated beats, had become her life, creating a faceless bond of trust and survival. Her husband was Detective Larry Wells—a thirteen-year veteran homicide detective. They met through law enforcement; they lived through law enforcement.

"Go ahead," Callahan sounded annoyed by the intrusion. "Is this a priority?" If the call needed an immediate response, Barb would advise him so and he would reluctantly back off of the eyes in the mirror.

"Negative, a neighbor problem," Barb answered calmly. "Do you have something working?"

"10-4," Callahan paused, " but, I'm not quite sure what. Can you get another unit for the call?"

"Ten-four. Keep me advised of your situation."

"You'll be the first to know," Callahan smiled back at the radio.

"What are you up to now, Callahan?" Barb said aloud, but not over the air. Turning her head from side to side she leaned back in her chair trying to relieve some tension.

"Callahan?" A voice came from behind her. "Why are they letting him out in the daylight?"

"He and Stark are in between training squads. The Lieutenant wanted them to teach some classes at the Academy and they have switched to day shift. But, wouldn't you know it, Callahan has been on days for less than a week and he's already up to something again."

"What a surprise," Durwood Walker, the civilian communications supervisor said sarcastically. Folding his arms across his chest, he said, "You know, Callahan could go to a Dodger's ball game and sit next to the Hillside Strangler. He's a magnet for that kind of shit."

Jordan's heart began to beat faster as they kept pace with the car in front, but he didn't know why. We're following the car instead of pulling him over for a broken taillight. Callahan told the dispatcher that something was about to happen, and she seemed to agree with him. What the hell am I missing?

Inside the car in front, the frightened man with the shadowed past slid his hand slowly down his right leg. Trying not to lower his shoulder, he extended his fingers, reaching into his sock. To the mirror, to the road, and back to the mirror again, the driver's eyes watched as the police car followed closely behind. Calm, I must be calm. I must not overreact, he said to himself. This is Tucson, not LA. This town is too far away and too laid back to know the truth. He carefully pulled a thin, delicate knife from his sock, tucking it between the floor carpet and the seat.

"Did you see that, Jordan? He just put something under the seat." Callahan hardly moved his lips.

"How do you know that? I didn't see anything!" the recruit said, totally bewildered.

"You'll learn to recognize the smallest of details, the slightest of movements," Callahan answered, his eyes still glued to the car in front.

What in the hell is he talking about? Jordan thought.

The car proceeded slowly through traffic. The driver checked that his speedometer coincided with the speed limit. He knew not to make any stupid moves, anything that could create a reason to be stopped. The plates were current and he didn't think he had committed any traffic violations. He hoped the cops would go away. Or did he?

"Jordan," Callahan half whispered, "if this is any consolation, I'm a little anxious, too. But, this is when apprehensiveness turns to skill. Mr. Mirror Watcher up there seems to be nervous about his past. We're a little concerned about our immediate future. This may be nothing or a whole lot of everything. Don't be afraid of the unknown. Make it your teacher."

Jordan watched Callahan as he spoke, studying his teacher's movements and his words. He began to understand the challenge of fear. It was a ten second lesson in life.

Time and space became a priority as Callahan watched the weathered Dodge Monaco move north on South Sixth Avenue toward the freeway. The offense had the advantage. The driver knew his destination. He also knew what the police wanted to know about him and his reasons for running.

Callahan needed to find out why he was here. Local knowledge was the Ace-in-the-hole. Come on Ace. Where are you going, little man? What brings you here?

"How long are we going to follow this guy?" Jordan asked.

"Just a couple more minutes." Keep one step ahead, just one step.

The left turn signal flickered white as it shined through the broken red lens of the taillight. The car made its way into the turning lane, directing it into Southgate Shopping Center, an aging strip mall that definitely showed signs of the economic struggle of the area. The row of often-renovated business spaces that formed the mall was anchored by a small-scale supermarket, one of the few businesses that had survived the test of time. At the confluence of South 6th Avenue and Interstate 10, both extremely busy thoroughfares, the mall was built with the anticipation that the area would grow and prosper. That wasn't to be. Many small enterprises had tried to succeed, but most had failed.

"Let him stop himself," Callahan responded. "That in itself will tell us a lot. Whatever he's hiding is not in that vehicle."

"How do you know that?" Jordan asked.

"Because he can't secure it."

"Why not?" The recruit had become frustrated.

"It's right there in front of you. The right rear window is broken and the trunk lock is punched out."

"Damn," Jordan said as he shielded his eyes from the sun and looked closely at the vehicle in front.

Once in the mall parking lot, the car suddenly made an abrupt left, accelerating as it raced to the rear of the buildings. As the vehicle turned, the first side view of the driver became visible. The profile revealed a small man, probably in his mid-forties, with a receding hairline that sharpened his features. Instantly, he turned his head towards the persevering police unit and again the eyes of both drivers met. His pointed nose and thin lips gave the appearance of a rat, with dark hollow eyes that darted back and forth. Like an animal in the wild, he possessed a fear, perhaps the fear of being trapped.

"This guy really doesn't want to meet us," Callahan said, "and that kind of offends me."

Behind the plaza was a large vacant lot, approximately two acres in size. It remained undeveloped, making it convenient for the needs of a sporadic, itinerant carnival. Presently, the large archaic wheels of the beat-up rides stood motionless. Most of the activity was coming from birds pecking at the remnants of last night's popcorn and peanuts on the dirt floor.

It was quite apparent now that the driver was viewing the confines of the carnival as his refuge. No human life was evident, but many pairs of eyes were felt. An internal law was about to be violated. An unwanted intrusion was being brought to their island. It was unforgivable and definitely unpardonable by the clan of carnies.

"This guy is more stupid than I thought," Callahan observed. "He put himself in a no win situation. He brought 'the man' into the uninvited area. His ass is grass, whether with us, or his "carny" friends. It just doesn't make sense."

The carnival workers that performed the day-to-day, town-to-town labor were breeds of their own. The love of their work was definitely an oxymoron. The reason they were here was quite obvious: to keep on the move and out of sight. The workers created few problems to the various communities for that very reason – their need for anonymity. Their logic was simple. If they weren't seen or heard, they didn't exist. They survived as a group, both as a workforce and a community within a community. They chose their friends and acquaintances carefully. It was a form of survival. An unwritten law existed — no one person was to bring attention to the whole. Like animals that hunted in packs, they found comfort in numbers and, as a group, sought solitude. Keeping secrets, not creating them, was the order.

A pair of Dodges, one behind the other became a chess game with real life pawns. A few seconds brought decisions that lasted a lifetime. Callahan knew this. Timing and luck. Skill and intellect. Knowledge and common sense. It went beyond survival. Behind the badge beat a heart and it continued to beat because of accurate split-second decisions.

Callahan slowly took the radio mike from its holder, and without taking his eyes off the car in front, he spoke, "One-Adam-Seven . . . we'll be stopping a blue Dodge, approximately a 1966 with California plates, One-Nora-Baker-Five-Two-Three-Six behind Southgate Shopping Center at 6th and I-10 . . . run a 10-28, please."

"10-4 Adam-Seven," Barb's voice responded. The rear of Southgate. What's there? she asked herself.

"This is going to take awhile, Jordan," Callahan instructed. "Out of state plates are tele-typed to San Francisco to be run through their computers. It's a slow process and the Superior Court has given us just twenty minutes to detain someone for the purpose of a records check. Let's pray that somebody has their shit together on the other end."

"What if the twenty minutes is up and we don't get a return?" Jordan asked.

"We'll worry about that if and when it happens."

The old, heavy car moaned as it veered into the alleyway behind the plaza of stark, deteriorated buildings. The vehicle was traveling faster now than on the street. Fear consumed the pale man with the apparently dark past.

"There's a good chance this guy is going to rabbit when he stops. We have no idea if he's armed, so let's treat him as if he is. Meaning, don't get in my way or his. Got it?"

Jordan nodded, swallowing hard.

Just ahead, behind the carnival setting was a single row of semi-trucks and travel trailers, the crude and familiar temporary homes for the workers. Once the trucks' forty-foot trailers were emptied of equipment and material for the rides, they became impromptu quarters for the laborers. The travel trailers, ranging in size, age, and comfort levels were examples of the caste system within the pecking order of carnival hierarchy. The better the job position, the better the housing.

The eyes left the rearview mirror. The driver sank lower in his seat. His head could barely be seen above the headrest. Quite possibly he realized his error in bringing the unwanted intrusion of the outside world to the solitude of the migrant carnival. The same authority that the occupants were trying to elude was now being escorted in.

The white light peeked through the hole in the taillight lens when the driver brought his car to a stop in the carnival parking lot. Callahan stayed left, a half car length back, to establish a clear view of the driver.

The driver's options had been drastically reduced, if not eliminated. He knew he had violated the unwritten code of the society of anonymity. His past was about to catch up with him, unmasked by an intuitive cop with a Motorola radio.

The driver lowered his eyes as his body sighed with relief. He searched the car's interior with a slight movement of his head. Is this it? Is this my last view of freedom? Was it worth the price?

Jordan watched the driver as Callahan cautiously, but confidently approached the now silent car. The door was closed, the window down. The driver's face was gaunt, giving the appearance that he had been much heavier in the past. His forehead was perspiring, dropping beads of sweat down a three-day beard. His unkempt, thinning hair was swept backwards, done with his hand rather than a comb. His once white T-shirt was soiled, and not just from today's work.

"I want to see both hands on the steering wheel. Now!" Callahan ordered as he approached the car. No obvious violation had been committed and a broken taillight did not qualify for a weapon-drawn felony stop. A gut feeling was not evidence.

Still staring directly ahead into the pitted windshield, the driver placed his shaking hands on the steering wheel. He was perspiring as his lips moved slightly, either rehearsing his answers to the upcoming questions or saying a prayer. Out of the corner of his eye, he caught sight of the officer. Still not moving, he knew he had run out of time and space.

"Keep your hands where they are and move when I tell you to," Callahan demanded, standing two paces back from the left shoulder of the driver. "I'm going to open the door and you are going to step out with your hands in front of you. Got it?"

The driver nodded. With some difficulty, Callahan opened the large, battered door and flung it wide, hoping the hinges would hold it open. They did.

"Step out, please."

"What did I do? I thought I was . . ." stammered the driver, his voice trailing off.

"Just get out and I'll tell you."

The driver swivelled around on the seat, bringing his sweating, shaking hands in front of him. One by one, he placed his feet outside the car and stood with both arms extended in front of him.

"Ah . . . a little LA influence, I see," Callahan mused at the frazzled man. Though the driver was slight in build, Callahan was quite aware that stature could be mitigated in a hurry by the presence of a weapon. "Now, turn around slowly and place your hands on the top of the car."

"Give me your name," Callahan demanded as he moved behind the shaking man.

"My name is, uh," the driver stammered, "Pittman. Nolan Pittman."

"You don't seem to be real sure of that, Mister Pittman," Callahan stated, moving closer. "Now show me a piece of ID that will verify that."

"Callahan!" Jordan whispered loudly, approaching his training officer. Callahan turned to find the recruit's eyes directed at another event. Approximately forty yards away, doors to the small travel trailers simultaneously opened.

"I see 'em." Callahan smiled as he patted down the outstretched driver for weapons. "No problem."

One at a time, carnival workers began to emerge from the cluster of trailers. At first, curiosity brought them from their self-imposed exile. However, as they came together, resentment became prevalent. Ten, maybe eleven, soon gathered to observe the vehicles that had entered the carnival compound. Their faces wore stares of concern and hate directed at the intrusion of the law and the betrayal of a peer.

"Should I call for a back-up?" the unarmed recruit asked nervously.

"Sgt. Stark has been watching us from behind the grocery store," Callahan answered, without taking his eyes away from the curious onlookers. "Just look his way and he'll know that we want him here."

Jordan paused, doubting Callahan's statement, then turned his head toward the rear of the discount market. Immediately, a squad car emerged and began to drive in their direction.

Sergeant Stark slowly pulled alongside Callahan, his eyes surveying the group of carnival workers in front of their trailers.

Victor Stark's appearance mirrored his personality, always in the background, soft-spoken, but effective. At 5'10" or so, and somewhat heavy, he looked more like a chaplain than a cop. He had spent in excess of ten years in the detective division prior to his promotion to sergeant. Once promoted, an opening for Training Sergeant in Team I occurred, providing him the opportunity to re-learn the nuances of front line duty. Stark didn't know Callahan before he took the assignment, but it wasn't long before a strong partnership between the two developed.

Callahan turned his attention to the gathering of carnival workers. The driver also turned to watch his peers. "Stay put," Callahan ordered him.

One man, larger than the others, began to shout at the officers, but was too far away to be understood. Wearing a black, sleeveless T-shirt and an attitude, he apparently wanted it to be known that he was their leader.

"Friends of yours, Thumper?" Stark inquired facetiously from his car window.

"Hand me your radio, Vic," Callahan requested of his supervisor. "And turn it to speaker for me, please." Stark complied and chuckled aloud as he waited for Callahan's next move.

Pulling his handcuffs from the rear of his belt, Callahan tossed them a short distance onto the hood of Victor's car. The distinct sound of metal on metal produced the effect he wanted. Court was now in session.

"What we are going to do here is run record checks on everyone." His voice echoed off the trailers. "Just as a public service to our community," he grinned.

Jordan stood to the side, trying to understand what he was witnessing.

"We value you as new members to our city and we want you to feel welcome. So, one at a time, if you would, please bring us a form of picture ID and we'll start the process."

The impromptu speech had served its purpose. The crew of curious carnival workers looked at each other without speaking. They shook their heads. One by one they turned and disappeared into their trailers. The large one in the black shirt stopped briefly and stared at the officers. Rolling his shoulders forward to exhibit muscles disguised by fat, he scowled and pointed a finger at Callahan.

"Do you have a problem, son?" Callahan asked, as he stepped in his direction.

The man turned and spit vulgarities in the opposite direction as he retreated into his travel trailer. A little intimidation went a long way for someone wanting to remain anonymous, Callahan thought. He watched the trailer doors close and window shades open slightly. Out of sight, but definitely not out of mind.

"Now, back to you, Mr. Pittman. I need your driver's license," Callahan demanded of the driver.

"I think it's in the car," Pittman said, attempting to step into the Dodge.

Instantly, Callahan placed his arm across the smaller man's chest and stopped him abruptly. "Not in this lifetime. License. Now!"

"But I can't remember where I put it. I'll have to look for it," the driver pleaded.

"You can't remember? Do you need me to help you with your memory?"

"No, sir," the frightened man asserted, trying to distance himself.

"Then why don't you just very carefully take your left hand and reach behind you and pull it from your waistband?"

He had to know that I would have touched it when I patted him down, Callahan thought. What in the hell is going on here?

Stark and Callahan exchanged glances. Stark got out of his car and stood in front of the suspect's vehicle. Slowly, the man's trembling hand reached behind him and retrieved the wallet, purposely hidden inside the gathering of his oversized trousers. He tried to remove a form of identification without revealing its other contents. His shaky hands fumbled with the cards. Suddenly several forms of identification flew from his wallet and fell to the ground like a game of 52 card pick-up.

"Damn it!" Pittman mumbled. He dropped to his knees, desperately trying to retrieve the contents of the wallet.

"Here, let me help you," Callahan's eyes focused on one particular item containing a photograph.

"No, please. I can do it." The frantic man crawled on his hands and knees across the ground, grasped the card and squeezed it, trying to make it disappear in his hand. Callahan grabbed Pittman's upper right arm and pulled him up beyond his full height.

"Your license, please."

Callahan took the laminated card from Pittman's open hand and recognized the photo as that of his captive. The typed information, however, showed his name as James Warren Downs, date of birth, Oct 12, 1940. Three more driver's licenses remained on the ground, all with different names, and none accompanied by photographs of the bearer.

"You realize," Callahan said as he released his grip, "that we are going to have a hard time believing anything you tell us now."

James Downs chose not to speak, shifting his gaze between the two officers.

CHAPTER THREE

"WOODY, COME HERE a second," Barb requested as she rolled her chair back from her radio dispatch console.

"What's up?" her supervisor asked, walking toward her.

"Something's not jiving with the plate Callahan ran a few minutes ago. The NCIC returned a plate on a Buick. But listen." Barb punched the replay cassette mounted at her console, until she found One-Adam-Seven's last transmission. "It's right here."

"One-Adam-Seven . . . we'll be stopping a blue Dodge, approximately a 1966 with California plates, One-Nora-Baker-Five-Two-Three-Six behind Southgate Shopping Center at 6th and I-10 . . . run a 10-28, please."

"10-4, I'll start the 28."

She shut down the tape.

"Did you tell him?" Walker asked.

"No. The information just came back," Barb stated. "I'll do it now."

"Thumper, radio has some info for you about his vehicle," Stark advised, handing Callahan the portable radio.

Callahan walked a short distance away. "1-Adam-7, go ahead."

"Can you give the plate again on the vehicle that you stopped? We need a confirmation."

"10-4. Hang on." He walked the few steps to the rear of the vehicle before he relayed, "One-Nora-Baker-Five-Two-Three-Six."

"10-4, the plate on the vehicle you have comes back as a 1970 Buick, not a 1966 Dodge, as you indicated.

"Got a name to go with it?"

"10-4, a Malcolm Watkins in Carlsbad, California."

"Can you run that name and see what you come up with?"

Barb's fingers and mind were immediately at work.

"Stand by, it could take awhile," she responded.

"Also, I need to run a 29 on the subject that I have. Let me know when you're ready."

"Give me his information and I'll run it as soon as I can."

"Mr. Downs," Callahan said calmly as he walked back to the car, "before we go any further in our investigation, the law says I must advise you of something. It'll just take a minute."

Fear struck the prisoner as his mind and body exploded with anxiety. Why would license plate information create an arrest situation? He had a question, but his past experiences with law enforcement told him that it would not be answered.

As with most seasoned officers, Callahan knew the Miranda Warnings from memory. However, countless testimonies in court taught officers many lessons. Read the suspect his rights from the typewritten card so that nothing could be left for dispute later. The rights card evolved from Miranda vs. Arizona, a sex offense case regarding the timely manner in which suspects were advised of their rights to an attorney being present during questioning. When the questioning became accusatory, the Miranda Warnings had to be read to the suspect.

Callahan pulled his laminated rights card from his left breast pocket, beneath his badge, and began reading, "You have the right to remain silent, anything you say, can and will be used against you in a court of law. You have the right to the presence of an attorney prior to questioning and during questioning, if you so desire. If you cannot afford a lawyer, one will be appointed for you. After being advised of these rights, do you understand them fully?"

"I know my rights, and I understand that you have an obligation to read me my rights." Suddenly, the prisoner changed his demeanor. "I don't want an attorney. I just want to know what crimes I'm accused of."

"1-Adam-7," the radio interrupted, "are you Code 1?"

"Give me a second."

The prisoner's face turned to stone as he watched the officer walk away. Taking a step toward Callahan, he tried in vain to hear the accusations that he knew were forthcoming.

"NCIC reports," Barb began, "that Malcolm Watkins has been listed as a missing person since July 24th of this year. They also advised us to contact the FBI with any info pertaining to him. We are doing that now."

Something wasn't right. He could feel it. What had gone wrong? Downs started to tremble as his body craved a substance to ease its pain. "Calm down," he thought to himself.

It took a few seconds for Callahan to return to his prisoner. Malcolm Watkins. Missing. Associated with plates that don't belong to this car. "Barb, check this VIN for me." Callahan looked at the Vehicle Identification Number inside the driver's side windshield and read the number into the mike.

"10-4," Barb replied.

"Is there anything you want to tell me, Mr. Downs?" Downs looked directly at the officer, but did not speak.

"Tell me about this car," Callahan instructed as he patted the roof. "Tell me how you happen to be in possession of it."

"I bought it."

"Where?"

"In California."

"From whom?"

"The owner. He said he didn't need it anymore."

"What was his name, Mr. Downs?" Callahan sternly asked as he glanced briefly at Stark.

"I can't remember." James Downs began to lick his lips nervously.

"You're lying. Tell me his name."

"Ok, ok, ok," Downs repeated. "I didn't buy it from the owner. It was left for me as a part of the deal. Excuse me, a deal."

"Deal. What kind of deal?" Stark asked.

Down's head looked between the two officers. "I drove a car to San Diego and in return they gave me this," he said, nodding toward the Dodge.

"Who is Malcolm Watkins?"

Downs reacted as if he were hit in the pit of the stomach. "I don't know a Malcolm Watkins."

"Bullshit."

"Oh, my God, look at this, Woody. Who in the hell does he have there?" Barb was reading the teletype as it appeared, line by line. "That guy's in possession of a vehicle with plates belonging to a missing person, and now this."

Walker stood behind her and read the teletype over her shoulder. "Send him a couple of units. This is getting serious."

"Stark is already there."

"I don't care, goddamn it. Send him some backup."

"Answer the Sergeant's question," Callahan demanded. "Tell us . . ."

Barb's urgent voice interrupted, "1-Adam-7."

"Go ahead," Callahan responded.

"Are you Code 1?"

"To hell with that. Give me what you've got."

"NCIC advises that there are seven current felony warrants for your subject. Can you copy the info?"

"Give me a minute."

The officers exchanged glances. The suspect now became a prisoner.

Downs' shoulders dropped. Seven warrants! All they could possibly have is a few minor drug charges. Downs went limp and leaned against the open door for support. Callahan stared at Downs as he stereotyped his thoughts and predictions. Thief. Robber. Embezzler. Probably all three. Con artist. Perhaps, murderer.

Barb just confirmed what his insides had predicted all along. Call it instinct. Call it police intuition, but never call it luck. It was a microcosm of life. You felt it.

"If you have information on the warrants, go ahead and give them to me. One at a time." Waiting for her response, he stared at Downs like a mountain lion facing a deer.

"One," Barb responded, "for unlawful flight to avoid prosecution, one for attempted homicide on a law enforcement agent, and five," she hesitated, "and five for child molestation."

The words exploded from the microphone. They carried the shock of a death notification, the disbelief and finality of a cancer blow.

Child molesting!

"No! No! That's not me they're talking about," Downs blurted. "I'm not what they say," and he stopped.

Callahan stood up straighter. He took a deep breath and responded with an eerie calm that was well known to everyone.

"Please confirm the warrants and advise the issuing agencies that the subject is in custody. Dispatch the ID unit. Notify the FBI and Homicide."

"Already in progress. Also, the force commander is en route. Anything else?"

"Yeah. When you ran the VIN, who came back as the registered owner of the Dodge?"

"No one. NCIC says that the number does not exist in their computer system."

Silence.

Callahan looked back at Downs. He stared into Downs' eyes and for a moment Downs tried to match his stare. But as seconds passed, Callahan's expression began to change. His deep blue eyes grew cold with hate.

With both hands, Callahan grabbed Downs' shirt and pulled him up to his height. The cloth tore under his right hand. Callahan re-gripped and pulled him up again so that his feet came off the ground.

"Don't kill me, please, oh please." Downs thought of running. After all, he was doomed anyway. But it was too late. He had nowhere to go.

"You fucking scumbag." Callahan's eyes were on fire.

Downs struggled for a breath. "It's not me. I didn't do those things."

"Thumper," Vic interrupted, "Stuart is here with the TWIX confirmation of the warrants."

Callahan glared into the eyes of his prey. "You're lucky, asshole." He released his grip and the prisoner wilted and collapsed, whimpering as he fell to his knees.

"Wait," Downs pleaded. "I have something more. Maybe we could make a trade?"

Again the eyes of the cop and the man with the mysterious past met. "A trade? What could you possibly tell us, Mr. Downs? These warrants tell us what kind of an asshole you are. I know who you are. I know where you're from. I know you are a child molester. What could you possibly have to tell me that would change what I already know?" A sour taste came up in Callahan's throat as he jerked Downs from the ground. The feeling was foreign to him. It was hatred and it was tangible. "You and your life are pretty worthless now. Out here in the real world you are despised. Inside prison you will be hated and even worse. If you have more to tell me, do it now. You don't have any options left."

Callahan knew time was of the essence. Anyone or everyone, including the media, monitored police radio dispatches. Any kind of outside interference could hinder or stop further investigation of Downs' migration to Tucson.

Lieutenant Stuart Gardner was the relief day shift force commander. He was an up and comer and he relished the climb. He needed these situations. It showed to the hierarchy that he was of command caliber.

"Nice collar," the Lieutenant said, walking up to Callahan, extending his hand. Callahan shook it merely as a gesture, but ignored his comment.

"Lieutenant, do you have the copies of the warrants?"

"Yeah, let me read them to you. They're beauts."

"Lieutenant, if you don't mind, I'd rather read them myself," Callahan broke in, his voice more harsh than he intended. "And at this point, let's keep it between ourselves."

"You're right. Do you want a screen unit to book this guy?" the Lieutenant asked.

"No thanks, Lieutenant," Callahan answered. "Not yet, I believe there is more here that we need to know."

"More, what more? What else do you have, Callahan?" Gardner shot back. "After all, I'm the Force Commander and I have the need to know."

"Soon as I know, you'll know, Lieutenant Gardner," Callahan replied with his plan taking shape. "However, you can get me a unit here to secure this vehicle. I don't want anyone coming near it. To answer your question before you ask it, I'm not sure if he is hiding anything in it, but I don't want it tampered with."

The man that carried a license identifying himself as James Warren Downs had been content to exist within the confines of a semi-trailer. He received minimal compensation in wages and living quarters with his job as a set up man for the carnival equipment. When the carnival was set up and functioning, the forty-foot trailer was his domain. In transit, he shared it with worn angle iron and rusty sheet metal. It wasn't home, but it traveled, in increments, away from California.

"Downs, you are under arrest," Callahan grabbed him by the arm and pulled him away from the car. "What is it you want to tell me? You'd better tell me now."

"Information . . . for my life?" the prisoner asked. Downs began to get desperate. "You don't know everything. There's more. I'll show you."

A car, then another, began to drive into the lot.

"Lieutenant," Callahan called, "can you stop those vehicles from coming in here?"

"Sure, and I'll get more units to help."

James Downs realized another situation was about to unfold. But, at this point, the only thing that mattered was saving a life.

"Vic, hand me my cuffs," Callahan nodded toward the hood of Starks' car. One at a time, he handcuffed the prisoner's hands behind him.

"My keys, what I need, uh, you need," Downs said.

"What?"

"My keys are in the ignition. The key you need is on a rawhide string."

"To what?"

"I'll show you. I'll take it, him, I mean you," Downs stammered. "I'll take you to the trailer. I live there."

Callahan motioned to Jordan, standing to the rear of Down's vehicle. "Carefully reach in the car and pull the keys from the ignition."

Jordan complied, making sure not to touch anything else inside the car.

"Is it on there?"

"Yeah, what's it to?" Jordan asked, holding the keys up by the rawhide string.

"We're about to find out," Callahan answered, glaring at Downs. Taking the key, Callahan held it before him. Downs knew it had special meaning. Maybe, just maybe, it was his last desperate attempt at decency.

"Jordan, stay close to Downs' car and don't let anyone near it." Jordan nodded and stepped in front of the passenger's door.

"Show me the lock that goes on the end of this key," Callahan directed to Downs.

"It's over there." Obviously flustered with both hands cuffed behind him, he nodded his head toward a tarnished gray and white semi-trailer.

Callahan abruptly picked up Downs by the shirt, staring directly into his eyes. "When you unlock the door, you are all alone. When it opens, if you have a surprise, you will be the target. Understand, asshole?"

James Downs nodded. "It's not what you think. Please, give me one more chance."

"One more chance for what?" Callahan asked within a few inches of his prisoner's face. "I have confirmed warrants telling me you molested at least five kids, you tried to kill a cop, and you want another chance? You talked about a trade, scumbag. What in the hell could you possibly have to trade?"

"You'll see," Downs asserted. "You'll see."

Two more police units pulled into the carnival lot as Callahan walked the handcuffed prisoner toward the row of tractor-trailers. He listened to the sound of the gravel crunch beneath his boots as he tried to sort out the scenario inside his head. A man, obviously on the run, in possession of a car bearing a license plate belonging to another vehicle. And the registered owner of that vehicle, Malcolm Watkins, was reported as missing. A third vehicle pulled up to the scene. This one was not a patrol unit and not from TPD.

Callahan watched as the "suit" stepped from the nondescript, gray Chevrolet and said a few words to the Lieutenant.

"Callahan," Lt. Gardner called, "an FBI agent wants to talk to you."

"Tell Weaver to hang on for just a few minutes." Callahan recognized the agent as Weaver Bailey, a long time friend from the policemen's Olympic basketball competition.

"He wants to see you, *now*, Officer Callahan," the Lieutenant shot back.

Callahan saw the distress in the Lieutenant's face, but he would have to deal with it, knowing Agent Bailey would understand.

"Tell me, Downs. Tell me what you have. And it damn well better be more than words. There's an FBI agent over there just waiting to get his hands on you."

"No, no, I have more. No one will hurt you. You'll see. Open the door," Downs directed his stare at the door. The three of them stood in front of a forty-foot trailer with the doors securely padlocked.

"Stark, unlock it, then stand back. Our asshole friend here will open it."

"I can't," Downs pleaded. Turning to look over his shoulder and nodding toward his hands that were cuffed behind him.

"We can take care of that," Callahan said. Unlocking one handcuff, he jerked Downs' arms in front of him and closed the open cuff around his bare wrist.

Both Callahan and Stark drew their weapons and their intended target was the same — the door and then, whatever was inside.

Downs struggled to slide the bar upward on the heavy trailer door. The latch released and the door screeched open. The vast trailer contained nothing of size or shape, until Downs spoke, "Andy, it's me, James."

With the sound of *Andy*, Callahan turned in disbelief to the handcuffed prisoner. "What? What are you . . .?"

Then the voice came, feeble and weak. It was the voice of a child. The voice of a desperate child asked, "Who's there?"

The ambient light was filtering into the space of the seemingly empty trailer.

"Vic, sit on him," Callahan shoved Downs towards the Sergeant. Taking a chance with the unknown, he holstered his weapon and pulled himself up inside.

He could not see clearly into the shadows of the rear of the darkened trailer. It was day shift and his Kel-light was back in the patrol car.

"It's okay," Callahan offered, not knowing to what or whom he was talking as he squinted into darkness. "I'm a police officer. You're safe now."

"Go away," came two words, barely audible, from a weakened child.

As Callahan's eyes adjusted to the limited light, he saw a slight, child-sized figure curled into a ball in the far end of the spacious cubicle. The large officer, made even larger by his silhouette, brought himself down to the level of the voice. He began to crawl slowly across the floor of the semi-trailer on his knees, stopping when he knelt on an object, a discarded bolt. He immediately felt the pain, but he cast it aside along with the bolt. His hands contacted the dirt and grease of perhaps a thousand origins, realizing that this was the forced domain of the imprisoned child.

"Andy, they call me Thumper," the officer said. His moves were slow and deliberate. Silence. As Callahan edged closer, he could hear the sounds of the child discreetly sliding himself away, seeking the solace of a corner. The distrust of the child filled the air like smoke without a chimney.

As the child stopped his retreat, so did the officer, allowing the boy his space. "I'm here to take you from this. I'm your friend. Here, let me show you."

From his chest, Callahan unpinned his badge and slowly extended it in an open palm to the child huddled in the faint light. "Feel my hand. Take my badge." Small, rough fingers found their way into the officer's hand and began to inspect the contours of the metal badge, but didn't remove it as requested.

"I know you're a policeman, but . . . but, that doesn't mean that you're good."

The statement stung. Callahan wondered what this boy had been through.

His tiny fingers found their way around Callahan's hand deliberately taking inventory, in search of kindness. The slowly moving midday sun had changed its angle just enough to give the child a glimpse of the Irish face and the American smile.

The frightened child found his way to the officer's arms and into his heart. Callahan held him as if his own children had a brother. He missed his own more than ever, knowing several angels were now at work.

"Thumper," Vic hollered into the trailer, "are you all right?"

"We're fine," Callahan answered, his emotions compounded by disbelief. He could feel his anger swelling as rational behavior hung by a thread.

Callahan pulled the trembling Andy into his arms. The child clung to the officer's chest. Underweight and gangly, clad in soiled underwear and a much too large T-shirt, his little body heaved with sobs of relief and despair.

Callahan stood and walked the length of the trailer and into the sunlight forcing Andy to cover his face and eyes. He knelt down at the edge of the doorway, softly saying to the quivering child of 9, maybe 10, "This is Victor. He is also a policeman. He's going to take you from me."

"No. No," Andy cried in despair and intensified his grip on Callahan.

"It's okay. You can come right back to me. It's okay."

With that, Andy loosened his hold. Stark was below him on the ground beneath the trailer and Callahan bent over and handed the shaking child to him. Before Victor reached for the child, he shoved his prisoner to the ground, not caring where he landed. Callahan's focus turned to Downs and once again the eyes of the captor and the captive met. Instantly, Downs bolted and began to run in an awkward stumble.

Callahan leaped from the rear of the trailer and in seconds tackled the out-matched and handcuffed James Downs. The force drove Downs' face into the barren dirt where he lay, feeling both the physical pain and the pain of a wasted soul.

"Do it. Kill me, you chicken shit. If you hate me so much, shoot me, SHOOT ME!"

"That would be too good for you," Callahan said slowly. "Who is Andy? Where did he come from? You worthless bastard. Tell me, before I rip your throat out. TELL ME!!"

Downs stared up at Callahan and clinched his teeth together. Then the unspeakable words hissed from his lips.

"I bought him."

"You what?" Callahan yelled, choking back the appalling nausea that slammed his body. "You bought him? What in the hell does that mean? Bought him? Where?" He looked at Andy for a reaction, but Andy's fearful eyes just watched. What kind of an animal would do this? Only the human kind.

Without hesitation, he jerked Downs from the ground and held him up like a dirty dish rag. His feet dangled from his idle legs. Staring into the eyes of the wretched man he issued a command that hung heavy in the air, "Take his cuffs off, Vic. Set him free."

"No, Thump, no," Stark responded with a plea. "It won't change what has already happened."

"This insufferable prick deserves to die." Callahan glared into Downs' bloodless face. He released his grip dropping him to the desolate soil.

Downs crawled away, trying to survive, or perhaps, attempting to die. All three of them knew the obvious intent of Callahan's actions. In the unwritten laws of a non-civilized culture, the killing of this desperate animal perhaps could be justified, but not here, not in this society.

Victor Stark suddenly became Sergeant Stark, placing a forearm to the chest of Callahan. "Back off," he yelled. "That's an order."

"Get away!" Callahan pushed Stark's arm aside. "I'm going to kill the son-of-a-bitch!"

"No!" Andy screamed, breaking free from Sgt. Stark's grasp and running to the fallen Downs. Kneeling next to him, the boy begged to Callahan.

"What he said is true. He bought me. He saved me."

It's not whether you get knocked down it's whether you get back up.

~Vince Lombardi

CHAPTER FOUR

IT WAS 8:45 PM before his shift finally ended, nearly fifteen hours after it began. Michael Callahan finished his portion of the written reports and slowly closed his silver pen. Under different circumstances, he would have embraced the quiet solitude that normally accompanied the end of a long and stressful shift. However, tonight this would not be the case. His emotional roller coaster had slowed down, but it was refusing to stop. This time it was riding the rails of his sad personal life.

Glancing at his watch, he realized his children were probably asleep, but the day's events involving Andy drove him to verify their safety. For a few moments he stared mindlessly at the telephone on the desk in front of him. Closing his eyes, he recalled a conversation with his wife Margaret in the wee hours of the morning after an extended shift at work, almost a year ago. She had met him just inside the kitchen door of their home with a stern announcement. Dressed in a nightshirt, she blocked his entrance and said, "Our life simply cannot go on like this. The kids and I hardly see you. You're not here enough to be a father or a husband. You spend ten, twelve hours a day at work, on your days off you're in court, and mornings at school. And when you are here, you wrap yourself up in building additions onto this house. I'm telling you, things have got to change. You have to decide what you care about most." Margaret looked away, trying to gather her emotions. Then she said quietly, "I mean it, Michael. This is not a bluff."

That was the beginning of the end. They never argued. They never fought. They didn't know how. There was no communication. Instead, they grew apart and soon divorced.

He slowly punched the numbers on the phone pad he knew all too well. Callahan was calling the house where his children were, the house that was once his home. Times such as these made him feel so helpless, so hollow. He had come to realize that guilt was not an emotion; it was a journey.

"Hey, it's me," he asserted as Margaret answered the phone, "I know it's a little late, but I wanted to, better yet, I needed to call before I left the Department."

"I thought you were on day shift?" she asked softly, keeping her voice from the sleeping children. "Did something bad happen?"

"Everything is fine," Callahan reassured. "Just one of those investigations that requires a lot of time and mountains of paperwork. Are the kids all right?"

"They're sleeping, and yes they're fine." Her voice showed the strain of separation anxiety and fear. Words did not seem appropriate or sufficient. This was not the time or place for questions or answers, assuming that there were answers.

"Sorry to trouble you, but I needed to hear that they're safe." The stress of the day, the week, and his present life was very much apparent in his voice and his choice of words. "Tell them that I'll be by tomorrow."

"No problem. I'll let them know that you called." Neither spoke for a few seconds. Words became difficult to find. "Talk to you later," Margaret said, and a click reverberated in Callahan's ear.

The receivers of both phones fell silent. Jumbled thoughts of 'why' created a collage of memories and despair. 'What ifs' replaced glad you're home safe and read me a story. He sat transfixed, trying to separate today from yesterday, and wondered about tomorrow. As he pulled himself from the chair, he felt old beyond his years.

For the first time that he could remember, Callahan wished that he had taken the elevator. Each step he took down the staircase required too much effort. The adrenaline produced by the day's excitement had left his body, leaving him mentally and physically exhausted. He pushed the door open to the lobby and the noise echoed throughout the building of high ceilings and concrete walls. Heads turned his way out of reflex. One couch and eight matching chairs were situated in a living room configuration that no one really bought into. Behind the twenty-foot long front counter an un-enthused desk officer forced a smile and mumbled "Later" as Callahan walked by. A thick Plexiglas shroud protected the personnel in the entrance area. It hadn't always been there.

In the not-so-distant past, the front entrance to the police station was unmonitored. The public as well as police personnel came and went without much notice or security. As usual, it took a catastrophic event to create awareness for change. A mentally deranged, middle-aged female entered the main door and walked to the front counter where the on-duty desk officer was seated. Without being noticed, she promptly produced a handgun and shot the officer, point blank. He survived. Policy changed and construction began.

The crisp, cool evening air touched his face as he stepped from the station and into the night. The sounds of the automobile traffic on South Stone Avenue presented a form of relief, easing the transition from a life of turmoil to one of relative solitude. Even though the segments were brief, he welcomed the periods of being just a citizen. However, he was never off duty. His badge, his firearm, his instincts remained with him twenty-four hours a day, seven days a week. It was the respite from the intensity that gave the mind the rest it required.

Tomorrow was a day off as if it were choreographed by the past day's events. A forty-eight hour hiatus from the rigors of an occupation was cherished by all, and police work was no exception. But while you could relax your mind and body, you couldn't relax your commitment. In many instances, the work created problems as well as solved them. Callahan was not going home. He had not had a home for the last three months. However, it was his choice. He made the decision to be alone. He had no one to blame but himself and his priorities.

Walking slowly down the steps, he noticed a lone figure sitting in the dim light on a concrete bench off to the side. He found it odd that this was the first time he had noticed the four-foot wide seat. Callahan felt the eyes of the person follow him as he came closer.

The shadowy light revealed a woman, possibly in her late twenties, sitting cross-legged under a light blue, full skirt. A sly breeze picked her hair from around her face and tossed it playfully about her shoulders. Her dark eyes were the color of the moonless night. She began to smile as Callahan walked closer.

"Good evening, Officer Callahan. Isn't it a beautiful evening?" As she spoke, her hands came together and floated onto her lap. "Did you have a good shift?"

"Not particularly. But it's nothing that I won't be able to deal with." Callahan stopped short of being in front of her, letting her voice create his smile.

"I'm quite sure of that," the attractive lady answered.

"Have we met?" he asked softly.

"Not formally. We've been at the same places quite often."

"Really," Callahan said, cocking his head to one side, "do you work here at TPD?"

"I'm in communications," she smiled. "I'm Angela. I've listened to you for a long time."

"You look very familiar, but I don't ever remember talking to you." Callahan moved to the side, trying to change the angle of a shadow on her face.

Her eyes stayed on him. "Oh, you have," she laughed. "Quite often, actually. Maybe, you don't recognize my voice. It seems to change, depending upon the circumstances."

"I'll start paying closer attention to the voices that I hear," Callahan said as he moved closer.

"I heard you tell someone once in the lobby of the station, 'To handle yourself, use your head. To handle others, use your heart.' That's very good advice."

"I have to remind myself of that from time to time."

"I bet you use that philosophy during every shift you work. You probably even did tonight, without even being aware that you had." Angela gently rose to her feet. "I have to get back now."

"I'm looking forward to seeing you again," Callahan smiled.

"You'll hear me more than see me, but I'm sure we'll run into each other now and then." Angela walked by him with a sideward glance of her soft, smiling eyes.

Callahan watched her graceful stride, again wondering where he had seen her before. A car door slammed shut in the parking lot. He glanced at the sound. When he looked back, she was gone. She's a very interesting lady, he thought as he pulled his collar up and continued on.

The short walk to where Callahan had parked his Ford pick up on a side street, half of a block away was accompanied by no thoughts, no emotion, just a bitter void. The quiet was appreciated, but the anticipated loneliness wasn't.

Michael Callahan's present home was a camper, the kind that extended over and behind the cab of his truck. The house number was his license plate. His address was where he turned off the key and parked. The amenities were few, but enough to create the atmosphere of identity. As minimal as it was, it met his needs and his moods.

The day's events starring Andy and Asshole had taken their toll. Callahan was tired, bone tired. Lack of nutrition and emotion began their battle within his body. He should be hungry, but his stomach acid refuted the thought. Tears began to flow down his cheeks without warning. He was not feeling sorry for himself, just sad about life in general. He soon sat motionless behind the wheel. Staring forward, his eyes found the reflection of streetlights bouncing to him from the hood of his "home." Get over it, he demanded of himself.

Callahan pulled out from his parking space on the lonely street. It felt good to drive without purpose and he began to relax, praying that it would last. The adrenaline produced by anger and emotion was leaving his body. The result was exhaustion.

This was only the second time in six years that Callahan had worked the day shift. However, when given the opportunity, he took it. He thought it would allow him the break that he needed. He was wrong. It just added to his frustration. Other duties within the department could release him from the rigors and violence of night shifts. But it would also take from him his passion — the teaching and training of new officers. He loved his work and position in spite of the pain it caused, past and present. Someday, he might choose a different path, a different destiny, but not now and hopefully not anytime soon, unless destiny had an agenda of its own.

Just when he needed it most, a smile came from his heart and lifted his spirits. Callahan thought of his dog, his companion. Rufus was a purebred, pedigreed, AKC registered, German Shepherd. The ninety-pound, black and tan animal could care less about his breeding. Rufus seemed to resent being referred to as a police dog because that would require discipline and conformity, neither being of interest to Rufus. He had to rule, be in control . . . not unlike his master. Rufus and Callahan were a match, and like all matches, they could be ignited. At certain times, the sparks and fur would fly, as Irish man and German dog clashed. In spite of their differences, they were both well trained and loyal. Obedient, well, that was a different story.

After the marriage separation, Rufus was left at home to be with the children. He was their protector. He put up with every child-to-dog situation in the book. However, separation from his mentor was too much for the broken-hearted animal to handle. For five days he ate very little, barely enough to survive. He missed his master, obviously fearing the worst. He had to go where Callahan went . . . and he finally did, perhaps saving both lives.

"John, I'm on my way over," Callahan said into the phone at the convenience market.

"Rufus hates you," John answered back as he stepped over the dogs lying on the kitchen floor.

"Pretty indicative of how my day has gone," Callahan smiled. "Tell him to get in line."

"You tell him. See you in a couple," John said as he hung up the phone. "Dad's on his way." He reached down to scratch an ear on Rufus.

John Francis was a fellow officer, and dog sitter. Rufus stayed with his buddy, Bonehead and shared John's large backyard. The dogs heard the truck long before it pulled into John's driveway. Both reacted with a bark just to let the world know that they were vigilant.

"Let him in, Bones," John instructed as he retrieved two Budweisers from the refrigerator. Bonehead slapped at the screen door handle with a well-trained paw, opening the door promptly for Callahan as he approached the steps.

"Someday that dog is going to let someone in your house

who is less than desirable," Callahan remarked as he walked through the wide open door.

"Let's hope it's a female, big fella," John smiled back.

Rufus watched from the kitchen doorway and then slowly walked to his master. Quietly, he collapsed to the floor, not wanting to waste too much energy on emotion.

Callahan sat back on the sofa with his hands behind his head and stared at the ceiling. There were rust color stains from where the roof had leaked around the evaporative cooler. The house was showing its age and he knew John wasn't exactly "Mr. Fix-it."

"Speak to me. What happened today?" John pulled the tab off one of the cans and placed it on the wooden coffee table in front of Callahan.

"Unbelievable," Callahan uttered with his eyes still staring upward. "Words can't describe what I saw today."

"That bad, huh?" John said as he began a slow circuit of his living room.

"I was going southbound on 6th. This vehicle was going north." Callahan said, chewing on his lower lip. "When he looked at me I saw something in his eyes. It was like some evil thing. You know the feeling."

John nodded in agreement as he spread a thumb and forefinger across his thin mustache. But it was a lie. He never felt the same instincts that Callahan often referred to.

"Something told me to pull this guy over. And don't ask me what." Callahan pulled the snap-on tie from his collar and unfastened the top button. "I turned around and started to follow him and he led us into that carnival behind Southgate."

Slowly, Callahan related the day's events. John found a recliner, but only used the front edge of the seat to sit on. The warrants, the trailer, Andy. Everything was told as if Callahan was being cross-examined.

"Did you get to talk to this guy alone after everything went down?" John asked.

"Not really. But, I did sit in on his interrogation at the station."

"And?"

"Downs joined the carnival as it pulled up stakes in Southern

California and headed to Arizona, Flagstaff to be exact. He began to frequent a small diner on the outskirts of town. Cheap food, simple people. He made friends with a waitress. He described her as being beaten up by her life. He said neither of them asked questions about the other. Guess he figured they wouldn't tell each other the truth anyway. But she did tell him that she had a child, a son."

"Andy!" John whispered out loud.

"Yeah . . . Andy. His mother wasn't married, but living with some guy. I guess the guy was pretty much of an asshole. It was obvious that he saw Andy as an intrusion and convinced her of the same."

John sat motionless, staring at the floor. His thoughts found memories of investigating child abuse cases and crib deaths, situations that even God could not justify. John's mind asked, "Why do we do this job?" But, he knew why. He just didn't know how. Just when police officers thought they had heard it all, a new horror appeared on the horizon.

"Oh, did I mention," Callahan continued, "that this live-in boyfriend of hers is one of us? A cop, a deputy sheriff!"

John's eyes rose to meet Callahan's.

"Also," Callahan continued, "this deputy was a hardcore drug addict and he used and abused his authority to get drugs. He worked the outlying areas of the county and found the lowlife pushers. In return for his indifference to their drug deals and other bullshit, they would supply him with his choice of illegal substances. He was a goddamn thug."

"And just how did this carnival worker end up with the boy?" John asked.

"Downs offered her money, all the money he had. Two hundred lousy dollars. She wanted more, but she was desperate. Much to his surprise, she took the money he had offered in exchange for her child."

"Incredible," John said. "She sold him to this carny guy? What in the hell was she thinking?"

"I don't know. Shit, she was an addict. I can't even begin to tell you what would go through her mind."

"But she sold her kid to a child molester." John looked at

him blankly. "Jesus, Callahan. Who is this Downs?"

"Hang on, it gets better," Callahan placed his hands on his knees, bringing him eye level with John. "He doesn't have any fingerprints."

"What?"

Callahan straightened, holding both palms in front of him. "The tips on all of his fingers were scarred. That's the evil I was talking about, John. I looked at his hands and he said to me, 'It's amazing what a little lime and a scalpel will do.' And then he smiled. This is a sick son-of-a-bitch. Who in the hell does this to himself? Just the thought of it makes me shake like a dog shittin' peach seeds."

"Know what else is strange here?" John sipped the last of his beer and studied the can before he continued, "How many other cops would have noticed this guy's look? Even if they had, would they have had the initiative to do what you did?"

Callahan shrugged. "Can't answer that. But, I can't help but think that he wanted me to find that kid."

"Why would you say that?"

"Why else would he lead me there? This guy could have kept going on 6th and we probably wouldn't have found out that he was with the carnival."

"You're probably right," John nodded.

"Yeah, but here's where it gets a little sticky." Callahan began to pace. "He was driving a beat up old Dodge with license plates that belonged on a Buick. The Buick's plates are registered to some guy named Malcolm Watkins. By watching his reaction, I'm positive that Downs knows him. He kind of mouthed the last name when he heard it."

Callahan paused, taking a deep breath.

John didn't speak. He just gave that raised eyebrow look of, 'go on.'

"Then Barb tells me that this Watkins guy is listed as a missing person. Downs hears this and his whole demeanor changes. He mumbled something about this not being a part of the plan."

"What plan?"

"Don't know. He wasn't about to tell me." Callahan stood and stretched, drawing Rufus' head from his paws in anticipation of going elsewhere. "But listen to this. In Downs' possession was a Bill of Sale that described the automobile and listed totally different plates – the plates that were actually issued to the old Dodge. So, somewhere along the way, those vehicle plates were exchanged."

"And there's something else that sticks out in my mind. Barringer was dispatched to transport Downs to 10-19. I watched him take Downs' arm to lead him toward the police unit when Downs said, 'Ahh,' and flinched in pain."

"Barringer let go, and asked, 'What's hurting you?'"

"'My shoulder,' Downs said. 'But, it's all right . . . chronic problem, a slight tear in the infraspinatas and some adhesions around the joint. Nothing serious.'"

"Huh?" John said.

"That's what Barringer said." Callahan continued, "And then Downs said, 'I said I have a slightly torn rotator cuff.' I asked him how he knew the name of the exact muscle in the rotator group. He wouldn't answer me. People aren't going to remember the names of muscles unless they have been schooled in human anatomy. I knew the name because Anatomy and Physiology was my minor in college."

"Shit, do you think this guy's a doctor?" John asked.

"I don't know if it's to that extent, but I'd bet my bottom dollar that he has, or had something to do with the medical field. Someday, I'm going to find out exactly who James Warren Downs is. Thanks for the beer. Sorry about the long day."

As usual, when Callahan was ready to leave, it was without hesitation. He pushed the front screen door open. Rufus followed behind, jumping the two steps off the porch.

"Hang on a second, Thumper," John followed him out the door. His words became chosen, rehearsed. "Sears called and offered me a job today."

"Why would they call you, John?" Callahan stopped and turned around.

"Because I applied there for a sales position."

"You did what?"

"I can't be a cop anymore; I'm totally burned out." John's voice hesitated as he suffered through the pain of his own words. "I've been a police officer for almost nine years and I dread going to work. This life is chewing me up. I can't laugh anymore. Hell, I can't even cry. Everyone I look at has to prove to me that he's good, or at least not an asshole. All I see is negative. It's not right, Thumper," he shook his head. "It's not right." John forced his hands into his pant's pockets and began to pace the porch.

John continued, "I don't know this person that I see in the mirror anymore. My only friends are other police officers and all we talk about is our work, who we arrested or who's out there running from us. Callahan, I have to get out to survive. I'm not even good at what I do anymore. And if I keep on doing what I'm doing, someone is going to get hurt. I couldn't live with that."

Callahan had seen this coming, but not in its entirety. John had been doing his job like a paint-by-numbers kit. He did whatever he was told to do, nothing more. Other officers had approached Callahan with concerns about John's job performance, knowing that the two were friends. Something had to happen. But he didn't anticipate this.

"Are you sure that you want to leave police work?" Callahan asked.

"I can't do it anymore, Thump." He squeezed his eyes shut. "Shift work, court dates, working weekends. I can't hack it any longer. I can't do what you've done." The corners of his mouth pointed downward making his face gaunt and stressed. John suddenly appeared much older.

"And what is that, John?" Callahan asked, his eyes narrowing. "What have I done?"

"You sacrificed everything. That's what. And that's exactly why you are so good at this fucking job. You eat and breathe police work."

Callahan stood silent, not having an answer. Not sure if there was one. But he felt John's words.

"Sorry, Thumper. I didn't mean anything personal by what I said. It's just," John's face instantly relaxed, "I've got to make a change." John turned back into the house, letting the screen door close behind him.

CHAPTER FIVE

WITH TWO LONG STRIDES and a leap, Rufus was inside the camper, inspecting its contents for intruders. His elevated bed was slightly below the booted opening into the cab. Mexican blankets and a quilt on top of three-quarter inch plywood, created a space to be envied by canine and human alike. He made two, then three attempts at getting his blankets just right, a figure eight, and then a plop. With a heavy, lung-emptying sigh, Rufus was ready to go anywhere.

Callahan sat on the edge of the window seat just below the wet nose of his companion. Staring at nothing, he began his usual routine by pulling his boots off, unbuckling the black leather gun belt, and removing the stainless steel, .38 caliber Smith & Wesson from its holster. He opened the cylinder and emptied the six rounds into his hand, placing the empty weapon on a shelf in the cabinet, hidden and secured under the bed. His thoughts stung with John's last words. I wonder what it would be like to lead a normal life?

On the same shelf was a smaller model .38, his off-duty weapon. Even in civilian clothes he must be armed. Not by choice, by law. Hoping to get another day's wear from his uniform pants, he held them up for inspection, but the day's events in the dusty vacant lot had taken their toll. The pants were relegated to the impromptu hamper that closely resembled a plastic garbage bag. The white dress shirt would soon join them after his badge and other paraphernalia were removed.

Old Levis and a University of Arizona sweatshirt now became the after hours uniform that would double as nightwear. Fatigue was beginning to make his body beg for rest, but his mind presented a different itinerary. Sleep was a must, but not an option, at least not anytime soon. He stepped from the camper into the cool, invigorating night air, supplying the elixir that he so badly needed.

Callahan took a deep breath and glanced back at John's place. He saw John pass in front of a window, then a light was turned off and the house darkened. He wanted to forget the words that John had spoken, but he knew he couldn't. Callahan pulled open the door to the cab. A well-intentioned paw found its way through the booted window as he turned the key and brought their home to life.

With no immediate destination, he began to drive using the road as a refuge and the engine noise as a counselor. Raindrops fell, touching the windshield like a moth kissing a porch light. The pavement glistened and the wipers did nothing but smudge, mixing inadequate moisture with unclean glass. The distorted view through an unclear windshield seemed to reflect his current situation.

Ten minutes later, the intersection of Wilmot and Speedway appeared in front of him. A left turn, heading north on Wilmot led towards Mount Lemmon and his hide-away. Waiting for the light to change gave him time to make a decision. A right turn on the same street would head him south in the direction of his sleeping children.

He turned right.

The hour approached midnight and traffic was light except for a small influx of automobiles leaving the Buena Vista Theater. Playing on the radio, a popular song suggested that freedom was just another way of saying you had nothing left to lose and he could not agree more.

This is not what I want to hear at this moment, Callahan thought, slapping at the radio knob making the cab silent. But he knew that he couldn't run from everything in life and reluctantly turned the music back on. Rufus noticed the right turn instantly and nudged his head farther into the cab, fully aware of the familiar route.

Five traffic lights, a left turn, then a right . . . and then a left on David Street. Many trips had been made there since the break-up, but none with this amount of sentiment. Rufus sensed that they would not be stopping and moved his head closer to his best friend. Many emotions welled up in his master's eyes.

In the driveway of the house, Margaret's sister's automobile now occupied the space previously reserved for his truck. Easing closer to the residence, he worked to decipher his feelings. How could a father love, yet leave?

The well-manicured lawn and the house addition that he had personally constructed meant very little now. They were merely garnishments surrounding failure. Rufus laid and watched with no movement. He too, saw it as a house minus the ingredients to make it a home.

Margaret and he had purchased the modest, yet attractive, rose-colored brick house because it was comfortable and situated in a well-established neighborhood. In his off duty hours from work and college classes he found time to add the family room. Looking at the structure now, all he saw was brick and mortar, wood and glass. The house now represented material assets only. And failure.

The truck passed the house and slowly rolled down David Street. At the intersection, he turned around. When he passed the house again, he closed his eyes, mentally tucked his children in their beds, and promised them that everything would be all right. Then he prayed that he was telling them the truth. Rufus raised his head slightly to acknowledge his former home and a family that had changed.

Without an itinerary, he drove. Appropriately, the rain continued to fall, ushering in fresh thoughts on old subjects. The rain increased, but momentarily he refused to interrupt the magical streams with the wiper blade. A large sign, illuminated by his headlights, informed motorists that the entrance to the Air Force Base was forth coming. With a slight smile, his thoughts took him back in time. After a brief stint in college, life changed quickly — much too rapidly for a man young in years and short on advice.

IT WAS AUGUST 31st 1967. A C-141 transport waited at Davis-Monthan Air Force Base, just outside of Tucson. The large aircraft sat in a hanger at the far end of the north runway. The top secret and highly sophisticated cargo was being loaded, ever so carefully, into the aircraft's enormous belly. The destination was an overseas location known only as 'OL-20,' presumably, South Vietnam. Its mission was surveillance.

The final piece of cargo made his way into the forward cabin of the aircraft, not as a part of the crew, but as a passenger. The young airman, barely twenty-one years old, strapped himself into a seat adjacent to the navigator located on the flight deck. His mind was flooded with thoughts of the unknown, both there and abroad.

Airman First Class Michael E. Callahan was about to depart to a war zone. He was two years removed from the cornfields of Indiana and ten thousand miles from a war. However, his thoughts were elsewhere. His wife of three months was presently sitting in a gynecologist's office waiting for confirmation.

The first letter he received from Margaret, approximately two weeks later, began with, "Guess what? We're going to have a baby!" With no qualifications other than circumstance, he was thrust into manhood and fatherhood . . . simultaneously. The realization that he was going to be a father had made the war experience bearable, but the distance from home much greater.

MICHAEL CALLAHAN CHOSE his spot to nest at milepost 11.5 of Mount Lemmon Highway for two reasons. The seclusion of Middle Bear Canyon provided him with both venues that his personality required — fight and flight. By parking his camper fifteen miles from civilization, Callahan could be reclusive enough to lick his wounds, yet remain a quick drive away from the world that he tried to control.

The small campground was vacant as he backed his truck into its habitual space at the edge of the pine trees. It wasn't that Callahan ignored the "Closed At Dusk" sign, he just used it to his advantage. It meant solitude, needed for his decision-making and his well-being. The forest rangers knew he was there, but they viewed his presence as an asset. If ever needed, he was one more agent of the law.

The rain had subsided, leaving the air clean and the night cold. Sounds and smells were magnified by the freshness of the moisture in the air. Rufus took his customary walk to the periphery of the light emitting from above the camper door, but no farther. He was quite aware of other creatures out on the prowl that were also enjoying the beauty of the night. After a couple of sniffs of the ground, he assumed his habitual sentry post under his favorite tree.

Callahan pulled a lawn chair from its storage place, positioning it next to his ice chest. Rufus' ears reacted to the cooler's lid being opened, but he stayed still. Callahan pulled out a carton of buttermilk. "Want some?" he offered. Rufus stared ahead. Yuk. Bring out the 'crinkle noise' stuff.

He opened the big blade of his imitation Swiss Army knife and pulled an open package of saltines from the tray in the cooler. Now you're talking.

"Did I see a drool? I better not see a drool. This is people food. You're a dog."

Rufus turned his head away and licked his lips, concealing the dreaded drool. He kept looking away until he heard the crunch. The unmistakable sound of that wrapping stuff they put around sharp cheddar cheese. He watched, drooling, as Callahan cut a slice, and then another, placing them on the top of crackers. Rufus' eyes followed Callahan's hand to his mouth. And again, until he couldn't take it any longer. A well-placed nudge under Callahan's hand would almost always cause the cheese to become airborne and captured in mid-air with snapping teeth.

"Are you sure you don't want some buttermilk?" Yuk. This meant the ritual was over for the night.

Callahan finally relaxed, allowing exhaustion to overtake him. After putting the chair away, he and Rufus went into the camper and collapsed, with one last ritual. Callahan would crawl into his bed with Rufus lying next to him on the floor. The dog would remain there until his master was asleep, and then move up onto his own bed.

I SHOULD HAVE ASKED her yesterday evening what would be the best time to go by, Callahan considered as he headed back down the mountain road. He stopped at a convenience store to purchase his customary cup of black coffee.

"I'll be right back," Callahan advised the vigilant Shepherd, digging for a dime in his pocket. "Watch the truck for me, and pay for the gas when the pump stops."

The dime dropped and he dialed the number. It's funny, he thought, how circumstance could change the sound of a ringing phone.

"Hello?"

"Hi. Everything all right?"

"Yeah, we're fine," she said tenderly, still hearing the concern in his voice.

"What time should I come by and pick up the kids?"

"You're planning on keeping them with you tonight, right?" She did not allow him time to answer. "Come by about 4. I need to talk to you about some things."

"See you then."

"Let's go get some food, Rufus," Callahan said, climbing back behind the wheel. "And then we can pick up your buddies."

"Could you pass me the sports page, Chester?" Callahan slid the ashtray down the counter; it didn't stop until it hit a napkin holder.

"Yep," Chester answered. After wiping his hands on his once white apron, he began shuffling through the sections of the *Arizona Daily Star.* Chester placed the folded back front page section inside the sports and moved his three-hundred plus pounds down to Callahan's stool. Chester's diner, called 'Mama's Kitchen,' seated twenty-two skinny people and fifteen, or so, people of considerable girth. So, a full house was somewhere around eighteen, if the thin ones sat at the counter for six.

"The Phoenix Suns won again," Callahan said. "Did I tell you that I once had a tryout with the Suns?"

"Really?" Chester made it quite obvious that he could care less. "Want something to eat or just coffee?"

"Yeah," Callahan said. "Why don't you rinse your apron out in a bowl, heat it, and bring me some crackers."

"Wiseass. Biscuits and gravy?"

Callahan nodded. "It was 1969. Right after I'd gotten out of the Air Force."

"What was?"

"My tryout with the Suns. They had put an ad in the paper. That was their first year, you know?"

"How did you do?" Chester asked through the pass-thru window into the kitchen.

"Made it through the first cut."

"That's cool."

"Not really," Callahan said, wondering if that moving 'dot' in his coffee was alive. "It seems that I didn't read the whole article."

"Meaning?" Chester slid the plate onto the counter. "Want some bacon?"

"Naw, this is good." Callahan didn't look up. "The tryout was for the team mascot."

"Are you shittin' me?" Chester belly laughed. "And you made it through the first cut?"

"After I had signed up at the front door, they motioned me in the auditorium. The place was packed. But right then I knew something was wrong. There was a one-legged guy, three fat girls, triplets to be exact, and all kinds of strange people in fur, carrying their animal heads around. I didn't go back. Don't tell anybody."

He moved his plate to the side, knowing he had eaten too much. Old farm habits were hard to break. 'Never fail' is what his dad called gravy, meaning that it never failed to be at the table for any given meal. Chester made the closest thing to homemade farm biscuits and his 'never fail' was excellent. One time Callahan thought of asking him what he put in it, but thought better of it. The visual of the apron always came to mind. He also thought of asking him who "Mama" was, but let that one go too.

Chester never gave Callahan a bill for the food, but Callahan always left four bucks. He told Chester that he would leave more if the service was better. Chester would make a rude gesture, and Callahan would return it. People would excuse it, saying it was some kind of a 'guy thing.'

Callahan was digging into his front pants pocket for his money when he noticed a young woman looking into the window. "I know her," he thought. "But from where?" He looked straight into her eyes, her face gentle as a mother's. She moved her head, with her stare catching his. She smiled.

"Thanks, Chester," and Callahan pushed the door open.

He moved outside, standing just a few feet from her. She

looked angelic. That's it, Angela. "Angela, right?"

"Yes, and how are you?' she asked.

"I'm all right." He looked over his shoulder, back into the diner. "Are you looking for someone?"

"Do you live around here?" she asked, side-stepping his question.

"No . . . I, uh . . . live, for right now, up the mountain a ways," he turned, holding his gaze toward Mt. Lemmon.

"Interesting. I was just wandering around a bit, you know, stretching my legs," she smiled. "I do volunteer work in the next building."

Callahan squinted his eyes, searching for a sign. "What kind of volunteering do you do?"

"I work with people that have suffered a major health set back. Something catastrophic that has altered their life drastically and left them wheelchair bound. Strokes, heart attacks, that sort of thing."

"That's impressive. What do you do with them? Therapy?"

"Oh, no. I don't have the education or training for that. I'm just kind of a," she paused, "support group. Just being there means a lot to people that have no one."

"People with paralysis? Non-ambulatory types?" Callahan took two steps to the side, trying to get a look inside of the white walled building.

"Exactly. Want to see?" Angela touched his hand.

"Sure. This is . . ."

"I know," she interrupted, "right up your alley."

"How do you know that?" Callahan took her hand, staring down at her delicate touch.

"You know how people talk around the Police Department." Angela was a step ahead, her hand behind in Callahan's. "They said you wanted to be a doctor at one point in your life."

"Well, kind of. I always thought it would be very rewarding to help people that are, I don't know how else to say it, beyond help." She was walking quickly, with purpose. "You know, after the medical community had given up on them."

"I knew it," she giggled. "You're going to love these people."

The inside of the 1,600 square foot building was hidden by vertical blinds that covered the large, plate glass window. Angela pushed the front door open and stood to the side, ushering Callahan to the inside.

The room was a white shell. Three chairs near the door were empty. A half moon counter in the corner to the left partially concealed a young girl receptionist. Along the far wall was a ballet bar, nothing else. Two couches and one chair sat twenty feet from the door, facing forward. Round balls of various sizes littered the floor behind the sofas. Two racks of small weights, two stationary bicycles, and a treadmill were against the back wall. A radio, playing an 'oldies' station was just loud enough to make your foot tap.

"There's no one here," Callahan said, creating an echo. "Where are the people you talked of?"

"Oh, they've gone," Angela smiled. "I did all that I could for them."

"But, you said they had problems. Serious problems. Where are the people that should be here helping them? This is a great place to work with these people. Why is it empty?"

"There is no one to work with them. It's that 'dark hole' that exists after they have used up their allotted physical therapy sessions. I can only help them so much with words. They need more. They need someone to give them hope by making them want to leave their wheelchairs. The guts to make them want to walk again. To stand with them, share their fears and desires. To be stronger than the pain, more caring than a prescription. Give them time, quality time. They need to learn to laugh at their past, smile at today, and beg for tomorrow . . . with a purpose. Do you know anybody like that, Michael Callahan?"

"I don't understand, Angela. How can someone have hope if there's no one to give it to them?" Callahan felt as empty as the room.

"I can't answer that, Michael. Even I have my limitations." Angela's eyes sparkled as she led him from the empty building. "But we all must keep dreaming. That's how we capture spirits."

Callahan started to speak, but she stopped him by gently placing a finger to his lips. "I have to go now. I'll talk to you soon."

"Where are you going?" Callahan had not felt her hand leave his.

"I have a large family to take care of. They need me."

"Are you married?"

"Oh, yes. Very much so. And it's a beautiful marriage."

Callahan watched as she walked away, behind the white building and out of view.

Keep your face to the sunshine and you cannot see the shadow.

~Helen Keller

CHAPTER SIX

"RUFUS!" THE KIDS heard the truck pull into the driveway and waited for ninety pounds of love to come flying at them.

"Watch out, here he comes!" Dog and kids met each other in the front yard, becoming a ball of fur, dead grass, and giggles. Callahan leaned against the fender and watched them play, enjoying the sounds. Margaret was standing in the front doorway, looking thinner than she had in some time. I must tell her I noticed, he thought, dog-earing the moment in his mind. She turned and disappeared inside the house without acknowledging his presence.

"Dad, I've got something in the house to show you that I did in school," Amy exclaimed, as she got to her feet and streaked toward the house.

"Me too," and Tommy was on her heels.

"Mind if I come in?" Callahan asked as he waited with the partially opened door in his hand.

"Mom, Dad's here!"

"Come on in," her response echoed from a distant bedroom.

Callahan felt strange entering the house from the front door. Something he never did when he lived there, always from the carport into the kitchen. A quick glance at the interior revealed Margaret's latest attempt at redecorating. The family pictures were no longer in sight, probably packed in a no-reminders box. The large beige and green couch, worn more on one end than the other, his favorite, was gone. The walls even looked different, the color had been muted with gray, the shade of a dove's feathers. Two pictures that he instantly disliked were on opposing walls. They were of two people, gender unknown, both unsmiling. He had not seen these before and frankly didn't care if he ever did again. I don't remember this feeling, he said to himself as his eyes continued to be confused. It was as if he had never lived there.

Rufus walked through the kitchen and to the hall, with nose in the air. The smells weren't the same anymore. He did remember how he could open the sliding screen door onto the patio. He turned and looked back, as if in disgust, and meandered out of sight. The dog was not fond of the house anymore. The feelings of comfort were gone for him.

Little fingers tugged at his hand, pulling Michael down the hallway and into her room. Amy's bedroom had subtle changes, although the little girl flowers on the walls and in the bedding were the same. Dolls and stuffed animals were being displayed rather than played with as she grew into different interests. Clothes and jewelry increased in importance, along with books and music. Posters of male musicians were tacked on the wall next to kitten pictures.

"See my book, Dad? I wrote it myself in school." Her soft blond hair bounced and her crystal blue eyes sparkled as she pounced onto the bed, patting a spot next to her for him to sit. "It's about us going fishing with Grandma and Grandpa in the White Mountains. And the lightning storm. Remember?"

"Sure do. That was some trip. We went to California first, to Disneyland. And then up through Nevada, back down to Northern Arizona. We camped for four or five days there, didn't we?"

"Yep. It's all in here," Amy smiled, flipping the pages. "And remember Mom got mad at you because you kept on fishing in a thunderstorm?"

"How could I forget?"

"You can have this after I turn it in for a grade. But you can read it first if you want."

"I'd like that," her dad smiled, kissing the top of her head.

"I'm pretty sure that we are going to get an offer on the house," Margaret said while sitting quietly at the kitchen table. "This couple seemed real interested."

"That didn't take too long," Michael leaned back in the chair and stretched his legs out in front of him.

"We knew it wouldn't. This is a nice house. The landscaping is beautiful and the room that you built. . ."

"*We* built," Michael interjected.

Slowly her eyes came to meet his, creating a language known only to her. She was an attractive woman, bearing the sharp features of her Welsh heritage. The once long, straight, dark brown hair was cut shorter now, curled up above the collar. She was tall, at five feet ten. Her weight seemed to fluctuate with her moods.

"You've lost some weight," he said, remembering his promise. "You look good." She chose not to respond.

"My picking the kids up tonight will give you a break and I really need some time with them."

"Yes, I could use some 'me' time." She stood to pour herself some coffee, and turned away before she spoke. This was easier for her and very much in character. "When are you going to find a real house to live in? It really worries the kids." She held the mug up to her lips, then added, "and me too."

"As soon as the house sells and I get some money. But I can't now, my money goes here. I don't need a lot of money to live in the camper."

"And you know I appreciate that," Margaret said. "And the kids, too."

"I know."

"Mom, where's my backpack for camping?" Tommy yelled from his room.

"Right where you put it. In your closet," Margaret shook her head. "I swear, that kid's room is a disaster."

"Like father, like son," Michael added. He stood and walked over to the door. Without speaking, he watched Rufus patrol the back fence, just like old times.

"Interesting, though," Margaret said as she turned and walked to his side. "Your gardens, your tool shed, your workshop were all immaculate. Wonder why the difference?"

"Individual space, I would guess. They were my nests. My own space. So personal, yet so meaningful to the family as a whole." Michael turned and surveyed the room. It was as if he were having closure with his former home.

"Why didn't we discuss these simple things before?" Margaret wanted to cry but could not. That was reserved for when she was alone. "We didn't communicate, did we? We never took the time to learn how to talk or to listen."

"We're ready, Dad. Let's go." Both children were laden with their backpacks and duffel bags, having mastered the procedure.

"Say goodbye to your Mother and get Rufus into the truck. I'll be right there." After hugs and kisses, the two children led Rufus out the front door, arguing their way to the camper.

"We never discussed what marriage meant to us. The give and take from a relationship and what we expected from a lifetime partner." Michael softly placed his hand upon her shoulder as he spoke. She gently laid her cheek on his fingers. They knew that they each had lost a mate, but would never lose a friend.

"I envisioned us growing older and better together," she added fighting back the tears, "but it's not going to happen."

"We aren't going far from each other. We will always have our children."

They turned and facing each other, wiped each other's tears and then held each other close, a closeness that would last a lifetime.

Both children occupied themselves with sketch pads and coloring books, as their father guided the truck from the city. The radio was silent. The only noises present were the soft scratches of scribbling crayons and the constant hum of the tires on the asphalt. Callahan curiously watched the normally chattering children content with the quiet time. Looking through the windshield in front of him, he reflected back to his own childhood when silence was a tool of punishment and a means of withdrawing affection. It was then that he realized the purpose for his retreat — it provided a time for healing.

Callahan took a deep breath and held it for a moment. He

exhaled slowly, feeling his body relax. He loved days like this. Days where the faint aroma of autumn leaves rode on the backs of soft southern winds. He loved the trees and the sounds they made when he drove by. The road was the same every time he made the trip to Bear Canyon, but the scenery was always different. The mountain shadows changed with the time of day or the assortment of clouds.

Rufus always knew when they were getting close to the campground. It was his spot and he loved showing it off, especially to the kids. The truck barely stopped before the children and the dog hit the ground running across the trickle of a creek and onto the rocks. Like place settings at a dinner table, they each had their own spot. Dad would be in the middle, Tommy on his left, and Amy on his right.

"Tommy, can you set my watch for me?" Callahan asked, slipping the Timex from his wrist.

"Sure can. Give it to me."

"Dad, may I ask you a question?" Amy said softly.

"It must be important if you need permission to ask it," Michael said quietly as he peered at his daughter.

"Sort of," she answered back, not looking at her father.

"Sure you can ask me a question. You know that. You don't need permission."

Amy pushed her hair back behind her ears, a nervous gesture he hadn't seen her use before. He gently moved his arm around her shoulder, knowing something was troubling his beautiful child. "Why did you go away? Why aren't you living at home anymore?" She now stared directly at him, looking far more mature than her nine tender years should allow. Amy didn't want just an answer. She wanted his answer and his reasons.

Tommy was busy programming his dad's digital watch, just the kind of endeavor he relished. He wasn't ignoring the conversation; it was just that his sister was very astute in her line of questioning. From the moment he had driven away from their home, Michael knew they would have a lifetime of questions, and regardless of the answers, his reasons would never validate his actions.

With his head bowed, he pulled his fingers through his hair, knowing his moment of reckoning with his children had arrived. He had played this scenario over and over again in his mind. He had dreaded this moment, but knew the reality of the situation must be confronted. Its effects would be felt for a lifetime.

"It's not a simple answer, Amy."

"Why not? It looked pretty easy for you to leave."

Callahan felt his heart explode and his breathing cease. "It wasn't an easy decision, it involved a lot of issues." After he spoke, he wondered if she knew what he meant by issues. She obviously did, but she didn't answer with words. However, her eyes spoke volumes. Michael looked up to the sky, afraid of what his eyes might reveal. For now, he must use words, if he could only find the right ones.

"Here's your watch, Dad," Tommy laid it on his father's lap. "What's an issue, and how many is a lot?"

"It's hard to explain, to put into words."

"Try, Dad. We would like to know your reasons. We need to know. You and Mom are our parents. You're supposed to be together." Amy's emotions were showing through and Tommy's were following suit.

Michael searched for words to say, to describe to his children what he didn't fully understand himself. He felt it was for the best — having his children come from a broken home rather than live in one. He wasn't getting along with Margaret, or Margaret with him, and it glaringly showed in the children's environment. Solitude was sought rather than loud verbal disagreements. How could he explain to them that he had a mistress and that the mistress was not a person? How could he explain to them that he had chosen his profession over his marriage? Could he make them understand that his job compelled him and simultaneously consumed him? He realized he would satisfy no one with his explanation, including himself.

"Well, your Mom and I weren't getting along and we decided it was best that we didn't stay together. . . married. . . anymore." Michael's words were getting very difficult to manufacture and it was showing in the strain of his voice, but it had to be done.

"Me and Amy fight and we're still together," Tommy said.

"Amy and you are brother and sister. That's a whole different kind of relationship. I will always be your Dad, and Mom will always be your Mom."

"Promise?" Tommy said, looking up at his Dad with tears in his eyes.

"Yes, I do," Michael said, placing an arm around Tommy's waist, pulling him close.

"But Dad," Amy interjected, "you said that to Mom and you promised and now you're not together. Didn't you mean it then?"

Both faces were upon him. Michael thought the only rational quick thought that was conceived for such situations — Oh Shit! He must answer and answer quickly, as any delay to a child was perceived as indecision.

"Yes, I did mean it. However, situations and feelings change. They can grow stronger, or if the relationship isn't right, the feelings weaken. And, no, I can see what you're thinking. It's not the same for the children." His work flashed in his mind. All too often this was not the case. Abandoned children, the aftermath of divorce, were growing in saddening numbers.

"I will always be here for you and your mother. That's a promise."

"Can we quit talking about issues now? I'm getting a head sore," Tommy said, rubbing his forehead.

"Headache, you're getting a headache," Amy corrected.

"It's my head and I'll call it sore if I want to."

"But you're wrong."

"Hey, c'mon now, no more issues," Callahan held his hand up and smiled. "I'll make a fire and we can tell ghost stories. And we have to get to bed so we can go hiking early in the morning."

"Not too early, though. Right, Dad?" Tommy yawned.

CHAPTER SEVEN

"STOP YOUR GROWLING," Callahan grumbled as he buried his head in the pillow. "Let me sleep." Rufus glanced at his master with a brief turn of his head and continued to growl, but softly, almost resembling a purr. Callahan opened one eye, then the other and tried to focus on Rufus' tail for an indication as to what was causing his concern. Slow moving tail, no drool meant kids were outside. Rapid moving tail, lots of drool meant girls were present, faster the tail, bigger the girl. However, this time was different, quick tail, no drool, large smile. He kicked off the cover and reluctantly rose. "This had better be good and worth my effort," he said in his best morning voice. Through the small side window, Rufus was watching a man, a man with a smile and a red tipped cane. He was standing alone with his hands to his face, the cane leaning against his thigh. Delicately and methodically his fingers caressed his eyes as he continued to smile into the mirror of his mind. The scene mesmerized Rufus and Callahan as they watched in stillness through the window in the camper. The gentleman gathered his long, thin, red tipped wand, and began to move about. Tapping a half moon arc in front, his every move was precise.

"Charlie," came a lady's voice from somewhere out of view, "we are going over to the restroom, be right back." He nodded in response, but said nothing as he raised his face to the warmth of the morning sun. He ran his fingers through his hair as if he were primping for a picture.

Charlie. Rufus liked the name Charlie and gave an appreciative lick to Callahan's cheek.

Charlie adjusted a pack that was secured around his waist. On his feet were hiking boots, politely touched by his Levis at the shoestrings. He took his denim jacket off, folded it neatly, and placed it on the rear bumper of a pickup truck. A tee shirt, somewhat snug, revealed an upper body that was not particularly defined, but obviously exercised. Not tall, but not short, and not overweight, Charlie looked every part the hiker, an outdoorsman. But that would be impossible, Callahan thought. The man is obviously blind.

"We're back," came the same voice as a tall female companion joined him. "Lead the way. You're the experienced hiker here. We'll follow and try to keep up." Charlie walked directly to the well-traveled mountain trail. He used his staff with the instincts of an orchestra leader and in an instant was out of sight. Rufus sighed a soft cry as he dropped to his belly, lowering his chin to his feet. He wanted to know more about the man he could feel.

"Rufus," Callahan said as he scratched furry ears, "Charlie may be blind, but he has more vision than most of us. In a way, he's like you, big fellow. You can't speak, but you say a lot." The large mound of love lay motionless as his master kissed him gently above both eyes.

The sun suddenly appeared above the mountain rim, with its warmth spreading to the canyon below. The sightless man had walked away into a world of his own creation. Man and dog sat there for a few moments, not speaking, letting the silence answer their questions.

Callahan opened the camper door to allow Rufus his space. Ordinarily, the obedient dog would sit and wait patiently for the release command before exiting. This morning was different. Rufus could not contain himself. He slithered in a belly crawl out the door and down the rear step to his backyard of nature. With his ears erect, the real life cartoon character tried to catch a glimpse of his special friend with the extraordinary senses.

The hiker and his friends were gone for now. Out of sight, but not out of scent. With his nose in the air, Rufus located their direction of travel. He first sat, then quietly lay down. He lowered his head, and with a snuggle, placed it on his paws. Callahan knelt down and stroked his companion, realizing why he loved him and other animals so much. They were intuitive, caring, with unconditional love, and no complications, similar to the way that Charlie viewed the world that only he could see.

"What's goin' on, Dad?" Amy yawned, peering down from the bed over the truck cab. "I heard you talking to someone."

"Rufus found a new friend and had to let me know about it."

"Who, Dad?"

"Just a hiker," Callahan smiled. "Maybe we'll get to see him again. I'm going to make us some breakfast and then we can go for a hike ourselves. Okay?"

"Good luck in waking Tommy up," Amy said, watching her brother pull the covers over his head.

Rufus heard the distinct rattle of his leash and knew that he had a hike of his own in the offing. He immediately rose and stood obediently by his leader, hoping with a glance that they would follow the same trail as Charlie.

"Not this time, big boy. Let's stay a little closer to our camp," Callahan said, sensing his dog's intent and desire. "Besides, they have to come back this way, and you wouldn't want to miss them."

The leash was attached with Rufus leading the way in front of the children. He first went left and briefly down, and after they crossed a trickle of a stream, they began to ascend up a small ravine. Critters scurried away as Rufus buried his nose in the trail of smells made from yesterday's feet.

"You're too strong for me, boy. Besides, you have your own agenda," Callahan said as he released the restraint. The ninety-pound German shepherd quickly found his way to the top first and waited, posing like a poster of Rin Tin Tin. Callahan followed, expecting the dog to continue on, but he didn't. Tracing the animal's stare, he found him to be watching the small figures of Charlie and friends, at least a half mile away in the ponderosa pines. Ten seconds later, they were out of sight.

"Why is Rufus being weird, Dad?" Tommy asked.

"Not weird, Tommy," Callahan smiled. "He's sensing something that only animals can."

"Now you're being weird, Dad," Tommy frowned. "Whatcha

mean?"

"That new friend," Callahan laughed, "that Rufus made, is blind. He's out there hiking in the woods, and Rufus knows it. He's just waiting for him to come back."

"For reals?" Amy asked, shading her eyes and looking off in the distance. "You suppose that me and Tommy can see him? You know, meet him?"

"I don't see why not." Callahan shook his head at his own choice of words. So many things we take for granted he thought, sight, speech, the ability to walk. "The people that were with him called him Charlie."

Charlie. The name made Rufus smile with several wags of his tail.

"We're almost back to the truck," came a voice that was not really known, but recently familiar.

With a soft cry, Rufus began a tail wag that invited his entire body to participate.

"I know," Charlie responded, "I can feel the dog."

"What dog?" another voice asked from the unseen people among the pine trees.

"The one that was watching us, along with his family, from inside a camper that parked next to where I was standing. I could hear him breathing, a large breed of dog." Charlie continued to walk and smile with the thoughts of his own companion stroking his mind. "We're almost back to the parking lot, Connie."

"You're amazing," she answered back, "truly a masterpiece by God."

Charlie honored her compliments with silence as he continued his skillful decent into the sparsely inhabited picnic area.

"Wait for us. Calm down," Callahan demanded of Rufus. "I need to put your leash on. And don't pull me. Stay next to me!" He had never seen the black and tan animal so excited before. "Hang on, Rufus. Let's go meet your friend, but I'm not going to be worth much if you drag me through these rocks."

Immediately, Rufus spotted the hiker and his whole demeanor instantly changed. It was as if the animal were among royalty. Stately and proud, he walked with his head at the left knee of his master. The leash was limp, its presence not required. Rufus knew he could be seen.

"Rufus. What a great name . . . Rufus," Charlie said as they approached. "It's English, you know. It means lion-like. And your name, sir?"

"Callahan. Michael Callahan."

"That's a great Irish name, sir," Charlie said. "And your children? What are their names?"

"I thought Dad said he was . . .?"

"Shh," Amy interrupted.

"May I?" Charlie asked, placing his hand in front of him, palm down.

"By all means." Callahan dropped his end of the leash from his hand. Without a word, the incredible dog met the incredible man, an amazing photograph of love. Rufus delicately licked the fingers of Charlie's hand, placing his nose into his palm.

The face of the man with the perpetual smile looked upward, staring into his own version of heaven. His hand now traveled the length of the German shepherd's body, painting a picture for his mind. Rufus smelled his arms, his clothing, and with a slight woof, asked Charlie for his cheek. They shared licks and nuzzles, and messages that no one else could hear. With an outstretched hand and no words, he asked for Michael's face to finish the sketch in his mind.

Callahan felt awkward, almost embarrassed, by the request.

"Go ahead," whispered Charlie's female companion. "He won't bite."

Charlie delicately touched each feature on Callahan's face, as if he were reading brail. Callahan smiled and it felt good. He realized it had been a long time since he smiled, really smiled.

"Ralph Waldo Emerson once wrote," Charlie said to his new friend. 'What lies behind us, and what lies before us, are tiny matters, compared to what lies within us.' I can feel your heart, Officer Callahan. Keep your smile forever. It shows your soul."

"Dad," Tommy blurted, "how does he know that you're a policeman?"

"My sister saw the Fraternal Order of Police sticker on the

windshield of your truck," Charlie laughed. "I was a police officer myself, until an accident took my sight."

"I'm sorry," Callahan said. "Where were you a police officer?"

"San Diego, and don't be sorry. I still do consulting work in law enforcement. I'm doing fine. You know what they say, once a cop, always a cop."

"And by losing my sight, Michael," Charlie continued, "I've learned to appreciate what I hear and not what I say. I've learned to hear what lies beneath the words, the moods, and the feelings around me, regardless of age or status."

Charlie bent down and gently shook the hands of Amy and Tommy. Knowing all too well what was coming next, he squinted his eyes up to receive the wet tongue from Rufus. The kids giggled and Rufus barked as Charlie stood and walked to his truck behind his wand.

"Take care of your Dad, kids," Charlie waved from the open window. "He needs all the angels he can get."

"Wow!" Tommy exclaimed, watching the truck drive away. "Can't wait to tell Mom."

As usual, their time together went quickly. When they arrived home, the kids rushed from the truck to tell their mother the details of their encounter with the unbelievable man they had met.

"And then, Mom . . ."

"Let me tell some," Tommy interrupted.

Callahan smiled, closing the door of the house on David Street behind him again.

When you come to the edge of all the light you know,
and are about to step off into the darkness of the unknown,
faith is knowing one of two things will happen:
There will be something solid to stand on
or
You will be taught to fly.

~Unknown

CHAPTER EIGHT

HIS DAY BEGAN WITH SUNSET. John Francis was not home when Callahan opened the old, slatted, redwood gate to let Rufus meander into the yard. He and John were taking different paths in life now, but he knew nothing had changed in their friendship. "I'll be back soon," he said to Rufus and Bonehead. Closing the gate behind him he studied his watch. It was 5:05 pm and time was about to take him into a different world. His shift was to begin in less than an hour and scheduled to end at 2 in the morning, but it seldom happened that way.

The world of law enforcement did not incorporate normal work hours or adherence to a Monday through Friday work week. Time for sit down dinners, perhaps a cocktail or two, something for all on television, and helping with the homework was often missed by the parent in uniform who patrolled the streets during the night hours. Getting ready for bed, story time, and some late night TV for Mom and Dad was for the stereotypical household. That was the other world. The community that law enforcement protected.

The hours at the end of a day were Callahan's world. They provided the dense emotional atmosphere that allowed for his detachment from other aspects of life. Working during the busiest, most stressful hours filled the void by creating diversion from his personal life. However, he was starting to realize that other passions in his life were suffering. Mood swings and solitude had replaced Barbie Dolls and catcher's mitts. He knew he couldn't go back, but where did the strength come from to go on? Pulling into his customary parking spot, he felt alone. Normally, a new squad of rookies would bring an excitement, an anticipation of the unknown. Not now. Not tonight. Pulling the keys from the ignition, he sat still. A rush of anxiety, no, more like a fear came over him. But, not the type of fear that caused the hair to stand up on his neck. It was more the kind of fear he felt way down deep inside. The panic kind of fear that tightened his chest and weakened his legs. The kind that took every bit of energy he could muster just to function.

He glimpsed his eyes in the rearview mirror. Instantly he looked away, but the message lingered. It was the gaze, the forlorn look, that he saw all too often in the vacant look of the homeless. Previously, the uniform had provided him strength, but even that wasn't working now.

For the first time, the walk across the street to the station required effort. His stomach produced an acid that climbed to his throat. He placed his hand in front of him to see if he was nervous enough to shake. His fingers were trembling. He pulled his hands behind him, out of sight. Callahan was used to being in control of his emotions, but presently his emotions were controlling him.

"Just the guy I've been looking for," greeted Callahan as he entered the elevator. "I need you to do me a favor." The voice and the hand that slapped him on the back was that of Al Molina, veteran sergeant and perennial pain in the ass.

Callahan stared at the elevator doors as they closed. He really wasn't in the mood for Molina right now and he let some time pass in silence before responding.

"Did ya hear me?"

"I heard you, Sarge. What can I do for you?" Callahan asked just as the brief ride ended.

Stepping from the elevator, Sergeant Molina peered up and down the hallway, making sure that they were alone. "I need your help in firing somebody . . . this worthless fuckin' rookie in my squad.

You're used to handling these dumb shits."

"If you've got a problem, Al, why don't you handle it yourself?"

"Because of all the paperwork and bullshit that goes with it, that's why. I ain't good at that kind of crap. Besides, that's what a training officer is for, to help us sergeants deal with the small shit." Molina's demeanor and command of the English language were as ugly as he was. He had an oversized head with eyebrows that resembled a pair of angry caterpillars. His face looked as though it had once caught on fire and someone had put it out with an ice pick. The Sergeant was definitely not a candidate for the next recruiting poster.

"So, you think terminating a new officer is small shit, *Sergeant* Molina?"

"Well, you know, if he can't hack it, let's get rid of him."

"What's so bad about your rookie, Al? What's he doing so wrong that you want to fire him?"

"You know, not one big thing, just a lot of little crap that he's been screwin' up," Molina said. "So, I'll talk to Johnson, and then you and Stark can see just how worthless he is. Then you fire his ass. He's just not up to standards."

"Standards? What in the hell do you know about standards, Molina? You've done things your own way for so long that you wouldn't recognize an operating procedure if it slapped you right in the mouth."

"This guy just doesn't have the balls to be a cop. He's a fuckin' wussy," Molina snarled. "You'll see."

"You got one particular incident in mind, Al?" Callahan was beginning to see the problem. The officer, whoever he was, was not one of Molina's good ol' boys. He didn't fit into Molina's veteran circle.

"Hell, I can't think of one right now. Maybe I just don't like him."

"Or maybe, he don't like you, Al."

"Ha! Everybody likes Big Al. Besides, I don't give a shit if some snot-nosed rookie don't like me."

"Yeah, Al. I'll talk to Vic. If the Lieutenant okays it, we'll take him."

"I owe you guys one," Sergeant Molina said as he hoisted up his pants and walked away.

"By the way, Sarge. What's this new officer's name?"

"Montoya . . . Alex Montoya."

"You're going to get hurt, my friend."

"What? What did you say?" Callahan asked.

They were alone in a room suited for forty. The pre-shift officer briefing had concluded, and as usual, Callahan waited for Sergeant Stark.

"And you just might get someone else hurt too," Victor said as his face took on new features. The often smiling, cherub looking face, suddenly became stern. He stared straight ahead, seeing nothing. The time had arrived for his observations to be heard, the one-on-one talk that he had spent restless nights dreading. Victor felt the eyes upon him. But, he couldn't turn his head to look. He pretended he was alone, just as he had rehearsed his deep thoughts to his dear friend, every night for a week.

"What are you talking about, Vic? You're screwing with me, right?" Callahan laughed, a phony laugh that dripped with fear and borderline anger.

"Your personal life is spilling over into your professional life. And, you of all people know that we cannot allow distractions, of any kind, to affect our work. It's a deadly mix."

"C'mon, Sarge, you know as well as I that . . ."

"Let me finish, Thump," Vic snapped as his eyes found their mark. "An example of what I am saying happened tonight. You sat in the back of the briefing room, arms folded, wearing your mood like a blanket. You were having your own private pity party. You have always preached unity, and the strength it creates, but tonight you presented a different picture. You say that you're 'one of them,' but you're not. These new officers see that and they perceive what you say as bullshit. And can you blame them? Think about it."

Callahan stared back.

"Believe me," the Sergeant continued, "this is so hard for me to talk about. But as your friend and supervisor, I have an obligation."

"Obligation to do what, Stark? Humiliate me? Or better yet, pull some fatherly bullshit." Callahan wasn't smiling anymore.

"You're on the outside looking in at your family . . . and you're doing it here as well. Your personal problems will work themselves out. But if you bring them out here on the streets, someone could get hurt."

"You're full of shit, Stark. I'm good at what I do. And I make you look good in the process."

They were face-to-face in the empty room.

"That's good, Callahan. That's real good. By attacking me, you get stronger. Give me a fuckin' break."

"You're the one that started this bullshit."

"Do you, for a second, think that you're the only person, the only cop, that's ever gone through this? Hell, no . . . and you know it. But what you are fighting, is control . . . or should I say, lack of control. It's eating your ass up and affecting your work and I can't let that happen."

"So write me up!" Callahan's eyes were on fire. "Fire my ass. If I'm not doing my job, then get rid of me."

"When I took the oath as sergeant, I swore myself to a sense of duty. You're making it tough on me right now. It's compromising our friendship. You're good at what you do, but . . ." Victor's voice trailed off as his emotions could only be put off for so long.

"But, what? Give me a break," Callahan kicked a chair, spinning it against the wall.

"Grow up, Callahan," Stark's voice sharpened as Callahan started for the door. "Or get the fuck out."

Callahan froze, his hand on the door.

"You're needed by everyone in your life," Stark continued, "all of you, not just parts and pieces here and there. Get your strength back, and walk like the man that you are."

Stark moved by Callahan pushing the door open. "Come on. We've got rookies to train."

"You grew up around here, didn't you, Alex?" Callahan said, pulling from the police unit parking lot and onto South 6th Avenue.

"About two miles from here, over by the base of A Mountain."

"Old area, huh?"

"The oldest. The Presidio, the beginning of Tucson, was not too far from this area. History tells that it was set up by an Irishman, Hugh O'Connor of the Royal Spanish Army."

"An Irishman?" Callahan asked as his eyes sparkled with the mention of his heritage.

"Yeah, they built a fort on this site. And a few years later, Apaches attacked the fort, but were turned away. From what I remember from school, it wasn't long after that they built walls around the presidio, and the city of San Austin del Tucson began."

"That's interesting stuff, " Callahan acknowledged. "This is quite a legacy that you live within. And you seem to know so much about it. How much education do you have, Alex?"

"Why? Would it make a difference?"

"No. Not at all. I was just curious as you come across as pretty intelligent."

"Thanks, it's just that I read a lot, history especially."

"No college?"

"No. After high school I had to go to work. It's what we did. Higher education was never considered."

"Maybe you should consider it," Callahan said looking directly at Alex. Their eyes met and a seed was planted.

Alex was quiet for a moment, but then continued, "My great-grandparents, even their parents, probably grew up here. Hell, everybody in the neighborhood and surrounding ones for that matter are related, in some way or another."

" I bet that makes for some great birthday parties," Callahan mused.

". . . and graduations and weddings. Sometimes, not in that order," Alex countered.

"That's not just exclusive to this neighborhood. It's everywhere," Callahan observed.

Callahan continued driving south. He had stopped talking, knowing that he had broken the ice. Looking from the corner of his eye, he noticed Alex had relaxed. This is good, Callahan thought. Now, to get his attention.

"You have three weeks. Three short weeks," Callahan remarked as he shifted in the seat.

"Three weeks." Alex held his breath. "To do what?"

"To become a cop, or seek other employment." Callahan stared directly into Alex's eyes.

"Should I just resign now?"

"That's entirely up to you. And if that's what you decide, let me know as soon as possible. I've got a lot of other officers to worry about."

"You sure know how to make a guy feel good," Montoya said, dropping his stare to the floor.

"I'm not here to give you a back rub. I'm here to save you from being terminated."

The patrol car rolled into traffic as Callahan lifted the radio microphone to his lips. "1-Baker-7, 10-8. We will be roaming Team 1 tonight."

The dispatcher acknowledged and Callahan stared silently at the microphone before placing it back. "You and Sergeant Molina didn't get along very well, I understand."

"Yeah, I heard that, too," Alex said, looking straight ahead, feeling the pain of the statement.

"What do you mean, you heard that? Don't you know?" Callahan snapped.

"No, I don't. He never talked to me. He never met with me in the field, except when he happened to be at a call that I was on. But that was very seldom. It was like I didn't exist." Alex appeared very weak. His voice quivered, as he fought back anger and disbelief. It was apparent that his present emotional state caused great discomfort for him.

"He didn't supervise you at all. Is that what you are saying?" Michael Callahan knew the answer because he knew Molina. He wanted Alex's answer.

"At debriefing he would correct my paperwork without any comment. When I joined the squad, he said, 'Don't call me. I'll call you.' And he wants to fire me because I'm not doing my job. Hell, to tell you the truth, I don't know what my job is. I'm really lost out here," Alex said as he looked away. And Callahan knew why. Big boys didn't cry, but, they could cry out.

"Did you try to talk to him about . . . ," Callahan stopped himself in mid-sentence. "Never mind. We're talking about Molina, enough said. How about the rest of the squad?"

"They're good guys, all of them, but they're Molina clones. All veterans doing their thing. Basically, they don't need that much supervision. They have the benefit of years of experience. Do you think it's too late? Think they'll fire me?" Alex's desperation was apparent.

"It's out of their hands now. It's up to you and how much you can learn in a very short time. The documentation on you by Molina was minimal. Nothing derogatory, just that you are not performing up to standards."

"Whose standards?" Alex asked. "His or the department's? There seems to be a vast difference."

Callahan was already impressed. The fire was there. There is a different person than the one that's been seen. Now, the question arose, how to save him in such a short time?

"Molina has told the powers to be that you are timid and weak. That remains to be seen. If you are, you won't last a week down here in the jungle. Does this mean that you are going to be under the microscope? You can bet your sweet ass you are."

Callahan took a deep breath and paused to look directly at Alex. Alex did not look back. Alex's jaw squared as he put a hand to his forehead and pulled his fingers through his hair to the back of his head, while still looking forward. It was as if many decisions were being made inside, from his heart to his badge. He was starting to realize that they were the same thing.

"You saw there was a problem, but didn't know how to address it or handle it. Correct?"

"Yeah, I knew there was a problem right from the start. I talked to a couple other rookies about their squads. They weren't having any problems with their sergeants. I began to think it was me. So I tried harder to become one of them. It didn't work. They just pushed me farther away, like an unwanted stepchild. I have talked more since I got in this car than I have in the last six months. Does any of this make sense to you, Callahan? I'm not a bad cop. I just don't know how to be a good one." Alex had made a statement. He had held his ground. He was ready to fight for what he wanted. Callahan did not answer Alex for a few moments. Weighing all that was said, he felt a hint of depression setting in. It was becoming immediately apparent that nothing in Alex's personality could warrant Molina's perceptions. The wrong person was on trial here. However, he couldn't defend Alex's actions nor condemn Molina's. What was done, was done.

"I can't change the experiences you had with the other squad," Callahan said, looking directly at the rookie. "Vic and I can help you now. But the bottom line remains: it's up to you. What do you want? Is this the life you want? It's not just a job. It's a way of life. You will become different than you are now, to everyone who knows you, including you. And sometimes, you won't even like yourself very much.

"And Alex, I can't feel sorry for you. There is no room for it out here. There is caring, plenty of caring, but no sympathy. Sympathy comes between shit and syphilis in the dictionary and that's all it's good for in our world. We must care, but we can't carry it. Emotion can kill us. It has killed us. So get over it. Go on or get out. Do you understand, Alex?"

Callahan held his breath, hoping and praying that he had done the right thing, hoping he had said the right words. It had to work.

"Tell me what I need to do," Alex said as he turned and looked directly at Callahan. "I understand what you're saying. Tell me what I have to do."

"How do you function when you are alone, one-on-one with yourself?"

Alex froze.

Callahan said nothing, sitting silently, waiting for Alex to answer without prompting. A minute or two passed with deafening silence. The mood and the criteria had changed.

"I . . . uh . . . answer calls and do what they tell me to."

"They?" Callahan asked sternly.

"You know, the dispatchers."

"So, what you do and your perception of police work is just that, 'Do what I'm told, nothing more, nothing less, and somehow

I'll get by?' Is that it, Alex? Is that what it's all about?" Callahan's bullet had found the target. "That's pretty much it, isn't it?"

"That's what I've been taught. In your first year, don't make waves, answer calls . . . the 'Yes, Sir,' 'No, Sir' kind of thing."

"Who are you, Alex?"

"Who am I? What kind of question is that? You know who I am. You read my . . ."

Callahan interrupted with flashing eyes, "Knock off the bullshit, Alex, and grow some balls. Everything has been comfortable for you, a neighborhood full of family taking care of one another. If you have a problem, go to your family, there is no need to go further. If they can't help, go to another part of your family."

"But . . ."

"Shut up, Alex, and listen."

He did.

"There is nothing wrong with that. In fact, I envy you. I wish I had that kind of environment, to a point. However, you need to be your own person to grow and to find yourself. I'm not telling you anything you don't already know. I can see it in you. You are not weak, or meek, or timid. You just give that appearance. You know who you are. So damn it, go there. And go there now."

CHAPTER NINE

THE SPEED LIMIT ON South Park Avenue was 35 mph and the speedometer on the police cruiser reflected 2 mph less. The street was all but deserted at 12:25 in the morning with just an occasional vehicle passing the squad car like a kitten on carpet. Callahan had his say. Whether Alex had heard or listened remained to be seen.

"Callahan, you don't know how bad I want to be a cop."

"1-Adam-44 . . . do you need a 10-84?" the dispatcher asked.

"Hold your thought, Alex," Callahan said holding his hand up.

"If you got one close by," 1-Adam-44 responded, drawing the words out like it was painful to speak. "If not, don't worry about it."

"1-Baker-7, we'll head over."

"Does that guy always talk like that?" Alex asked, looking like he'd just smelled something foul.

"O-n-l-y o-n t-h-e r-a-d-i-o," Callahan answered, imitating the voice. "Strings is a bit different."

"Strings?'

"That's what everyone calls him. He's a musician, world-class guitar player. Without a doubt, the best I've ever heard."

"What in the hell is he doing being a cop?"

"We went through the Academy together. When I found out how good he was at the guitar, and the banjo, and all kinds of other instruments, I asked him that. He said he wanted the excitement." Callahan switched lanes, shoving the accelerator to the floor.

"He doesn't sound real excited," Alex smiled.

"Strings has worked Beat Four for at least five years I know of. He knows every crook and cranny in the area. I don't know how he does it," Callahan said, turning off on Park Avenue and onto 36th Street. "Every nationality and a hundred head of livestock live in his boundaries."

Strings' God given name was Stephen Sinclair. He was barely over six feet, with a head not matching his body. He was a dark-haired man with a receding hairline, dark brows and a broad, flushed face. His body was thin, except for a small paunch above his belt line, not expected on a man with a slight build. Long fingers extended from large hands and oversized forearms. Strings looked like he was put together by a blindfolded person playing Mr. Potato Head.

Callahan drove east and started to slow as he approached Forgeus Street. He made a right, looking for Cochise Avenue. Finding it, he made another right. The street was only one block long and then it stopped. It wasn't a cul-de-sac; it just stopped. In the middle of the street, forty-feet from the end, was a squad car. It wasn't at the curb, but in the middle. No emergency lights were on; it was just sitting there.

At the same time, Callahan and Alex saw them. Six or seven people were fighting, throwing punches, kicking at each other. "Can you see Strings?" Callahan asked.

"Yeah," Alex answered, not believing what he was seeing. "He's sitting on the hood of his car."

Callahan turned his overhead lights on, stopping behind the parked police car.

"Kill those lights, Callahan," Strings ordered. "You're goin' to piss 'em off."

The emergency lights went off. Strings was sitting cross-legged on the hood of his police unit when Callahan and Alex, bearing night sticks, ran to his car.

"Slow down," Strings smiled. "There's eight fools fightin' over there. If you joined in, that would make ten. Just stay cool. When they get done beatin' the shit out of each other, we'll take the winners to jail and the losers to the hospital." He was now laughing. "Looks like the League of Nations, doesn't it Callahan?"

Shouts of, "you motherfucker, I'm goin' kill your ass," or "wha'cha got, somebitch, show me," came from back-pedaling, fist-throwing people.

"That guy over there has a gun!" Alex shouted, placing his hand on his revolver and taking a three-point stance.

"If he aims it at you, shoot him," Strings said, without looking at Alex. "If not, relax. They all have guns, brother, and you can't reload fast enough to shoot 'em all. Just calm down."

Callahan watched as two males took center stage and squared off. He looked at Strings.

"I'll bet on the smaller one," Strings smiled.

"Damn it, Strings!" Callahan yelled. "You can't just sit and watch them."

"I would if you weren't here. This shit happens all of the time." Strings threw phony punches into the air.

Two more joined in the fight, one being a female.

"All right, all right. That's it." Strings stood from his car. "Is anybody hurt?" he asked the group.

"Fuck you, Strings," a voice answered.

"Ain't no time for romance," Strings yelled back. "Now, get your asses out of here before someone calls the cops."

"You da the man, Strings," a large black man hollered. "And so's those dudes witch ya."

"See, you've gone and done it," Strings said, walking in their direction. "Go on home."

The street emptied. Music began to blare from every direction. Strings began to sway back and forth, walking slowly, his hands on a guitar made from air.

"Can you meet me down by the Circle K?" Strings asked Callahan.

"Sure. C'mon, Alex."

"I'm not believing what I just saw," Alex said, shaking his head. "I've lived here all my life, and I still ain't believing it. Strings is nuts. He's crazy."

"I hear ya," Callahan smiled. "But, that's police work, Alex. That's what I was talking about. Being able to adapt. That shit you just saw can't be taught in any Police Academy."

"Alex," Callahan continued, pulling behind the convenience market. "That's not normal what you saw, and not everybody can do that. Strings is not accepted by other cops. He's a loner. Other cops don't like loners. He doesn't hang out with them and practice shooting. He's got his music, and most of them can't understand that. He doesn't go to 'titty bars' and all of that other bullshit." Callahan stared out the window. "We have a lot in common."

The headlights of another police car bounced through the vacant lot behind the store. Strings did not pull next to Callahan's vehicle, as customary, but instead, parked to the side. He got out, walked to Callahan's car, and leaned in the window.

"Nothing against you, Buddy," Strings said, "but I need to talk to Callahan alone. It's kind of personal." He winked at Alex. Alex nodded and smiled.

"What's up?" Callahan asked, walking with Strings away from the cars.

"Tell that other Mexican guy in your squad that he doesn't have to try so hard to be a bad ass."

"Padilla?"

Strings nodded. "That guy's going to have a short career if he keeps doing what he did tonight."

"What happened?"

"Padilla was a backup to me on a 10-31. There wasn't any violence, just a bunch of yelling and screaming and finger pointing. The usual crap at family fights. I told him to take the husband aside and calm him down, but just the reverse happened. Your man started shoving this guy around, to the point that he pushed Padilla away from him, and Padilla went berserk. I stepped in and pulled the husband away, telling Padilla to get the hell out of there. I told him that he was over-reacting and that's how cops get hurt. He said something under his breath and stormed out. Asshole."

Shaking his head, Callahan looked past Strings, visualizing what he was being told.

"I have a lot of respect for you, Thumper. I wanted you to know what's going on with this kid, just in case it's some sort of pattern with him. We're here to stop problems, not create them."

"Thanks, Strings. I appreciate you telling me this. This isn't the first time someone has told me about his temper, or whatever it is." Something had to be done, Callahan thought, knowing now that others were aware of Richard Padilla's tendencies. But what?

"Oh, one more thing, Thumper. You got some time tomorrow? You're off, right?"

"Yeah, sure." Callahan watched Strings paw at the ground with the toe of his boot. "Something must be really bothering you."

"I need to talk to you, that's all. I kind of need some advice."

"I'm not exactly the best guy to get advice from these days, Strings."

"The hell you're not. You know me," Strings said, looking at Callahan.

"I'll be over at Stark's house."

"Nevermind. The Sarge doesn't like me, I don't think."

"That's not true, but even if it was, he's not going to be there. I'm watching his house for him the next couple of days. Come on over. Bring your guitar."

"You sure?"

"See you about 6 or so tomorrow night. I'll write his address down for you."

Walking out into the night, Callahan pulled his keys from his pocket, looking at them as if they were to provide him some sort of entertainment. The moment began to blanket him with loneliness. He glanced over his shoulder at the parked patrol cars as if he were leaving friends. They represented violence, but they also presented authority. It was control, his control. He was good at what he did because of confidence. But now, the doubts began.

Slowly he found his way up the insignificant grassy hill behind the station, ignoring the concrete walkway. His normally confident walk was less than assured and he knew weakness, his silent adversary.

As he walked towards his truck, the man that could visualize everything saw nothing. He began to shuffle, his head down, not observing the headlights approaching from a remote side street.

The old truck slowed down, recognizing that the pedestrian with his head down was not about to yield. The driver's eyes watched intently from the idling vehicle as Callahan passed by.

"Hey, Callahan!" Alex shouted from his window. "Are you all right?"

"What?" Callahan turned, shielding his eyes from the glare of the headlights.

"It's Alex, man. You OK?"

"Oh yeah. I'm fine. See you tomorrow." Callahan turned, waved a hand, and continued to cross the street with a walk of determination.

"Thanks, brother. I won't let you down. What you said tonight made a lot of sense. I was feeling sorry for myself. I was weak. You gave me the confidence to become strong again. You won't regret what you are doing for me . . . and my family."

The truck shuddered as the worn clutch released, taking Alex back to the barrio. Callahan took a step onto the curb and felt a little embarrassed as Alex's words began to seep into his brain. Physician, heal thyself. With his next step, however, Callahan became taller, his moves, athletic. God had whispered. Callahan had heard.

Do not go where the path may lead
Go instead where there is no path
...and leave a trail.

~Ralph Waldo Emerson

CHAPTER TEN

THE STARK'S HOUSE was anything but. Simple design and small square footage made it appear at first glance to be a run of the mill neighborhood dwelling. But, a larger than normal front yard, landscaped to perfection, gave the house its own distinction. The eclectic interior, mirroring the personality of those who lived there, was homey and comfortable. Color, lots of color, most of it reflecting the culture of the Southwest, shone throughout the home. A small guest house, situated just a few steps from the main dwelling, served as a party room with a pool table, TV, and wet bar. Wrought iron railings and indigenous plants bordered a flagstone patio surrounded by an impeccably manicured green lawn, kept that way the year round. The house itself was small, but the home was large.

Rufus and Sam, the Stark's oversized Basset Hound, were lying next to each other in the comfort of the grass quilt. Totally opposite by breed and exactly alike by nature, they shared the same philosophy: cause no problem, be no problem.

The temperature was changing as the wind escorted a predicted summer monsoon into the valley. Callahan's bad posture in a good patio chair, plus the breeze and two less than aggressive dogs set the stage for a very relaxing evening. If only his thoughts would permit him to enjoy his surroundings. He knew his mind wouldn't allow him to get comfortable because the environment wasn't his. It was borrowed. Signs of a child at play littered the backyard, adding sadness to anxiety. He missed his children and he missed his home. But, at least for the present, he couldn't afford to be weak.

Jennifer Stark was a kind, gentle woman, masked in a physique suited more for a lumberjack than a critical care nurse. Her square, stout body and short, boyish haircut did not suggest the gentleness of the angel inside. Police wives were in a special class all their own, continuously hardened by what might happen every time their loved ones walked out the door with gun belt and badge. And Jenny's own chosen profession presented a double-edged sword of stress. She was a nurse in the burn unit of St. Mary's Hospital, dealing with the critical of all critical. The pain that she felt ran deep. It was seen in her job and lived in her life. She was special. Callahan knew it and from her he drew strength.

"Sara said that she ran into you in the grocery store this morning," Jenny said, trying to conceal a smirk.

"Did she?" Callahan said, his face beginning to redden. "Jenny, I've never been so embarrassed in my life."

IT WAS SATURDAY MORNING, about a quarter past ten. He had slept late, having spent the night parked on the side of John's driveway. John was up and gone, but his front door was ajar, an invite for Callahan to make use of what he needed. He took a quick shower and drank a shot of way too strong coffee. Whether he wanted to or not, he realized he needed to eat. He remembered seeing a grocery store just a few blocks away.

"Stay cool while I'm gone," he requested with a kiss to the forehead and Rufus slithered from the cab to the camper.

Once inside the store, Callahan realized he had no idea what he was looking for. Slowly he began to cruise the aisles. Something that came in a can and something else that went between bread. That would work. Beans, lunchmeat, and bread that didn't get soggy when you put too much mayonnaise on it. Pure genius, he thought.

In the next aisle he heard a child, a girl of maybe seven or eight, talking about anything and everything, and all at once. That reminded him so much of Amy. He paused. That's the kind of stuff that hurts. At the end of the row containing potato chips and dips, he saw the child as the child saw him. They smiled together, in one of those "You're OK" looks. Callahan then froze and backed behind the canned vegetables. Sara! That child was talking to Sara!

Sara Conners moved on to the next aisle as he watched her from in between the 'new and improved' creamed corn and the French cut green beans. The uniform was absent. She was wearing a colorful full-length skirt, and a long sleeve, white cotton blouse, ironed to perfection. As she turned to search the shelves, she bore a hint of a smile that complimented a face that was exquisitely highlighted with just the right amount of make-up. Her hair was pulled back in ponytail fashion, but the small descending curls gave her simple appearance a touch of class. She really was very soft, he thought.

Why did I duck away? Way too old Levis, a sweatshirt that used to advertise something, and whiskers. That's why. As he turned the corner a large lady piloting a shopping cart filled with items that gave cardiologists job security, ran directly into his thighs.

"I'm sorry," she said with a wink. "I didn't see you."

"No problem," he answered.

Sara hadn't seen him. Thank God for small favors. He quickly exited the store, and walked directly to the camper, trying to separate emotion from desire. He started his truck and drove past the front of the store to perhaps catch one more glimpse of her. Why am I doing this? Jesus, I feel so juvenile. "Let's get out of here," he said aloud to Rufus. He accelerated away from the store as he shook his head, ashamed at his actions and perplexed by his thoughts.

Rufus was looking and sniffing the cab with his head protruding from the camper. "Calm down. I'll get you something to eat when we stop." The dog continued to search, not finding much in the way of an appealing odor. And then Callahan felt his stare.

"What? It's over there in the bag," he said, pointing to the floor, but there wasn't a bag. "Oh, Shit. What in the hell is wrong with me?" he said. Disgusted, he directed the truck back into the lot.

"Like you've never made a mistake," he snarled at Rufus. He was sure he heard the dog laugh as Callahan disappeared into the store.

"Mommy!" The word welcomed him as he came through the automatic door. It brought fear, because he knew whose voice it was. "That's the man that smiled at me through the potato chips."

"Fancy seeing you here again," Sara smiled politely, delicately extending her hand to him.

"Again?" he asked, letting her fingers fall into his hand.

"Yes, again. I saw you watching me before. You should really work on your surveillance techniques." Sara studied him for a reaction as Abigail tugged at her skirt.

"Who is he, Mommy?"

"This is Mr. Callahan, dear. He's also a police officer."

He followed her eyes as she did a quick inventory of his clothing. "Sorry I look like this, but . . ."

"Don't worry about it." Sara was far too nice to be condescending, but he got the feeling that she was somewhat disappointed. "And by the way, your cart is over there." She smiled. All he could manage was an embarrassed grin. He had no idea what to say or feel.

Abigail stood looking up at them both. She tried to understand their conversation, but gave up. Instead, she gave a tug on her mother's skirt and leaned toward the door.

Sara gave in to her daughter's demand and began to walk. "Give me a call," she said softly. "Quit jumping over your shadow."

Sara squeezed his forearm as she walked away. She continued to smile, but this time it was somewhat forced. He didn't watch her leave, but he felt her go as her words hung heavy in the air.

"What are you looking at?" Callahan asked Rufus as he climbed into the cab. "Yes, I've got your food. As if you would starve to death if I didn't. Let's go up the hill. I've had enough of this city life for awhile." He drove, but his mind remained with Sara's touch, producing yet another guilt. When she placed her hand on his arm, an excitement that was dormant came to life. He fought to replace his feelings of exhilaration with the rules against fraternization. But, we're officers of equal rank. There's no impropriety. I have to get her out of my mind. But I can't. I need to talk to her. I'm tired of listening. I want someone to listen to me. Someone soft. Someone caring.

To hell with it. Keep driving.

"SHE'S HERE AND she's coming out to say hello, so don't

go acting weird on me," Jenny said, punching him playfully. You guys knew each other before the Police Department, I hear?"

"Yeah, I met her when I was going to the U of A. Small world, isn't it?" Callahan watched her step from the patio to pick up her son's toys.

"Or fate," Jenny smiled. "She's going to watch Willie this weekend. The two kids play so well together and it will be good to get away. Well, better go. Thanks for watching the place for us. Sam really likes having Rufus around."

"He could give a shit, Jenny, and you know that."

"I know, see ya later." With an armful of toys, she nudged open the sliding door and passed Sara, who was on her way outside.

"Twice in one day," Sara said, walking to an old wooden cable spool that Callahan was using as a chair. "What a coincidence."

"Jenny says it's fate and that I should sweep you off of your feet, pull you up onto my big, white horse and ride into the sunset." Boy, am I glad I changed clothes, he thought.

"Really?" Sara raised an eyebrow and smiled.

"Well, kind of," Callahan shrugged. "I added the part about sweeping and the horse."

"So, the only part she contributed was about it being fate?"

"Pretty much."

"It seems like a long time ago, doesn't it? But, it's only been, what, two or three years?" Sara smiled.

"More like four or five," Callahan answered. "I remember you asking a lot of questions about police work and what it would take to become an officer."

"Who would believe that I counseled you in what classes to take at the University, and now the roles have reversed, with you giving the advice."

"Somehow, I don't think it's quite the same, Sara," Callahan smiled. He turned and pulled a chair to her, inviting her to sit. "A bit more intense, wouldn't you say?"

"Just a bit," she smiled. She sat in the chair, one leg crossed beneath her. Rufus wandered over to her, sniffed, and then turned in circles before curling up by her side. "The job seemed so intriguing. It all seemed so fascinating, so glamorous."

"And now, after being on the job for awhile, what do you think?" Callahan knew her answer. He could see it in her face. Her softness was there, but beginning to be tainted by uneasiness. "It's cruel, Michael. And exhausting. The job consumes you, but, I like the work."

Callahan studied Sara as she spoke. I love her looks, he thought. And her honesty. She likes the work, but not the pain.

"I have to go now, Michael. But, could you call me sometime? I would love to talk more with you. You have a great sense of humor and I need to laugh more."

Callahan looked surprised.

"Was I being too forward?" she asked.

"No, not at all. I'm flattered. And I need to laugh more, too."

Just as they stood, Vic stepped from the doorway, followed by Strings, with his ever-present guitar case at his side.

"I hope I'm not causing you to leave," Strings frowned.

"Oh, no," Sara smiled, touching his arm. "I'm taking the kids for pizza."

"Why don't you come back with the kids after you eat?" Callahan asked.

"Thank you, I just might do that."

"I need your advice in making a decision," Strings said nervously.

Vic looked around, wanting to be somewhere else. He knew this conversation was going to get too personal and that always made him uneasy. Vic looked to Callahan for help. Callahan nodded slightly toward the house and Vic stood from his chair. Teamwork.

"Gotta go, Strings."

"Later, Sarge." Strings half stood, extending his hand.

Jenny waved from the kitchen, as did Sara. Strings picked up his guitar case and placed it on his lap. He flipped open the latches and pulled the cover back to reveal his beautifully designed guitar sitting on a bed of blue velvet. As if he were lifting a newborn from a cradle, he gently raised the guitar from its case, placing the case at his feet. He pressed the back of the guitar against his stomach and began to lightly strum it with his ear close to his fingers. His fingers moved the six strings with the precision of a surgeon.

Callahan felt the goose bumps form on his arms as he witnessed his friend's transformation into genius. Effortlessly, Strings brought the Spanish guitar to life with each gentle stroke. The same few notes seemed to be repeated over and over, but gaining intensity. After a brief pause, he stroked his fingers across all of the strings and repeated the original quick notes. Faster and faster, his fingers moved like lightening. His incomparable rendition of "Leyenda" was mesmerizing. The intensity of his talent was present in every note. It wasn't fair, Callahan thought, that he only had an audience of one. Strings continued, until the song softly closed with delicate notes, much like "Amen" at the end of a prayer. Strings bowed his head over his guitar, showing the love he possessed for his music.

"Incredible, Strings. My God, you have an amazing talent. I've never heard anything like that in my life." Callahan was in awe. "That's not just music that can be heard. It touches you."

"Thank you," Strings smiled. "That is a beautiful compliment."

"Where did you learn to play like that? Did you study music in school?"

"Yeah, I did, but my mother was a music teacher and an accomplished musician herself."

"Spanish guitar, also?" Callahan asked.

"No. The piano."

"What got you interested in the Spanish guitar?"

"When I was young, my mother took me to a Carlos Montoya concert," Strings grinned. "I was hooked. And then I studied the music of Celin Romero and Julian Bream. They are incredible masters of the guitar."

"And so are you, my friend." Callahan nodded.

"Nah, I'm not to their level, but thanks just the same."

"What's on your mind, Strings?" Callahan leaned forward in his chair. "What do you need to talk about?"

"My father," Strings began, "was a captain in the Philadelphia Police Department." Strings glanced at Callahan expecting a response, but didn't get one. Somehow, his father's credentials failed to impress.

"He was married, but not to my mother," Strings continued. "Thirty-three years ago, he had an affair with a woman from a prominent local family. She was married to an influential politician. This woman became pregnant with me and tried to keep it hushed, knowing the obvious problems the situation could cause. My father insisted on an abortion. She refused, and subsequently, their indiscretion was brought to light. My father's wife divorced him, taking everything he had. My mother stayed married to the politician, however, to avoid scandal, nothing was made public. But the politician put a thumb on my father's advancement within the department. When I was born, a dear friend of my mother's immediately adopted me. She was a single woman who was a Professor of Music at Temple University. The arrangement was for us to relocate, somewhere far away, and we did — to Flagstaff, and here I am. My new mother never married; she devoted her life to me and to music."

"Have you had any contact with your biological mother?" Callahan asked.

"No, just my father. About twelve years ago I called him. It was his fiftieth birthday and I wanted to let him know that I was thinking of him. Big mistake." Strings carefully placed his guitar back in its case. He did not look up.

"Why was it a mistake?"

"Because he said that allowing me to be born was a mistake, that he should have insisted on an abortion. He said my birth ruined his life. He's a bitter man. And somehow, he figures it's my fault." He rose to his feet and took a few steps away. "But, that's enough about him."

Callahan stared at the grass in front of him. He knew there were no words he could say to Strings that would ease his pain. 'I'm sorry' would be useless. The conversation wasn't a conversation anymore. They didn't notice the sleepy evening with the cooling breezes. The environment hadn't changed, but the atmosphere had.

"I need to talk to you about my girlfriend," Strings said, taking his guitar from the case and sitting back in his chair. "We don't live together."

"Is that the decision that you have to make? Whether you should live together or not?" Callahan asked with a smile.

"No," Strings answered quickly. Turning, he spoke softly as he lightly strummed the strings of his guitar. "She's pregnant and I don't know what to do."

Callahan remained seated, digesting String's statement. "What do you mean, 'advice in making my decision'?" Callahan asked as he stared at Strings.

"I have that conversation with my dad from 12 years ago in my head. I'm kind of in the same situation."

"Is your girlfriend married?"

"No, but we've never talked about marriage. What if I have the same feelings about the child that my father had about me? You know, that we had to get married because of .... you know." Strings nervously massaged his guitar.

"What does your girlfriend want to do?"

"She wants to have the baby."

"I'm not going to ask you if you're going to get married. That's something that you and . . .?" Callahan paused, waiting for a name.

"Elizabeth," Strings smiled, his entire face lighting up.

"Marriage is something that you and Elizabeth will have to decide. But my question to you is, 'do you love her?' That's more important. And you can bet that your father didn't love your mother. It sounds like to me, that she was more of a trophy."

"You're probably right, Thumper," Strings nodded. "I've never looked at it like that before."

"And I can also guarantee, just from the look of you when you said, 'Elizabeth,' that you love her very much. You already made your decision, Strings. That's why you're here. You just wanted some validation, and you got it. From what you have told me about your father, he has created his own problems. Let him figure them out for himself. You are a man, and soon to be a father. And a damn good cop. Don't worry about what you have no control over. You have your own concerns." Callahan put an arm around String's shoulder as Strings looked to the ground and nodded.

"Thanks, Thumper," Strings said, apparently relieved. "Your words helped a lot. It's good to have a friend. Especially now."

"We're in this together. That's what friends are for. You have to keep your circle tight." Callahan pushed Strings playfully away. "Are you hungry, Strings?"

"Sure. I'm always hungry."

"Good. A trade, food for music." Callahan took the baseball cap from his head and held it in front of him as he folded the bill inward. Now that it was just right he placed it back on his head and moved closer to the grill, joined by Rufus. Callahan opened the lid on the grill and moved his finished product to one side, away from the intensity of the heat.

"You don't teach, Michael Callahan," Stings said in a much different tone. "You explore. You reach into others and pull out what they want to be, whether they know what that is or not. And that is your gift. You play music in a different way. That is your calling."

Callahan smiled, but did not say anything. He slowly twirled a glass in his hand, studying the ice cubes. It was as if his mind were thousands of miles away, and it was.

Sara Conners had heard their conversation in its entirety. She didn't mean to. It just happened that way. She had left the children in front of the television and was walking to join them when she observed the intensity of their discussion. Off to the side, she spotted a chair under a tree and sat. The dialogue was not for her ears, but she could not leave. She had heard too much and her departure would be noticed, so she remained within the shadows. However, both Strings and Callahan had been aware of her presence.

"It's okay, Sara," Strings said as he sat in his chair. "I'm glad that you heard."

"I didn't mean to overhear. It's just . . ." Sara started to say, but stopped.

"What, Sara?" Strings asked. "What were you going to say?"

"I was going to say," Sara was on the verge of tears as she stared at her hands. "That I know what it's like to feel alone and need someone to talk to."

"I know," Strings smiled. "It's amazing how you can feel alone in a room full of people."

"And sometimes how crowded you feel being by yourself," Sara added.

Strings nodded, taking a deep breath. "How about you,

Thumper, you ever felt like that?"

Callahan took a few seconds to answer. "Have you guys ever watched ice?" he asked, his eyes fixed on his clear water glass containing several cubes.

"And how many beers have you had?" Strings asked as he winked at Sara.

"No, no, I'm serious. Have you?"

"Yeah. Hasn't everybody?" Strings answered. "What in the hell are you getting at?"

Callahan reached for the glass as he pulled his slouching body to an upright position in the chair. "I was twenty-one years old when I landed in Vietnam."

Sara and Strings again exchanged glances, but this time they were not smiling. Neither officer was aware that their coach had suffered that experience.

"A handful of us were crouched inside an 8x8 concrete bunker during a mortar attack," Callahan continued as his face hardened and his words became careful, "the explosions came in spurts. Thirty, forty seconds at a time. But the blasts were not as stressful as the silence in between. When you heard the bombs hit, you knew that you were alive. But the silence came. Your mind, your ears would be searching for noise. Some guys would hum softly, barely audible. Others would pray."

Neither of Callahan's friends moved as he set the glass down and fished a cold beer from the cooler between the chairs.

"But one night, during an attack, a soft spoken voice asked that question, 'Have you ever watched ice?' No one answered. We all sat still, wanting the voice to continue. And it did. It was so dark. Unbelievably dark."

"'Ice,' the voice continued, 'is strong, as long as it remains frozen. It can cut and it can hurt. It can destroy. But once warmth comes, it starts to change forms. Its harshness begins to melt and the ability to be harmful trickles away.'"

"Just then," Callahan paused for a drink and then continued, "another mortar hit and we heard it. And this time it hurt us. Concrete and dirt flew everywhere as the darkness was interrupted by flashes and screams."

"And the last words that I heard from the voice were, 'to melt the ice, you must hold it close, and dance with it. You must dance with the ice.'"

"And those of us that could, ran. Ran to ditches. Anywhere, trying to find someplace safe, even if it was temporary."

"I never saw the person that spoke those words," Callahan said softly. "I don't know if he lived or died. But, even after all these years, when I am all alone, I will sit still and wish the voice would continue."

CHAPTER ELEVEN

"IS STARK HERE YET?" Callahan asked Sergeant John Donahue, the front desk Sergeant. Donahue was approximately two months, three weeks, five days, four hours and twenty-one minutes from retirement. He didn't see much and what he did see, he didn't care much about.

"Nope, I haven't seen him," was Donahue's response, not bothering to look up.

"You're going to miss me when you retire, aren't you Sarge?" Callahan smiled.

"Yeah, Callahan. I can already feel the pain," Donahue answered with a smirk.

It was shortly before 5 p.m. on Tuesday evening, almost an hour before his shift began. This was customary. Being punctual was one of his trademarks. His military background was a reason, but his upbringing was the cause. Being late just wasn't tolerated.

Callahan pulled himself from the stimulating conversation with the sergeant and walked to the supervisor's area to retrieve the incoming paperwork for Team One, Squad Seven.

"Donahue said you weren't here." Callahan chuckled, finding Vic perusing the departmental mail.

"He did it again," Vic answered, not looking up, "he got me confused with himself. John is the one who's not here. How long is it before he retires?"

"About two years ago," Callahan mused.

"You're with Hoyt tonight, right?" Vic asked as he laughed at Callahan's last statement. "He's doing a good job out there, don't you think?"

"Yeah," Callahan answered. "Four weeks ago, I would have said no. It took awhile for him to lose that chip on his shoulder, but since then, he has done really well. He works with a kind of quiet arrogance."

"What changed him?" Vic asked. "It happened all of a sudden, didn't it?"

"JUST DO MY JOB, and don't make waves." David Hoyt turned his police unit onto a side street and stared straight ahead. I don't want to be super cop. Just a cop, one of many. And to be left alone, he reasoned to himself. Raised in a family with brothers much older than he made him basically an only child. His sport of choice was long distance running. Again he was alone.

"Damn hair," Hoyt said aloud as he tilted the rearview mirror toward him. "It's never turned out the same way two days in a row in my life." He harshly readjusted the mirror as if it were the mirror's fault that his hair had its own agenda. Out of the corner of his eye, he caught sight of a loud, black Chevrolet as it accelerated through a red traffic light. That guy could hurt somebody driving that way, he thought as he turned his police unit in the opposite direction. Hoyt detested the thought of creating a confrontation. He would respond to adversity, but disdained the idea of instigating controversy. Solve problems, don't manufacture them. His education, his college, had taught him that very principle. Until he quit.

"1-Adam-7 to 1-Adam-33."

Callahan's calling me! What's he want? *Shit!* I couldn't have screwed up. I haven't done anything. "Go ahead."

"What's your 20?"

"Irvington and Liberty." Damn!

"10-45 me at 12th and Ajo, northeast quad. In the shopping center next to Walgreens."

Michael Callahan studied his fingers as they tapped the

steering wheel of his idling vehicle. Nine days ago he had teamed with Hoyt for their first shift together. It had been uneventful in terms of police activity as well as personal interaction. He had written it off as the new officer being cautious and apprehensive. But now, after even more time had elapsed, why hadn't he loosened up?

Hoyt had backed his unit at an odd angle, taking up two parking spaces in front of an empty shop for a reason. He wanted to make it impossible to get close. He just loved to irritate the shit out of people, Callahan thought as he stopped several feet from Hoyt's vehicle. In a voice louder than he cared to exhibit, he requested, "Move your unit over to the front of Walgreens, park it, and come with me."

"Why?" Hoyt asked without looking up. He was ignored.

Callahan was upset, and Hoyt couldn't care less. *Just who in the hell do you think you are?* was in the minds of both. But no words were said, at least not yet.

"Do I need my stuff?" Hoyt asked defiantly.

"Everything but your citation book. Hell, you don't use it anyway."

This guy is good, Hoyt uttered under his breath as he gathered his stuff, leaving his *Sporting News* behind.

"Do you want me to drive? I know this area like the back of your hand."

Ten thousand comedians out of work and this guy insists on being one, Callahan smiled, but not with his face. He didn't want it to be shown that he thought the comment was excellent.

"Does Daddy know you're taking me out for a ride?" Hoyt again offered humor.

Callahan waited for Hoyt to get situated within the police unit before he initiated more conversation. Any inability to function together must get settled tonight or something else must be done. Personalities must not get in the way of performance. This was not a playground or an office disagreement. Nor was it about them. The people that they had sworn to protect must be their only concern.

"Why police work, David? What made you choose this as a career?" Callahan asked as he watched Hoyt buckle his seat belt.

"Who said it was going to be a career? It's just a job, like any other job." Hoyt didn't look up when he spoke. He just talked, putting words into space.

Callahan left the car in park as he continued the conversation. "What's going on, Hoyt? Give me a little hint here. Why the wiseass attitude?"

"Comes natural, I guess."

"You resent authority," Callahan's voice raised. "You don't want to conform to a group, or in this case, a squad. This is quasi-military work, son. We have to work as a unit to function, to survive."

"So, is that it, Callahan? I wasn't in the military and that in turn makes me a lesser person. Is that it? Do you consider me a draft dodger?" Hoyt still refused to look into Callahan's face.

"Draft dodger? No. But, what did you dodge, Hoyt? Tell me that."

Hoyt stiffened. "Callahan, what do you know about me? Or should I say, what do you think you know about me?"

"Nothing more than a little local knowledge would lend to."

"What is that supposed to mean? You lost me," Hoyt said as his eyes searched Callahan's face for a clue.

" I think you'll understand after I tell you that I was born and raised in Indiana. Southern Indiana."

David Hoyt swallowed hard. He did not know what to say or how to react. But, he did perceive exactly what Callahan was making inference to. "You have obviously checked my personnel jacket and found that I went to college in Indiana. Correct?"

"Yep. For three and one half years," Callahan answered. "At St. Meinrad's, I believe."

Hoyt nodded, expressionless.

"That's all you listed on your education history. St. Meinrad's," Callahan said as he smiled at the new officer. "But wasn't the full name of the school, St. Meinrad's School of Theology? A Catholic seminary?"

"You have known this all along haven't you, Callahan?" Hoyt asked as he looked up.

"Aren't you going to ask me why I didn't finish?"

"David, when I went into the military one of the first things that they taught me was the 'need to know.' Which simply meant, if you have a need to know we'll tell you. And that applies here. If I have a need to know, you will tell me," Callahan said. "But in the mean time, that is your business and will stay that way as far as I am concerned."

"I never lost my faith, Callahan," Hoyt said sternly, looking into Callahan's eyes. "My belief in God will always remain strong. It's just that I lost my conviction to become a priest. I knew I couldn't provide what was to be asked of me. My commitment was gone. I probably should have left sooner, but I wanted to give it time. I wanted to allow time for my mind to change. But it didn't. I had to leave."

"I DON'T KNOW, VIC," CALLAHAN SHRUGGED. "I can't tell you why he changed his attitude. I'm just glad he did."

Stark paused to look up and agreed with a slight nod. "By the way, there's a phone message in here from a Carrie at the Circle K at 12th and Valencia. It's marked 'Urgent.' Came in at 1620. Is that the girl that was sexually assaulted by a customer a couple months back?"

"Yeah, that's her. Does it have a number?"

"Here. Take it," Vic said as he handed the message to him. Callahan briefly stared at the piece of paper before he picked up the phone to dial. He purposely stopped into her store nightly, sometimes engaging in small talk, but more often than not, just a passing wave letting her know that he was around. The number stared back at him from the paper creating an anxiety of sorts, but also an excitement. Maybe her attacker had reappeared, something Callahan desperately wanted.

Callahan dialed the number and listened as Carrie answered the phone. After identifying himself, he became silent as her words were concise and to the point. "I'll be there shortly," was his only comment before he hung up the telephone.

"What was that all about?" Vic asked as Callahan stared into space.

"She says she saw the guy who attacked her. It's the first time she's seen him since the incident."

"Why didn't she call the emergency line and get a unit dispatched?" Vic asked the obvious.

"You know why," Callahan answered sternly. "This was an assault that occurred three weeks before she reported it. It's about trust. She doesn't trust cops because of something that happened previously in her life. She trusts me because I used her store a lot. A clean restroom and a phone I could use made us friends. Calling the emergency line would mean relying on a new set of strangers. Remember, Vic, she was forcibly raped."

Vic nodded.

"I'm going to go see if Hoyt's here yet. I need an early start, if you don't mind," Callahan said as he got up to go.

"Hoyt's never early, you know that. He's always going to be just one red light away from getting his ass chewed out. Go on out. I'll bring him to you. When you find out what's going on, let me know where to meet you."

Carrie was twenty-two years old, but appeared older. Her life's struggles had aged her like faded paint on an automobile. Even when she smiled her face would not allow her to appear happy, as sadness had formed her features. Carrie was of medium build, leaning toward small, and much too thin. Her brown hair was to the shoulder and straight, obviously styled by someone not in the profession. She was not overly attractive in physical appearance, but this meant nothing in sexual assaults. She was female, and in most cases that in itself qualified her as a victim. Raised by a single mother, distrust in the opposite sex was obvious and now, the feeling was greater than ever.

The convenience market was situated approximately two hundred yards from a major intersection. The parking lot to the front caused the store to set back from the street it paralleled. Without business, the store could be considered mildly secluded. Her attacker knew this and apparently had used it to his advantage.

Standing behind the counter of organized clutter, Carrie observed the police unit pull to the front of the store. She could not see the occupant clearly and glanced at her watch. She realized it was too early for Callahan to arrive, being well aware of his shift hours and days off. Her manager was kind enough to keep this in mind when scheduling her times and days to work.

Callahan sat patiently and waited for the four patrons to make their purchases and exit as Carrie was the only clerk and he needed her to be alone for their conversation. The last one was at the register when he entered and his appearance took her by surprise. He stood to the side waiting for the door to close. She spoke first.

"When we talked, I assumed you meant you'd be here at six," she said, forcing a smile.

"Yeah. Well sometimes I can't wait to get to work," he winked. Callahan wanted to hear what she had to say and he didn't have much time before someone else would enter the store. "You mentioned on the phone that you had seen the person that attacked you. When and where, Carrie?"

"Yesterday at Walgreens."

"Why did you wait until today to call?" Callahan realized what he had said, but not soon enough. He knew why. He was off duty yesterday. She trusted no one else.

Carrie did not answer.

"Did he see you? Did he recognize you?"

"I think so. That's why I called you." A car pulled to the front and Carrie began to hurry her speech. "He saw me looking at him and I ran. I ran away. I wish the hell he would just go away." Carrie bent, but she did not break. A slight quiver in the lip was the only hint of emotion.

Three young girls entered the store saying hello to Carrie as they bounced to the cooler for a beverage. Callahan's eyes followed them until he was sure that they could not hear his questions. "Did he follow you?"

"I don't know," Carrie answered, turning her hatred-filled voice from the customers.

He wanted to ask, "Why did you come to work?" He didn't. He so much wanted to ask, "Are you afraid?" He didn't. Instead he wanted to comfort with his badge and his ability.

"I'll be around as much as I can."

"I know," Carrie said shaking her head to clear the tears.

Callahan walked away from the counter, allowing the

distressed clerk to do her job. He moved to a display of stacked up Coca-Cola cartons, situated to the side of the large, front glass windows. Peering across 12th Avenue he observed a vacant lot, engulfed in shadows. More than likely, he thought, this was the spot used by her attacker to surveil and stalk. Maybe, just maybe, he could return the favor.

Other customers began to arrive, but Carrie's eyes searched for Callahan, seeking comfort. He nodded towards an opposite counter and she excused herself from the patrons to join him.

"Remember, if you see him, hit the alarm. We won't be far away."

Her response to him was a smile. Then back to work.

Callahan started for the front door, but stopped and suddenly walked to the rear of the store towards the restroom area. Once out of public view, he grabbed the receiver from the wall mounted telephone and dialed.

"Tucson Police Department. May I help you?" came the female voice.

"This is Officer Callahan. Could you get the Comm Sergeant for me?"

"Stand by, please."

Two, three minutes went by and he was starting to become impatient. "This is Sergeant Patterson. What can I do for you, Officer Callahan?"

"I know this is somewhat unusual, Sarge. But will you have Sergeant Stark meet me in the parking lot of the A.J. Bayless at 12th and Valencia? I can't use the radio frequency right now. I've got the feeling that it is being monitored by someone wanting to know my whereabouts."

"I thought that was what our communications system was all about, Callahan. You know, you call us and we'll call you." Patterson laughed. "Yeah, sure. I'll have F1 tell him. Fill me in later."

*I think somehow we learn who we really are
and live with that decision.*

~Eleanor Roosevelt

CHAPTER TWELVE

USING AN OBSCURE ROUTE through alleys and parking lots, Callahan slowly moved the patrol unit into the empty lot. Instantly, he was amazed at what he could observe. The brightly lit convenience market appeared as a stage to a darkened audience. He could easily see the sign of the AJ Bayless supermarket from where he was, meaning that he wouldn't have to travel far to pick up Hoyt and he could also observe Stark's vehicle when they arrived.

As he waited, Callahan pulled a small notepad from his breast pocket and flipped through the pages until he found the description of Carrie's assailant. He had read and reread the words a thousand times before, but he wanted it fresh in his mind.

White male
Approx. 35 years of age
5'10, 170 pounds.
Slender, athletic build
Close cut, light brown hair
Light colored eyes
Dark colored workout or jogging suit

Callahan stared at the page for a few more moments as if he expected it to come to life. This miserable bastard lives or works around here. I'm almost positive of that, he mumbled to himself before folding the notepad back into his pocket. Carrie had seen him in the store before the attack, but had never heard a name.

Callahan placed his darkened Dodge in gear and idled silently out of the vacant lot through an apartment complex to the east as he observed a police unit sneak into the Bayless parking lot. The sun was setting now and automobile headlights were being turned on, not to see, but to be seen. He drove onto Valencia, then turning left at 12th Avenue into the supermarket parking lot.

Pulling close to the driver's side door of Stark's unit, Callahan placed his car into park as he spoke. "Something tells me that our friend will show up tonight, Vic. She ran into him at Walgreens yesterday." David Hoyt grabbed his equipment bag from Stark's rear seat and joined Callahan. He was quite aware of the incident involving Carrie as his normal working beat was just to the north.

"Do you honestly think that he will be stupid enough to come back here?" Stark asked through his window. "Don't you think that he would wait until she leaves and . . ." He stopped, letting the others do the assuming.

"No, I don't. Maybe I'm stupid, but I believe that this asshole feels comfortable with the fact that he attacked here once and got away with it and can do it again. It's just a guess, and I hope we're here for it."

"Do you need some help watching the store?" Vic asked.

"You know, it probably wouldn't be a bad idea if you could get ahold of TAC and see if they could sit off on the store. This guy will check the area and more than likely spot our marked unit, but he's not going to recognize the vehicles that they drive," Callahan answered as he nodded his approval at the idea.

The Tactical Operations Squad was a unit that was called on for nearly everything involving police work of an undercover nature. Narcotics, to vice, to surveillance, to God only knew what. The group was elite and the acceptance into it was considered quite an accomplishment. Only a few were selected and the procedure was rigorous. TAC was made up of twelve officers, two sergeants, and one lieutenant. Needless to say, they were kept quite busy and their assignments were often extremely dangerous. This situation seemed to be right up their alley.

Vic's right hand keyed the mike as he took it from the dash, "1-U-7, is TAC 2 available?" he asked, trying to find the availability of a TAC Sergeant.

"Stand by, 1-U-7," came the familiar voice of Peggy as she asked the other dispatchers to search for the sergeant.

"We're going back across the street, Vic, and watch for awhile. Let me know later if TAC can sit on it by mentioning a ball score. OK?"

"Do you honestly think he'll show up at the store?" Hoyt asked as Callahan pulled into the vacant lot from the apartment parking lot.

"I don't know. I wish I knew what that asshole was thinking. But nobody does. I do know he's scared now. He knows she saw him, and that makes him even more dangerous, and that's what scares me," Callahan said, occupied with his own thoughts, still catching Hoyt studying him as he talked.

They sat quietly in the darkness of the shotgun unit. Its occupants poised for anything, hoping for one thing—the appearance of the hunted. The silence had its own personality. The constant drone of the voices coming from the radio frequency created a noise that was listened to by Hoyt and selectively heard by Callahan. Not that the importance of the dispatch to other units lacked importance, but tonight more than most, they were prioritized.

"Did he take her somewhere, or did he assault her here?" the rookie carefully asked. "I don't really know much about this case, other than the suspect's description."

Without answering, Callahan pulled from the inside of his clipboard a copy of the case report relating to the Sexual Assault/ Type Rape, with the victim being Carrie. The narrative on the report stated only that the victim had been assaulted. The actual details were on supplement sheets. All police personnel involved in an incident dictated the supplements after information was gathered and facts verified. The supplement made by the on-scene investigation at Carrie's assault was attached to the case report, commonly known as the face sheet. It contained blocks and squares of questions asked of the officers for pertinent information.

"Read it," Callahan said, pushing it towards his partner.

"I wish I could, but it's dark," Hoyt tried to see the print as he pulled the report up to his face.

"Lean forward. Read it from the lights of the radio."

Hoyt did and instantly he could see the words on the page, proof that experience was the best teacher. He went straight to the narrative and read:

At the above date and time, the victim was exiting the store at the above location through the front entrance. No customers were present in the store at the time and her relief clerk was to the rear of the store in the enclosed refrigerated cooler. As she walked to her vehicle, which was parked to the south, approximately 24 feet from the entrance, she was approached by the suspect. She recognized him as a frequent store customer and was not alarmed by his presence. After a brief conversation (see victim's statement), she again walked towards her vehicle and was, unknown to her, followed by her assailant. The suspect then grabbed her by the arm, bringing it behind her, stating, "I have a gun, do what I tell you to or I'll hurt you real bad."

The suspect then placed something made of cloth over her head and forced her around the outside of the store and into a vehicle of unknown description. The victim was then sexually assaulted.

NFI

Hoyt replaced the report back into the enclosed portion of the clipboard. But he had one question, "How can she come back to work after that happened?"

"Survival."

"How so?"

"She needs to show herself she can and she obviously needs the job."

Carrie knew she was being watched from the vacant lot across the street. Callahan had turned his vehicle's spotlight on with a very quick 'blink,' and another 'blink,' until she acknowledged his presence by raising her left arm, straight up, over her head. Their pre-arranged signal was her security, the least, the very least he felt he could do. This was one of those times when cops felt very helpless.

"I HAVEN'T SEEN HER in here before," the bartender said.
"Who are you talkin' about?" the man at the bar asked.
"She looks like she's lookin' for someone."
  The man turned on his stool and squinted into the dim light.
"Oh, shit. What in the hell is she doin' here?"
"You know her?"
"Yeah. She's my fuckin' wife."
"You're on your own, Louie." The bartender turned to walk
away. "But no problems in here. Take that kind of shit elsewhere."
  Louie Beldan nodded slightly, staring at the label he was
tearing away from a Coors bottle. Every night after work, for over a
year, he stopped here to have a 'couple of beers.' It was to relax,
unwind from hard days of laying concrete, he told her. And that's the
way it was at first. Just a couple. But a half hour turned into an hour.
Then it was two hours before he left and went home. Or sometimes
he didn't make it home at all.
  "Louie."
  "What in the hell do you want? Did you come here to
embarrass me?" he didn't turn around.
  She stood at his shoulder, pulling herself tall as she spoke, "I
just stopped to tell you that I can't handle this anymore. I have the
kids in the car with me. We won't be home if and when you decide
to go there."
  "Fuck you."
  And she left.
  "What was that all about, Louie?" another patron asked from
three stools away.
  "I can't believe I've put up with her shit for so long. On my
ass constantly. I work my ass off for her and she pulls this shit. To
hell with her. I'm better off without her."
  "Let me buy you a beer," his friend offered. "I know what
you're going through."

  "WE HAVE COMPANY," Callahan whispered. Why he
whispered he didn't know. Maybe because of the darkened silence
of his vehicle and the Chevrolet Caprice that crept, ever so quietly
into the vacant lot, twenty yards from them. The car entered the lot

from behind the Jack-in-the-Box, an angle that would not, and did not expose the police unit with four eyes watching it. With the use of headlights, the Caprice would have caught sight of vehicle #397. However, it did not.

"Is that the guy that we're looking for?" David asked as his pulse increased rapidly.

"Doesn't appear so, unless he's brought friends with him," Callahan answered.

"How do you know that?" David asked as he squinted at the old Chevy.

"As they came from the Jack-in-the-Box lot, the headlights from the car behind them illuminated the inside of their vehicle and it appeared to be occupied by two #3 males and a #5 male."

The numbers indicating their race were being identified from using the MINOW system. Law enforcement used this method to expedite radio transmissions: M = #1, indicating that the person's race was Mexican; I = #2, or Indian; N = #3, or Negro; O = #4, or Oriental; and W = #5, or White.

"Really," Hoyt said, annoyed at himself, "what was I watching?"

"Don't know, can't watch you and them at the same time. But I think we are about to have a problem."

"What?"

"It appears these idiots are about to target Carrie's store." Callahan couldn't believe his own words. "And I hope I'm wrong. And God knows I've been wrong before. But my gut tells me I'm not this time. However, it's their move."

"Do we get back-ups and stop them now?"

"For what, or from what?" Callahan asked. His attention was directed to the car . . . to the store . . . to the car . . . to the store.

"What are they waiting on if they are going to rob it?" The rookie felt his heart pounding in his throat.

"C'mon, Sherlock, look at the store. What do you see? You don't have to be a veteran, just smart." As he talked, he placed binoculars to his eyes for a better view.

"You've got the binoculars. You tell me."

"You don't need them. Use your head. Think like them.

Would you, if you were going to rob that store, do it right now?"
Callahan asked, not taking his eyes from the car.

"I fail to see what you are. . ."

"Vehicles and people, Hoyt. That store is too busy. Think,
damn it. They want money, not witnesses. If and when that store is
empty, they move. And so do we. Right now it's just a waiting
game, and a rare one at that. You most likely will never be in this
position again in your entire career."

"Two cars just left. That leaves one. Hang loose and watch.
Don't talk for a minute. Just watch," Callahan demanded. The 'casing
car' was approximately thirty yards from the cop car. Only one saw
the other; the other only saw the store.

"1-Baker-7," Callahan spoke into the mike clutched in his
right hand. The left held the binoculars as the dark blue or black
Caprice started moving.

"1-Baker-7," Peggy answered back.

"Is Patrol Two available?"

"Go ahead," came the slightly muffled voice from the
helicopter.

"Can you head over to the area of 12th and Valencia? If so,
ETA." As Callahan spoke, the only remaining vehicle at the Circle
K was leaving.

"Heading your way. Be there in a couple," came the voice of
Ron Tomy, the helicopter pilot. Ron was a poker buddy of Callahan's
and knew when he was bluffing. He also knew when Callahan was
holding a pat hand. This was one of those times. "Watcha got,
buddy?"

"A gamble, just a long shot, but hang around," and Callahan
smiled.

"1-Baker-7, copy partial California plate: Two-Union-David-
One. . .can't read the rest. It's on a dark blue, late 60's Caprice. It's
occupied by two #3 or dark skinned males and one #5 male. I'm not
real sure what we've got, but I need some units to start moving this
way, just in case. I'll advise further."

"10-4," Peggy acknowledged. She immediately located three
more units to head into the area. Peggy took charge dispatching them
into quadrant areas — north, south, and east of the scene.

"YOU'RE ON A ROLL, LOUIE." The man in the western hat laid his cue stick on the pool table. "That's three games in a row that you've won. Let me buy you another shot of tequila."

"Naw, I think I've had enough of that goddamn stuff," Louie said, rubbing both eyes with the heels of his hands. "Just bring me a beer. Last one."

"Pussy," the man in the hat shot back.

"Man, I gotta work tomorrow. Not like some of you low-lifes that sleep until noon 'cause you ain't got a job."

"What you worrying about, Louie?" his friend hollered from the bar. "You ain't got no ol' lady to go home to anyway."

They laughed.

"Yeah, well maybe that's why I want to go home."

They laughed again.

THE DARK BLUE CHEVY started westward out of the not so vacant lot. Heading toward the patronless vacant Circle K.

"They're turning their lights on," David exclaimed.

"Of course they are. They don't want to be noticed," Callahan shot back as he pulled the Remington 410 from the dash rack. "If they drive up to the store without using their headlights, they run the risk of being noticed, by cops, clerks, anybody. Here, take this. Do you remember how to use it? You'd better. You might need it." Callahan thrust it within inches of Hoyt's face, forcing him to take the weapon. The thought of something this deadly, this violent in his control revolted Hoyt. When it comes to using resources, I will choose my own, not something that I fear, he thought.

"Do we stop them now?" Hoyt asked as the car with California plates started into the market parking lot.

A look from Callahan gave him his answer. "I know, for what?" Hoyt replied.

Callahan took a deep breath and created words, and a prayer, "Here again, we roll the dice, buddy."

He turned the spotlight toward the store and gave a quick "blink," hoping Carrie would catch it on the first effort. She did, and apparently no one saw it but Carrie. Her arm was raised above her head and brought down as if she meant to straighten her hair.

"Watch and remember everything you see. You will be writing it down later," Callahan said, glancing at his partner.

The dark blue Chevrolet with a dented left front fender and partially cracked back window, pulled up to the Circle K store. The two occupants of the front seat opened their doors and stepped from the vehicle, looked in all directions, and started toward the store.

Callahan slipped the patrol unit into drive and began to creep forward. With the binoculars pressed to his eyes, he watched as the driver's right hand pulled a small handgun from his waistband. "The driver has a weapon in his hand, Hoyt. Here we go!" Instantly, the male in the back crawled over the seat and slid behind the wheel.

"Radio," Callahan said into the mike, "we have a 43 in progress."

Peggy hit the ALERT tone, advising the whole frequency that a major crime was in progress. The constant 'beep, beep, beep' that the field units heard told them to keep radio traffic to a minimum — or not at all. Quickly she advised, "10-43, 12th and Valencia, officers have it on-sight," then she became silent, releasing the air to 1-Baker-7.

"Two #3 males are both in the store and have handguns," Callahan reported. "Suspect vehicle is now driven by a #5 male. Clerk's hands are in the air. One suspect leaned over the counter and pushed the clerk aside. If there is violence we are going in. It doesn't appear so at this time. I don't want a hostage situation . . . I want these assholes out on the street," Callahan recited.

"They're running out of the store and into the vehicle. I'll give you a plate when I can see it." The police unit was placed in gear and slowly drifted toward the street and the obvious chase that would ensue.

Callahan could not see Carrie.

The getaway vehicle hit the pavement of the street with tires going faster than the automobile. The Chevrolet was momentarily going sideways as smoke billowed from the screeching tires.

"Hang on, Hoyt!" Callahan screamed to his partner as he hit the overhead lights.

"Get a unit to the scene," he ordered to the dispatcher.

A quick head jerk from the passenger told the occupants of both vehicles that the police unit had been seen. Callahan exited the dirt lot and shoved the accelerator to the floor, causing the 400 cubic-inch, high performance police engine to scream to life, directly behind the vastly out-matched Caprice.

"Hoyt, give radio the plate," Callahan yelled over the wail of the piercing siren.

"Radio, copy plate," Hoyt directed into the mike, "California, Two-Union-David-One-Seven-Five."

The darkness of the night was immediately filled with the colors of the emergency lights, as the siren shocked the stillness. The floodlights of Patrol Two soon bathed the suspect's vehicle in instant and intense light.

"We got 'em in sight," the pilot said as the chopper preyed menacingly above the northbound, ill-fated Chevy.

"You've got 'eyeball,' Patrol. You've got the play-by-play," Callahan advised, as he knew the chopper had a better view of the entire scene.

"Roger," was Tomy's only response.

Inside police communications, the on-duty force commander, Lieutenant Gaylord Johnson, joined others to monitor the pursuit. "Is the 10-43 confirmed, yet?"

"Yes, sir," Peggy answered.

"Is the clerk all right?" the Lieutenant asked.

"Yes, sir."

"Then tell them. It'll make their ride a little more enjoyable."

"It's confirmed 10-43," Peggy advised. "We made contact with the Circle K and the clerk is Code 4."

Callahan grinned. "So much for a quiet evening of surveillance," he shouted to his partner.

LOUIE SAT BACKWARDS on the stool, his elbows resting on the bar. "She's gonna be so fuckin' sorry that she left me."

Nobody heard what he said. His friends were gone and only one table of people remained in the far corner. Half falling, he removed himself from the stool and started for the door. The bartender was not to be seen. I'm fucked up, he mumbled, bouncing off a chair. He pulled his keys from his pocket and dropped them as he leaned against the door. The door opened quickly, too fast for an impaired person. Louie fell, lying half in, half out, of the doorway. Rising to his knees, he located his keys on the floor, and with the second attempt managed to pick them and himself up.

"Just let me get into my truck," he said aloud. "Then I'll be all right."

THE CHEVY SHOWED NO SIGNS of slowing as it continued northbound, changing lanes and dodging vehicles. Suddenly, with no lane to switch into, it sought the sidewalk as it violently jumped the curb and slammed broadside into a much smaller vehicle parked next to the walkway. The driver's side rear door jerked open, a dazed figure emerged, and dashed behind the car and into the neighborhood.

"We have a suspect running into the residential area, east of 12th, at Lincoln," came the transmission from the helicopter. "Vehicle 370! He's right around the corner from you. He sees you. He's hiding under some shrubs. To your left. He's right in front of you." This was exactly why they painted car numbers on the top of police units, the pilot thought.

"Radio. Be advised, the suspect is in custody. Give him another unit."

CHAPTER THIRTEEN

OFFICER RICHARD PADILLA was at the right place, at the right time. He had observed the old blue Chevy slow, then stop. He watched the door open and his heart began to race. A subject emerged and began to run, just a few yards from him. Padilla heard Patrol Two call his unit number. He saw the desperate man crawl under the bushes. The adrenaline rush was incredible. This was what police work was all about. The asshole trying to hide was a felon. A fleeing felon. He would try to resist arrest. They always did. Just like his brother had.

Padilla shouted to the suspect to remain still. The frightened would-be fugitive, prone on the ground, complied. Padilla drew his weapon and aimed it directly at the suspect's head. The eyes of the young black man, with his face in the dirt, bore his fear. He did not move, nor did he have any intention of doing so. His older brother, still out there somewhere, had talked him into the crime. He closed his eyes. He just wanted the whole nightmare to end. The handcuffs were a relief, until they were tightened and tightened some more. He cried out. The young man tried to fight off the pain around his wrists. Then, in an instant, he felt a fire in his head. And again.

"Keep fighting me, asshole, and you'll get some more." Padilla had felt him resist the cuffs and slammed the revolver against his skull. Again. The blood began to run down the suspect's face, and he screamed, and he cried. Padilla saw it too, but his reaction

was to look for witnesses. He saw no one. And he smiled.
But, someone had seen him. From a few hundred feet up.

The driver of the ill-fated Chevrolet was not about to quit running as he shoved the accelerator to the floor causing the vehicle to lurch away from the unoccupied Toyota it had slammed into and back out onto 12th Avenue. "Shoot the motherfuckers, goddamn it! Shoot. Now!" the driver shrieked at the passenger as the car spun sideways in front of 1-Baker-7.

"Get down!" Callahan screamed as he watched the passenger's firearm swing toward them. Callahan jerked the steering wheel to the right just as the weapon was discharged. The first slug from the large caliber handgun struck the windshield just above the rearview mirror with the second skipping off of the engine hood.

"What in the hell is he doing?" Hoyt yelled as he bent forward under the dash. "Stupid bastard is shooting at a police car!"

"He's trying to kill us," Callahan answered as he swerved the car quickly from side to side.

"Should I . . ." Hoyt began as he pulled his service revolver.

"No! No!" Callahan ordered. "You can't afford to miss."

The driver of the suspect vehicle tried desperately to maintain control as the damaged vehicle again contacted the curb. "Tell them to block off Ajo. This guy is not going to stop until we stop him," Callahan told Hoyt as the passenger in the car in front was desperately trying to get in position for another shot.

"Units, we are approaching Ajo," Hoyt said. "Block all four ways in the intersection!"

"Now, son of a bitch," Callahan said as he drove onto the rear bumper of the getaway car, "just give me one little opening."

"Damn it, Callahan," Hoyt yelled as he watched the passenger try to get into position for another shot. "Are you nuts?"

"*Right now!*"

Both vehicles where entering the intersection of 12th Avenue and Ajo Road when Callahan pulled to the left and slightly pushed down on the accelerator. The right front bumper of the police unit made contact with the left rear of the suspect's vehicle. Instantly, the old Chevy twisted sideways and Callahan jammed the accelerator to the floor.

"Holy shit!" Hoyt screamed as their automobile was burrowed into the driver's door of the robber's car, pushing it sideways through the intersection. Callahan's eyes were frozen upon the driver of a car that he could not control. An abrupt jolt raised the driver's side of the sliding vehicle off of the ground. The deafening screech of metal told Callahan's trained ear that both passenger side tires had been torn from their rims, illuminating the night like Fourth of July sparklers.

Callahan continued to force the getaway car sideways and towards a pair of concrete pillars that guarded a traffic signal. Without warning, he quickly removed his foot from the gas pedal and slammed his foot on the brakes, separating them from the careening Chevrolet. The battered car rolled up on its right side and slid until its roof made violent contact with the concrete structures just north of the curb. The windshield instantly blew out as the vehicle's top crumpled inward. Both occupants struggled inside the wreckage as broken glass and debris pummeled them.

The area surrounding the two vehicles was littered with law enforcement vehicles. Callahan and Hoyt crouched close to the ground with their weapons drawn as they used the open doors of the squad car for a barricade.

"Throw your weapons out and place your hands up over your head. Now!" came a command from the loud speaker atop a police unit. "And don't try anything stupid."

"A little late with your advice," Callahan smirked. "Hoyt, watch the black guy. He's starting to come out where the windshield was. See if he still has his weapon."

"Throw your weapons out before you exit the car!" the PA voice insisted.

Two hands appeared from the car, but no weapons. A tall, thin black man, screaming, "Don't shoot! Don't shoot!" began to crawl out the opening at the front of the overturned car.

"Watch him, Hoyt. You have a better angle than I do," Callahan instructed. "He just might try to 'rabbit' on us."

Scrambling to his feet, the suspect immediately started to run. *"Get him, Hoyt!"* Callahan bellowed. The armed robber stopped briefly to try and locate an opening between the emergency vehicles, but briefly was too long. Hoyt was on him in seconds, tackling him just above the waist. Instantly, two more officers were there to subdue the desperate prisoner.

The driver, a six-foot-something, white male remained inside the car, shouting obscenities and refusing any order. This was in spite of the fact that Callahan was pointing the shotgun that Hoyt had left behind, directly at him.

"Fuck you, pigs! Go ahead and shoot me, you chicken shit bastards."

"Hands up, asshole."

"Fuck you."

"One more time, asshole. Get out of the car or my friend will come in and get your ugly ass!" Callahan hollered.

"Fuck you and your friend!" the suspect shouted back.

The criminal within the car did not see Officer Mack unsnap the leash that held back "Thor."

Thor was a three-year-old German shepherd, the only 'pure-bred' police officer on the Tucson Police Department. His personality and demeanor matched his handler's, all teeth and no patience. Thor, however, was more esthetically pleasing to look at than his partner.

Officer Richard Mack did not appreciate anything that didn't behave. Mack didn't even like himself. He had eighteen years on the Tucson police force, with nine of them as a dog handler. He should have been rotated out of the dog unit, but they couldn't find anyone who would volunteer to tell him that. Richard Mack was not extremely large, six feet or so. He was suspected of being a little crazy, but no one really wanted to know for sure. Mack loved dogs, disliked people. The K-9 unit was a perfect place for him.

"Watch him. Easy," came the command. Thor didn't like the 'easy' part as he started walking toward the suddenly silent suspect. One growl with a snarl and bare teeth, many teeth, many long teeth, and the highly trained animal began his crawl toward the overturned vehicle. Several officers directed their firearms at the armed robber within the car.

"My friend is coming to see you, now. I suggest that you crawl from the car as soon as possible," Callahan ordered again.

"Thor wants to bite him," Mack smiled. Callahan swore later

that he actually saw the handler drool.

Before the suspect could begin another tirade of profanity, he saw the large, snarling head appear inside the automobile. "Holy shit! Get him off of me! Call him. Call him off. I'm coming out. Here, see my hands."

"OUT!" Mack ordered and the obedient animal began to back away as the prisoner crawled from the vehicle onto the pavement uttering, "Nice doggy. Real nice doggy."

"There will be other times," Callahan said as he put an arm around Mack's shoulder in mock comfort. Thor failed to see the humor in it. He already had reason to dislike Callahan as he had previously met Rufus.

"1-Baker-7, you can clear the air. The suspects are 10-15. Dispatch ID please."

THE FORD PICKUP TRUCK lunged forward from the parking lot of Jerry's Lounge and onto S. Park Avenue. The driver of an oncoming car leaned on the horn as he swerved to miss the truck.

"Asshole," Louie slurred. "Watch where you're going."

Closing one eye, he aimed the truck between two of the many pavement markings that he was seeing. The vehicle began to gain speed as alcohol forced the accelerator to the floor.

"I hope she didn't wait up for me. We'll fight and it will be the same old shit," Louie slurred.

PEGGY HIT THE BUTTON, releasing the *'beep, beep'* from the frequency. "10-4."

"Also," Callahan continued, "contact the robbery detectives and have them respond. Get me an ETA also. I got a feeling these boys have been down this road before."

"It's been done. They were notified at 2235 hours and are en route," Peggy advised and then gave the present time of 2242.

SQUAD CAR #370 SAT SILENTLY, waiting patiently on the perimeter of the chaotic scene. The driver's eyes stared intently at the two captives as they were being led to their transport units. He glanced up at the rearview mirror as he heard the heavy breathing of his prisoner. The young man's mind was fighting the aftermath of the recent events. The wounds he had received were superficial, but the scars of the officer's intent would remain forever. Padilla had gone hunting and had his trophy.

"You really shouldn't have tried to resist, you know. It wasn't real smart on your part. You did try to resist, didn't you?" Officer Padilla's eyes glared into the mirror as the helpless, handcuffed man's lips barely moved as he spoke,

"Yes, Sir. It wasn't real smart for me to try and get away." He had just arrived from L.A. He had seen enough of the game to realize that he could not win. So why try?

Padilla smiled as his head lowered a bit, but his stare remained on the mirror. "That's a good boy. You have learned well."

LOUIE WAS CONFUSED. He could not remember taking this road before. He had to hurry and get home. Everything was a blur. Including the street sign that read, Park and.... "*Oh, Jesus!*"

THE SEAT FELT GOOD as Callahan stepped into his vehicle. Leaning back against the headrest, he took a heavy breath, releasing a slow, long sigh. It was all a crapshoot, he thought. One error, one minor error, and the scenario changed from hero to victim. Life to death, or somewhere in between.

"Did you see Padilla's prisoner?" Hoyt asked as he opened the car door. "He must have put up quite a fight before he was cuffed. He's beat up pretty good."

"Where? Where is he?" Callahan asked as his eyes searched the area. "What do you mean beat up pretty good?"

He didn't wait for an answer as he observed Padilla's vehicle pull slowly to the side. "Start the face sheet," he directed. "I'll be right back."

"Nice work, Richard," Callahan said as he joined the officer. "Has he said much to you?"

"Thanks," Padilla responded, wearing a cocky, confident smirk that appeared eerie, almost ghostly. "No, Callahan. Our man here isn't very talkative. He tried to 'rabbit' and then fight me, but he found out who the man was. He paid the price."

Callahan watched the subdued suspect intently while Padilla was talking. The young man stared blankly into the plexi-glass shield in front of him.

"You read him his rights, correct?"

Padilla nodded.

"What is your name?" Callahan asked the prisoner. No response. "Where are you from?" The frightened suspect turned his head slightly to look at Padilla, but said nothing. Padilla smiled.

"Padilla, tell radio that you need another unit to respond here to transport your prisoner. And go over to my unit and give Hoyt your prisoner's name." Callahan needed a few minutes with the man in the backseat of Padilla's car.

As Padilla walked away, the handcuffed young man's eyes followed him. "You have blood on your face. What happened?" Callahan asked. "How were you injured?"

Slowly he turned his head to the questioning officer. *Why is he asking me these questions? If I tell him that asshole beat me for no reason, will he beat me some more, so I'll shut up forever? I know their games. See just how much the 'nigger' will say, then drag his ass somewhere else and fuck him up good!*

"Forget it, man. Nothing happened. I fell down, or something. Get me out of here. Book my ass. Do what you got to do. That's it. I ain't saying nothin' else." Robert Wyatt Williams turned his head to the side, to be with his own thoughts, reflecting on his own bad decisions.

"Any unit that can clear, 10-25!" Peggy's voice was urgent. "We have a possible 10-53 at Park and Benson."

"What was that?" Callahan shouted to Hoyt.

"They're looking for units to respond to Park and Benson. Possible 53."

"Grab your stuff and get out of the car. You're in charge of this scene," Callahan ordered, running to his car. "Get another unit to help you. Padilla, get that prisoner downtown."

"1-ADAM-36, I CAN RESPOND." Sara Conners' voice came across the frequency.

"Start over. Code 3."

"1-Adam-7, en route." Callahan hurriedly got behind the wheel. Hoyt pulled his equipment and stepped aside.

The emergency equipment was once again engaged. Once past the police induced traffic jam, Callahan shoved the accelerator to the floor. Park and Benson. Three minutes, maybe two, he thought.

IN A VACANT DIRT LOT across from the Circle K, a pair of eyes watched the winding down of the police investigation and saw the young female clerk wave good night.

CHAPTER FOURTEEN

SARA FLIPPED THE SWITCHES for the overhead emergency lights. Reflections of blue and red filled the darkness. The piercing sound of the siren added to her fears. She could feel her pulse pounding inside her head. She was less than two minutes away.

The situation was happening too fast for her to comprehend. Sara could feel her body tighten as the fear of the unknown attacked her brain like awakening from a nightmare and finding herself alone. Sara's heart was in her throat as she thought of the dispatch. The code 10-53 meant death. *No! Don't let it be true. It's too soon. It can't happen this fast. I'm not ready for this. Please! It's not fair.* She instantly felt the nausea of the unknown. She felt lost and inadequate.

Controlled apprehension and energy surged into Callahan's brain. The surface streets were not adequate. He must use the Interstate. Immediately he was on the bumper of a vehicle entering the freeway. The driver saw the police car in his rearview mirror and froze. The vehicle slowed and almost stopped. Callahan didn't. His foot buried the accelerator to the floor. The tires resented the curb at first, but then yielded to the speed of the automobile. The rear wheels dug into the soil of the off road landscaping, throwing a rooster tail of rock and dirt behind the powerful vehicle. The trip on the freeway would be brief, as the deadly intersection was twenty seconds ahead, at the bottom of the Park Avenue exit.

"Oh my God," Sara screamed as the unbelievable scene came

into view. One vehicle was on its top, wheels still spinning, touching only the air. Torn sheet metal and broken glass littered the area like a Beirut bombing.

"*This is Patrol Two. We have at least five vehicles involved, two ejections on the roadway — give us all the help you can get,*" screamed the chopper pilot.

"I'm 10-23," Callahan advised as he swung his unit around to seal off the perimeter of the scene. "Notify the traffic investigators. This is a nightmare."

Paramedics and fire personnel were on the scene almost instantly from a nearby station house. Wasn't enough — more were needed and needed badly. The ejections were from vehicles yet to be determined. Two people — one large person, one very small, were lying motionless on the roadway.

Sara saw Callahan arrive. She ran to his car.

"Michael, what do . . . ?" Sara asked.

"Stay with me!" Callahan anticipated her question. "It's triage time, Sara. We have to find the most seriously injured." As he bolted from his vehicle, he began a desperate search, attempting to match the screams with a person.

Two police units were on the scene, not nearly enough for the control of the split second tragedy. The intersection was a convergence of high volume and high-speed avenues. Hotels, filling stations, and restaurants were adding their patrons to the confusion. Traffic re-direction, crowd control, and preservation of the crime scene required more personnel than one sector could provide. Any officer's nightmare was to have more problems evolve from an existing one.

"*My baby, my baby, where's my baby?*" came a frantic plea from inside a mangled mass of sheet metal with spewing engine fluids. "*I want my baby, oh God, oh my God.*" The female voice came from a blood soaked face belonging to the apparent driver of what was once a Chevrolet. The windshield was shattered into a million little pieces in every direction. The entire front end of the automobile was completely obliterated. The firewall to the engine compartment remained; everything forward of it was ripped away.

The bleeding torso of a thirty-something woman was held intact by a restraint system that had done its job. Her hands squeezed the steering wheel as pain and fear gripped her body. The driver's door was gone, thrown somewhere. The top portion of her seat was laid back against the rear seat. However, she remained in a sitting position with nothing to support her except her unrelenting grip on the steering wheel.

"*My baby, my baby,*" she chanted, refusing to drift into unconsciousness.

"Patrol Two . . . about a hundred yards to the southeast . . . there's a subject stumbling through the desert. Get a ground unit over there!"

"Sam 5 . . . I see him. He appears injured. Give me a paramedic unit."

Emergency medical vehicles were continuing to arrive from surrounding hospitals and fire stations, but the flashing red lights and the mournful wail of sirens drew humans to tragedy like ants to a picnic. The more gore, the more onlookers — a despicable flaw in human nature.

With the wide spread area of the trauma, normal triage procedures were difficult. You looked until you found someone to help and then stayed with them. Michael Callahan and Sara became one with the desperate mother and the non-existent child.

"How bad is she, Doyle?" Callahan asked of the paramedic, as he knelt next to the woman in the carcass of the Chevrolet.

"Head trauma, lacerations to the scalp mainly — can't tell how serious. She took a good whack from the steering wheel. Internals maybe. BP is all right under the circumstances," Doyle said as he unwrapped the blood pressure cuff. "What's this about a baby?"

"Not sure," Callahan responded as he climbed behind her and into the rubble to apply more gauze to her forehead. "There's an infant carrier secured to the passenger seat by a seatbelt, but it's empty. Even the safety strap in the carrier is belted and intact. The back of this seat stayed up, not like hers. Something's not right."

"What do you mean?"

"When you take a baby from a car seat, you wouldn't re-lock the belt, would you?"

"No, you wouldn't," Sara answered.

"Maybe she's just so used to having her kid around . . ." Doyle started to say.

"I don't think so," Sara interrupted.

"You don't think what?" Callahan asked.

"She knows where her baby is," Sara asserted with confidence.

"The baby is not here, Sara, we have looked everywhere — she's hallucinating. Her body is in shock. She wants her child. She doesn't know where her baby is. She . . ."

"Exactly," Sara said, cutting Callahan off. "She wants her baby, *now* . . ."

"The child is not here," he shouted.

"Yes, yes it has to be," Sara shouted back. "Damn it, Callahan, try to take her hands from the steering wheel. Go ahead! She's not leaving until she sees her child."

Callahan tried. She would not release her grip from the steering wheel.

"You're a good cop. You're a good man, but you're not a mother," Sara cried out. "I am. That baby is here. Somewhere. Somewhere in this mess. I know it Michael; I know it."

"Sara, all that's left in this car is right here, bent dash board, folded seats and . . . and bent metal. See? See, nothing is here." Callahan froze.

"*Oh my God! Oh God,*" he screamed as he pulled his hand from the radio speaker on top of the dash as if it were a hot burner.

Looking down on the still intact dashboard and inside the grid of the radio speaker, he saw a finger. He saw a tiny finger. He saw a tiny finger . . . *move*!

"I need some help . . . *now*! *NOW*!" Callahan hollered.

"*Jesus, how . . . Doyle, get the jaws . . . under the dash, there's a baby in here.*" Sweeping glass and debris aside, Callahan didn't wait for help. He grabbed under the dash with both hands and yanked it upwards — again and again and again. It moved. Barely, but it moved just enough for him to force his hands up and under until he could feel the child. The baby was not wedged, but instead, moved freely as he placed his hands around the small, warm torso. Desperately fearing what he would find, he carefully pulled the child from under the mangled dash. A child of nearly twenty pounds, a child that was alive . . . a child that was unhurt . . . a child that was a miracle.

The officer delicately brushed his fingers across the infant's smiling face. The baby grabbed Callahan's forefinger, and in one motion, tried to stick it into his mouth. "A little hungry, are we, little buddy?"

The miracle child smiled; the mother felt him do it. With a battered glance, she saw her baby. The baby she knew was there all along. The mother released her grip on the wheel, as the officers released their grip on emotion. With the infant's cheek next to Callahan's, he squeezed the child tightly before handing him to 'Officer Mom.'

Sara immediately inspected the baby, finding nothing but minor scrapes. "Your baby is fine. He is unhurt. He is beautiful." She placed the baby's forehead to his mother's lips.

She smiled and slipped into a very peaceful, muted cry of relief — joined by Callahan and Doyle. One myth destroyed by two big men — big boys *do* cry.

"Sam 5 . . . this person is not severely injured. Just extremely intoxicated. Are we missing a driver of a vehicle at the scene?"

"10-4," one of the on-scene officers broke in. "We can't locate the driver or occupants of the Ford pickup that apparently caused this mess."

"10-4," Sam 5 responded. "I have a driver's license indicating this person to be a . . . hang on I'm having a hard time reading it. It looks like a Louis Beldor or Beldan."

Paramedics slid the ambulance gurney under Marie, as she was lifted from the wreckage of the family automobile. Sara placed eleven-month old Carlos on her chest for the ride to St. Mary's Hospital. One was battered; both were fine. Make that — the whole world was fine, even if for a moment, a very precious moment.

Ambulances came and left. Two dead, seven injured. One large tragedy, one small miracle.

"Mommy, why is everybody stopping? How come there are

so many red lights and fire trucks? Did people get hurt?"

"I don't know, Sweetheart. But Mommy is going to have to take a different way to get us home." Marcie Beldan drove toward the intersection. An officer with a burning flare was directing her onto a side street and away from Park and Benson. She began to feel sick to her stomach. While at her mother's, she felt she must return to their home. She was not one to run. One more time, she thought. I'll give him one more chance.

"Will Daddy be there when we get home?"

"I hope so, honey."

"Michael," Sara asked, "how did that baby end up under the dash board? And better yet, why didn't he get hurt?"

"A good guess is that the force of the impact was so great that the child was virtually catapulted out of the secured infant seat. How he ended up under the dash is going to be quite the job for accident re-constructionists. Both vehicles moving, one at an extremely high rate of speed, anything, I suppose, can happen."

"And put the suppleness of that child with the physics involved. . . who knows? But hardly a scratch on that baby. Incredible. I guess no one knows for sure or ever will."

"Only the big guy upstairs," Callahan said smiling, "and mothers."

*He who fights the monsters might take care
lest he thereby become a monster.
And if you gaze for long into the abyss,
the abyss gazes also into you.*

~Neitzsche

CHAPTER FIFTEEN

THE CAR SAT idling, but the heart of the driver was far from it. He could almost hear his pulse as the anxiety of the pending events tightened his chest. As the sweat beaded up on his forehead, thoughts of leaving entered his mind. No one knew he was there. No one would know if he left. To him, however, it had become a matter of survival. So, he kept watching, waiting for just the exact time. It would be a gamble. But it was a bet he could not afford to lose.

The front door of the Circle K had been locked, refusing customers while the crime scene evidence was processed. Potential customers and curious onlookers peered into the store windows. When no guts or gore were evident, one by one they left, disappointed.

"Wasn't much of a robbery," was said by someone.

Carrie's store manager had arrived and had been there for almost an hour. She was a middle-aged woman and a struggling single parent. Harriet Kline knew the pain and felt the helplessness. During her tenure as an employee of convenience markets for the past twenty years, she had been robbed four times. Harriet knew the fear and the nightmares to come. She also knew how clerks had resigned after the experience of an armed robbery. She hugged Carrie, whispering that it would be all right. Carrie smiled and hugged her back, appreciating the concern. The door was opened, and Harriet followed the ID Technician from the building.

Carrie's replacement, a short, forty-something, plump woman, wearing a Circle K polo appeared next to the officer tending the front door. After exchanging words, she threw her cigarette aside and smiled, as the door was unlocked for her. She then rushed to Carrie's side.

"Did the sons-of-a-bitches hurt you, dear?" she asked, extending her hand.

"No. I'm all right, Vera. Thanks for coming in early."

"No problem."

The officer in charge closed his note pad and turned to Carrie. "The men who robbed you are in custody. I hope that relieves your mind. They definitely picked the wrong store this time." He smiled and touched her shoulder. "The detectives will be contacting you. I'm sorry you had to go through this ordeal."

She smiled back as he left and the door was unlocked, making the store open for business once more. It was as if nothing had happened.

Carrie walked into the back room to get her purse. Her legs suddenly felt weak and she sat down on a stack of boxes. It was quiet. Almost too quiet. She was alone with her thoughts. She was breathing quickly, and realizing it, she tried to slow herself down. It was over. But how many more can I take? How much more will it take to break me?

She remembered that night. His eyes, his breath. His fingers digging into her flesh, forcing her against the wall of the building. He laughed as his hands tore at her clothing. She tried to fight back, get him away from her. The more she fought, the stronger and more determined he became. She tasted her own blood, but she couldn't swallow.

"You, bitch," he had said. "You know you want me. You want to feel me. Because of how you look, you could never have anybody like me. Until now." And he bit her cheek and tore at her breasts. He hit her beside the head and above her eye. And then he dragged her to the car.

"No," she found herself saying aloud, standing up from the boxes.

"Are you all right, dear?" Vera asked from somewhere out of sight.

"Yes, I'm fine. I thought I had misplaced my keys," she lied and walked to the front.

Carrie found it curious as she peered out the front window of the store that the sudden violence of an armed robbery could give her a measure of security.

"Do you want me to walk you to your car?" Vera asked.

"Thanks, but I'll be fine," Carrie said, shouldering the door open.

The night air was cool and very refreshing to a body that had been perspiring nonstop from stress. Carrie walked without hesitation out the front door in the direction of her car. Tonight, for some reason she couldn't explain, she had no fear.

A Volkswagon and a pick up truck were parked in the lot to the north, approximately forty feet from hers. She glanced back into the store. Vera looked up and waved a final goodnight. Carrie waved back and Vera turned away.

James Laudermilk sat for over an hour in the darkness and witnessed the aftermath of the robbery. Watching the activity at the store, he pulled the leather glove onto his right hand, flexing his fingers, again and again. No one would be around when he pulled her to the back of the store. And he would hit her, over and over again, until she was unconscious. He would head west out of the city, and then take the desert roads on the other side of the mountains. Anywhere. He could dump her body anywhere out there and it would be months before her remains would be found. If ever.

The small electronic box blinked on the seat beside him. Its rows of red colored lights flashed back and forth across the face of the scanner until it picked up a transmission. The Circle K would now be all but forgotten. The police could only be in one place at a time. And tonight there were many places to be. He couldn't ask for a better scenario.

The stalker, rapist, and potential murderer carefully guided his one-year-old Ford Crown Victoria into position directly behind the building. It was virtually impossible to see it from any street, the main reason he had picked this store for his assault. It was tricky getting in, but he knew it by heart. He had driven for forty minutes to get there as he had done so many other nights to watch his prey. Laudermilk had a mental illness. He was aware of it, but he didn't care as long as it went unnoticed by his wife, two children, and his fellow aerospace engineers. Carrie was his third venture into the reality of his sickness. The other two, both young, financially struggling women, chose not to report their attacks and disappeared into society. Carrie reported her assault and did not disappear. If he had his way, she would disappear now . . . tonight. This would be his last trip to the Circle K at Valencia and 12th Avenue.

He had not used his automobile's headlights as he came from the alleyway. However, with the aid of the light of a half moon, he saw an old abandoned Plymouth parked in the corner of the lot. Probably stolen, he thought, noticing the partially opened hood. To be sure, Laudermilk walked quietly to the empty car and peered inside, finding nothing but two opened beer cans lying on the front seat.

Laudermilk was athletic and looked the part in his dark blue, nylon jogging suit. He wore no under clothes. They were in the trunk with his change of clothes. His jogging suit was purchased earlier in the day on the far eastside of Tucson from a liquidation sale at a discount store. With the tags removed, they were virtually untraceable.

He was in the darkness with his back to the south wall of the Circle K building when he heard footsteps, the same footsteps he had heard before. And when they stopped, he held his breath.

Carrie stood still as she listened for any noise out of the ordinary. She heard nothing and took a soft deep breath as she placed her key into the lock of her car.

Suddenly, her head snapped backwards as an arm slammed across her mouth. The skin on her lips tore. She tasted the acid of her own blood mixed with the salty sweat that did not belong to her. An odor found its way into a compartment of her brain. His smell. A smell cataloged by personal fear. He lifted her from her feet, and with a half dozen steps, carried her out of the light. His arm dropped as his hand grabbed her jaw and slammed her into the wall. Her attacker's face came close to hers and she begged for strength.

Callahan, please be out there somewhere. You said that you would be here for me. You promised.

Even in the dark, Carrie could see the fire in her attacker's eyes. His tongue surveyed his smiling lips as he forced her head against the gray wall of the building where she worked. She closed her eyes. His breath repulsed her. *I can't cry. I must not cry. Please, someone help me.* He placed his mouth close to hers. So close that she could taste his words as he began to accuse.

"You could have quit working here, *bitch!* But you didn't." His tongue found her lips, stopping when he tasted her blood. "Oh, did I hurt you? Again?" His breathing became heavier.

"I can feel your heart beating, wanting to leave your chest," he whispered as he pulled harshly at her breast. "This is what I've fucking wanted. Finally. This is my excitement. Can you feel my excitement?" he asked as he forced her hand down his leg.

Carrie tried to fight, but the more she struggled, the more fuel she added to his unthinkable passions. He was crazed, a monster. His right knee was between her legs, forcing upward, as if he was punishing her for her gender.

"Why?" Carrie pleaded. "Why did you come back? Haven't you hurt me enough?"

"Because you saw me. And you recognized me. I should have ripped your fucking heart out the first time. I fucking hate you!" he said. And then he calmed, suddenly. "Now, I'm going to make you disappear."

Laudermilk squeezed her throat. "We're going to take a little walk."

Rich Childers and Joe Parelli were Tactical Operation Officers — officers that had just heard James Laudermilk's admission. Earlier, they had held their breath as the rapist had peered into their old undercover car with the beer cans on the seat. Parelli crouched down next to Laudermilk's vehicle. He had removed the keys from the Crown Victoria. Childers was flat against the building wall, around the corner, some fifteen feet from the assailant . . . waiting for the right time. It came as the suspect came to him.

A huge right fist from the six-foot-six, 270-pound Childers landed full force against the side of Laudermilk's face. He dropped to the ground immediately, releasing Carrie the moment he was struck. Parelli instantly grabbed the screaming Carrie, pulling her away from the two men. The attacker now became the attacked. The second Laudermilk's knees hit the ground, Childers was on him, pulling his arms behind him to be cuffed.

But the rapist was far quicker and much stronger than the larger man had assumed. The fact that he was hurt mattered not. In fact, it gave him an added push, the internal chemical rush produced by fear. Before Childers could react, Laudermilk twisted from his grip and with a trained kick, slammed his foot into the side of the officer's head. Childers screamed as he grabbed at the air while going down. Parelli shoved Carrie to the side and reached for Laudermilk. He was too late. The attacker disappeared around the corner and into the night.

"This did not happen! This did not fucking happen!" Childers clutched at his jaw as his face found the dirt. "The little son-of-a-bitch! Does he know who he is messing with?"

"Get him, Joe!" Childers reached behind and pulled his weapon from his waistband. "I'm gonna kill that little bastard!"

Carrie began to crawl and cry. She pleaded as she screamed, "Get him! Get him! Please don't let him get away. Please!"

Parelli sprinted around the corner taking the same route that Laudermilk had taken, but it was too late. Laudermilk was gone.

"Get back in the store!" Parelli screamed at Carrie.

"Damn it, Joe! How did this happen? This has never happened to us before!" Childers yelled, blood gushing from his cut.

"TAC 12," Parelli screamed into the radio. "A 10-44 suspect is running from the Circle K at 12th and Valencia. Give us some units here!" The officer's voice displayed fear and embarrassment. He then saw the gash above his partner's eye. "Also dispatch a 10-72 unit."

Laudermilk was a superb athlete trained in martial arts. He actually felt a victory as he sprinted from the Circle K. This was a new thrill, a new excitement. He began to laugh as he ran.

"Weak," he shouted, "Tucson's elite are weak."

He slowed and turned to look back. No one was chasing him. He would run briefly into the neighborhood, he thought. And then circle back for his car.

And then his feet left the pavement; everything went blank; his body slammed into the bricks. The rough texture of the block tore into his face. He tried to move, but he couldn't. Someone very strong was forcing him into the side of the building. He tried to struggle free, but froze when he heard the sound of a revolver being cocked very close to his ear.

Laudermilk was pushed to his knees, but his face remained firmly against the wall. They were next to the side door of Checker Auto, two buildings away from the Circle K.

"Where did you come from? Who are you?" the rapist asked painfully.

"I came from the *barrio*, asshole. A place where men do not rape women. You don't deserve to live."

When Laudermilk tried to break away, a knee was forced between his legs and he screamed.

Parelli had heard the voices as he ran to nowhere. He stopped. He listened, trying to determine where the voices were coming from.

"But I'm not in the neighborhood anymore, white boy. Give me a reason, come on now! Give me a reason to . . ."

Parelli crouched beside the auto parts store. And then he moved around the corner, his .40 caliber automatic held in both hands at arms length.

"Freeze!" he screamed. And then he saw a uniform. And a revolver shoved into the back of a person's skull.

"Are you looking for this piece of shit?" Parelli saw Laudermilk's face as the officer grabbed his hair and pulled him from the wall.

"You fucking asshole!" Parelli grabbed the prisoner and threw him back against the wall. "You fuckin' puke, I'm gonna kill you."

"Be careful. We're drawing a crowd," Alex said, nodding toward two automobiles stopped on the roadway.

"Cuff the bastard." Parelli relaxed his grip. "You're lucky," he said, spitting at Laudermilk.

"Where did you come from?" Parelli asked, staring at the officer cuffing his prisoner.

"I was across the street, in the vacant lot. I was taking a chance that our scumbag here had figured that the store had been forgotten."

"Really." Parelli was embarrassed, but relieved. "I haven't seen you down here before. What's your name?"

"Montoya. Alex Montoya."

CHAPTER SIXTEEN

PATROL TWO CIRCLED IN THE AIR above the police station like a hawk on a mouse. The frequency was going nuts with activity and more than likely so was the rest of the city. So why would he be landing? Callahan wondered.

The chopper was on the ground by the time Callahan entered the lot. Parking his unit in the "No Parking Zone," he watched a lone figure exit the helicopter and lower his head as he ran under the rotating blades. The officer in the flight suit looked around until he spotted Callahan's vehicle and immediately ran towards him stopping short, waving him off to the side.

"What's up, Ron?" Callahan asked as the pilot put an arm around his shoulder and directed him away from the noise of the aircraft.

"You may have a problem with one of your rookies. I've got to get back up in the air, so I'll be brief. During your chase, I observed the first suspect dive under some bushes. The unit that was there, #370, found him instantly. The subject was on the ground, prone, and not moving. I saw the officer cover him, cuff him, and then, God as my witness, it appeared that he began pistol-whipping the guy. I can't be sure. I was too far away. If your chase weren't on I would have stuck around. I thought you should know, but I didn't want to say anything over the air. It's your baby, Michael. I'm no Mother Theresa, but that was bullshit. Know what I mean? Gotta go. Call me later. Sorry."

The pilot took several strides then turned and stopped. "Did

you hear about the Circle K at 12th and Valencia?"
        "Is this a joke, Ron?" Callahan asked in disbelief. "I was
there, remember?"
        "No, after the robbery."
        "What are you talking about?"
        "The rapist came back."
        "Goddammit! I knew it." Callahan swung his fist into the
air.
        "Hey, it's all right. One of your guys got him after he assaulted
a TAC officer."
        "One of my guys? My squad was involved in the chase."
        "All but one, it seems. Later."
        Ron Tomy ran quickly back to the helicopter and with a lift
and a tilt, he was airborne.
        Callahan stood frozen. He had no idea what to think or what
to feel.
        "Shit!" he said out loud as he walked back to his unit. Padilla's
vehicle pulled into the lot and drove to the rear and parked. Callahan
began to walk slowly through the nearly unoccupied parking area.
The evening's events swirled in his mind like a dream with many
characters. Requests for decisions were being made to a brain that
was overloaded with anxiety and fear. But they were his points to
resolve, and only his, and he knew he must first listen to be heard.
He had made that promise to Padilla and every other new officer that
he had trained in the past.
        Padilla swallowed hard as he watched Callahan's shadow
move towards him. He felt his pulse quicken and his mouth become
dry. Padilla had pulled to the curb before he entered the lot and
watched the Bell helicopter lift quickly from the asphalt pad. They
couldn't have seen me with the prisoner he thought. Even if they
did, they wouldn't say anything; it's an unwritten code among police
officers. It was a code of silence held within the unspeakable ethics
of street justice. As a child he had witnessed firsthand the brutal
treatment of prisoners within the harsh environment of the *Barrio*. It
was acceptable, almost expected.
        The pilot of Patrol Two had landed to make Callahan aware
of my fine police work, Padilla surmised. He could see the pilot

telling his training officer that the young officer had used instincts and skill exceeding his brief tenure and limited experience in dealing with the capture of a fleeing felon. And now his training officer was going to pass on the praise of the pilot, adding some of his own. Perhaps, as the account of his ability was forwarded up the chain of command, a commendation might be in order. However, more than that he thought, was the recognition of the veteran officers, the seasoned street-wise cops who knew how to dispense justice at the lowest level. Like a child on Christmas Eve, Richard could hardly contain himself. He smiled as he thought that it was only the beginning.

"Tonight is what police work is all about, isn't it, Callahan?" The rookie stepped from his automobile without taking his eyes off of his mentor. "Man, I looked up and that asshole was right there." Padilla couldn't quit smiling as the evening's events flashed in his eyes.

"Yeah, Richard, that's what police work is all about. The good guys get the bad guys. And without anyone getting hurt. Everybody in control of his emotions. Right? Isn't that what you saw?" Callahan said as he stared intently at the officer, searching for a sign, the slightest gesture that would indicate that he knew he was in the wrong.

Padilla's smile began to fade, as his face presented new suspicion. "Yeah, sure. The chase. The arrests. Everything was handled really well, don't you think?" And he tried to fish into Callahan's mind as fear began to rise. "And Patrol Two! Christ, what a tool for the ground units. He can see damn near everything from up there."

Callahan didn't answer at first. He let the words seep into his brain. Slowly, he sat on the fender of Padilla's vehicle, trying to suppress his anger and calculate his questions. He studied his boots and brushed at his pants, feeling the silence and hearing his thoughts. There is something going on here that is out of my control he feared. Matters far more serious than the training of a law enforcement officer. But there was very little room for error in an occupation of mortality. After all, we are dedicated to the good of our citizens, not the bad of our profession.

"Tell me, Richard. Tell me what Ron Tomy saw from above when you located the suspect hiding under the bushes." Callahan continued to sit on the car as he watched the officer begin to pace. "I asked, or should I say ordered the suspect to lie still." He swallowed hard and his hands became nervous as his mind went back to the side street with the heavily breathing man at his feet. *The helicopter didn't see anything. He couldn't have. They were turning away; they were leaving.* "The suspect refused. He started to get up and then his hand started toward his waist." Richard licked his lips as his mind was creating words faster than his tongue could speak them. "Then he attempted to get up, to flee. I forced him back down to the ground and he resisted."

The blood began to surface in Callahan's face as he pushed himself up to his feet from the fender of the patrol car. He was angered and he was hurt and Padilla's lying was adding to his misconduct. His growing abuses of authority were apparent, now becoming criminal. He had to be stopped. His depravations were becoming more serious with each incident. He was beginning to involve other officers, affecting their careers, and more importantly, their lives. "And how did you stop him?" Callahan was now standing in front of Padilla, staring into his desperate eyes.

"We struggled," Padilla answered as he took a step backwards. "I took control of him, forced him to the ground. And then I cuffed him. Is there a problem?"

The blood! I forgot that Callahan had seen the asshole's face.

"Oh, yeah, he must have scratched his face up a little when we fell back to the ground." *Goddammit! He's going to see right through what I just said!*

"Damn it, Padilla!" Callahan slammed his hand down on the hood of the vehicle. "I told you the first night, along with the others, that I wanted to keep certain situations at the officer level, handle and solve our own problems. But you have violated that. You have a serious problem! Richard, you have crossed the line and you know it!"

"I see what you are doing now, Coach. You want details, off the record accounts of what really happened." Padilla's eyes flashed with fire.

Callahan watched him in silence as he felt nausea growing inside. He had listened to each word, not knowing whether to pity him or to be ashamed.

Padilla continued, "I told him to not move, and he didn't. But then he called me a fuckin' pig. And when I told him to shut up, he said, 'Fuck you, wetback!' And then I pulled my revolver and I hit him. And he started to yell something else, so I hit him again with the barrel of my weapon. It was then the asshole realized that we don't fuck around here on the Southside. I then put a knee on the back of his neck . . . and, I . . . ah, cuffed him."

Callahan watched the face of Richard Padilla as he shared his latest version of what should have been an event without incident. It appeared that he was searching for an acceptance into a world that he did not yet understand. But the young officer's deep-rooted problem had created a situation that had to be dealt with.

"Was he cuffed when you hit him? Answer me, Padilla. Was he cuffed and on the ground when you used your pistol as a weapon?" Callahan demanded.

"No! I told you that I handcuffed him after he tried to escape and put him down." Richard's voice was distressed, almost becoming a whine.

"I don't believe you, Padilla. It's all bullshit! Just what are you trying to prove?"

"So, what if he was cuffed? What the hell difference does it make?" The officer stared at Callahan.

"You beat a defenseless prisoner. Once you handcuffed him, you became in charge of his welfare. That's what the problem is, Padilla!" Their eyes were locked on each other like radar.

"And to compound matters, you lied. You have given me no choice. I have to report this. Your abusive behavior keeps raising its ugly head. Sgt. Stark has talked to you about it and so have I. But, you kept denying that you had a problem. That's all I have to say. Get your stuff from the car and go do your reports."

Callahan turned and started to walk toward the police building. He did not want his anger to get in the way.

"Nobody cared that my brother was beaten, asshole."

"What did you say?" Callahan turned around, not clearly

hearing what was said.

"My brother was beaten by cops, lots of cops. And I watched. I watched him fight back. I saw him get one of their weapons." Richard Padilla's hands were trembling as the tears started to flow. "He raised his hand while he was still on his back. My mother screamed. His eyes went to her just as they fired. Again, and again, and again. She grabbed her ears, and fell motionless to the ground. For a moment, I thought she had been hit; I cried out, and watched my brother die."

Callahan watched, but said nothing. Padilla backed slowly away, his hands behind him searching for the hood of his patrol car. As he made contact he fell backwards, sliding to the ground, rolling onto his knees.

"I was eleven years old when I watched my nineteen year old brother get shot to death. He was into drugs, using and dealing. He disgraced my family. My mother was never right after that night." Richard didn't bother to wipe away the tears, nor did he see Callahan wave other officers away from them.

"I hated my brother then, and I still do." He looked up to find Callahan's eyes. "And I hate everyone like him." Officer Richard Padilla had just spoken volumes. His life, his hatred were one in the same. At age eleven he had quit growing.

"Why did you wait to tell me this, Richard? Are you seeking a justification for your actions? Your own abuses?" Callahan spoke softly through his words. How do you discipline hatred? he wondered, as his eyes fell upon Richard's face.

"No! I'm not making excuses. I'm not even giving a reason. It's just — never mind." Padilla pulled himself up to his feet, not bothering to brush the dirt from his uniform.

"If you have something to say, Richard, say it," Callahan said. "But just remember, you're not eleven anymore. It sounds cruel, but not as cruel as answering violence with violence."

Padilla bent over, his hands placed on his knees, as he seemed to direct his thoughts at the asphalt. "I guess I wanted to make right my brother's disgraces. I wanted to bring pride back to the Padilla name."

"By what? Bringing more disgrace? Creating more shame?

What if you were arrested for assault while in uniform? Man, that would really bring the family name back to respectability." Padilla suddenly stood straight as Callahan continued, "You said that your mother was never the same after that night. Neither were you, Richard. And it's quite apparent that you are in need of help, the kind of professional help I can't give. But for now, we have work to finish."

"I'll be up in robbery if you need some help with your report." Callahan did not look back as he walked away.

Richard's words then came as ice. "I've heard about you and your brand of street justice." Padilla's stare was drilled on Michael Callahan's back. "What makes your methods right and mine so terribly wrong? Is it the fact that I am on probation, or are you trying to correct some of your own abuses?"

Callahan turned to answer, but did not have one. Richard Padilla did not have an answer either, but he did add to his statement. "I hope and pray that you never have to watch someone die, Callahan."

Callahan froze. Richard had unwittingly crawled inside his mind. He wanted to be angry, but he couldn't. He wanted to go back and choke the little bastard. But he couldn't.

"If I had waited to be a good 'ol boy, would it have mattered? But because I am a *rookie* and haven't been initiated yet, I am wrong?" Richard's voice became louder with each thought. Slowly, he stepped toward his stationary mentor. "You, and the other 'so-called' veterans play by different rules. Right? Your own fraternity of lies, and cover-ups. But, I fucked up because I wasn't accepted yet. Or never would be."

Richard moved to his vehicle and began to gather his equipment. The night suddenly seemed different. No intensity. No pretense. No lies or cover-ups.

"You're right, Richard." Callahan wanted to add more, but was interrupted.

"No, I'm not. But, neither are you." Richard walked by as his training officer stood in the darkness. "But, you were right about one thing Officer Callahan. It is about survival and only the strong survive."

Padilla walked on, leaving Callahan with new thoughts and past decisions.

I hear the sound I love, the sound of the human voice.
I hear sounds running together, combined, fused, or following.
Sounds of the country and sounds of the city,
sounds of the day and night.
Talkative young ones to those that like them,
the loud laugh of work people at their meals.

~Walt Whitman

CHAPTER SEVENTEEN

FROM THE ROAD leading up to Mt. Lemmon, an abrupt left was required to gain access to the small, but sufficient campground of Middle Bear Canyon. Only a few knew how to enter the first time without going up the road and then turning back. And some knew it by heart. Like the green truck that pulled in as Callahan watched. Rufus was lying close by under a tree and raised his head upon Jake's arrival, but did not bother to get up. With a heavy sigh, he laid his head back down, stretching his long body out in his favorite sunspot.

"Callahan," Jake asked as he stepped from his Forest Ranger pickup, "do you know a police dispatcher named Angela?"

"Yeah. Why?" his mind searched back.

"She wanted to know if I had seen you today. I said 'yeah' and she said that if I saw you again to tell you she was coming up here."

"When did she call?"

"This morning, a little after six."

"Did she tell you when she was coming up here?"

"About 4 or so."

"Thanks, Jake. Appreciate you coming down to tell me."

Jake wasn't an attractive person to look at. He was all knuckles, including his forehead. It was as if his large eyes were blessed with an awning. Jake had false teeth, but only wore the bottom plate, allowing his chin to come close to his nose whenever he chewed. And that was pretty much all of the time, with Mail Pouch being his choice of chewing tobacco. He was slender, almost skinny and tall, but would be even taller if he had better posture. This mountain was his life and any other mountain that required his services.

"She sounds pretty, Callahan. Is she your girlfriend?" This was the first and only time that Jake had ventured into his friend's personal life. Jake figured whatever brought Callahan here was his own business. Besides, the police officer might have a few questions regarding Jake's past and that wouldn't be good. Too many questions could be asked of an ex-clergyman. Jake had a saying, 'if you have one foot in the past and one in the future, you're pissin' on the present.'

"Think about your question, Jake," Callahan said, looking down at himself, "what self-respecting female would ever be my girlfriend?"

Jake laughed and nodded his head like one of those bobbing dog statues found on a dashboard. "Gotta go. See you all later."

Callahan sat on the rear bumper, leaning forward, hands on his knees. Why would she be coming up here? I hardly know her. Hell, I don't know her at all. Oh well, it might be good to talk to somebody different. Callahan stood, scratched the two-day-old growth on his face and walked to the side of the camper. Peering into the glass window, he found his reflection, looking at it with a mixture of self-pity and distain. He smiled several different ways, trying to determine which one Angela would find attractive. None seemed to work. That's it. Rugged. She goes for the masculine look. He looked back into the window glass. Shit, even that needed some work.

"C'mon Rufus. Let's go up to the store at Summerhaven. I love that drive and I need to make a phone call."

"The phones are out. Can't help ya, Callahan," Marty said.

"How long have they been out?"

"Since yesterday."

"When do you expect them to be working again?"

"Do I look like a phone repair man?"

"That would make you too respectable. Those guys work for a living."

"Get out of here," Marty ordered, not looking up, but trying to sweep whatever he had in front of the broom at Callahan. Marty ran the general store/restaurant in the village. Summerhaven sat 9,000 feet in elevation and twenty-five miles from the base of Mt. Lemmon. That meant a round trip of twenty-nine miles for Callahan from his niche in Bear Canyon. Twenty-nine miles of switchbacks, changing terrain and a climb of four thousand feet. He and Rufus loved it because the higher elevation meant much cooler temperatures.

"Got any sandwiches made up, Marty?"

"Yeah, in the deli-case. Take your pick and leave your money on the counter. Good seeing you again. Come up more often." Marty still hadn't looked up.

"Thanks."

Callahan glanced at his watch; it was just before noon. He had enough time to drive farther up the mountain towards the ski lift. He loved the Ponderosa Pines and the smells of the Coronado Forest. Especially now. It was the second week of May. Bees covered the flowering buds. The air was filled with pollen and barbecue smoke and sounds of people having fun.

Rufus jumped in front, not wanting to waste the view. But instead of sitting, he stood, with his head fully extended from the passenger's side window. Without the warning of a growl, he barked, repeatedly, those deep-throated barks that only a German shepherd can produce. Someone or something was nearby, causing Rufus' hair to stand on edge.

"Calm, boy," Callahan said, placing his hand on the dog's hip. "It's okay."

Callahan backed slowly from the front of the deli. The barking stopped, but a long, toothy growl ensued. Callahan looked to his right and found the subject of Rufus' attention. He applied the brakes and abruptly stopped. A person was smiling. A young, dark skinned man in a camouflaged jacket. He smiled and raised a knife. A large knife. He drew it above his head.

Callahan turned the engine off and placed his right hand on the revolver in his waistband. His heart pounded as his mind began to play tricks on him. His hands began to shake and he placed them upon the steering wheel in an attempt to steady them. He saw a walkway that led to a room. No, a small apartment. Callahan heard screams. The knife, the gunshots. The sirens. He heard, "You killed him. You killed him. You killed him," from a desperate young woman's voice.

The words, 'You have a real nice dog, man,' brought Callahan back to Mount Lemmon.

"What?"

"Your dog. He's cool." The young man turned away, cutting the frayed end of a rope.

Callahan watched him tie the knot and pull the ends tight to secure his camping gear to the top of his Jeep, then folded up the knife and put it in his back pocket.

"Let's go, buddy," the man in the camouflaged jacket said to somebody. "We're ready to go."

"Who were you talking to?" a young mother asked, obviously pregnant, walking down the wooden steps.

"Some guy in a truck," the young man said, looking back over his shoulder. "He's kinda strange," he extended his arms. "Here, let me take that bag."

"Thank you, David. Is Tony in the truck?"

Callahan took a deep breath and forced a smile, but the young man was looking elsewhere. Why did my mind do that, he thought? He watched the Jeep back away from the parking space. He pulled onto the roadway and started back down the mountain. He had forgotten about going up higher. He drove down the sunlit road with no cars in sight. The pine trees towered above him on both sides and he began to calm.

Well, I'd better find some way to look presentable, Callahan thought, backing his truck into its customary slot. The Levis that he was wearing weren't bad. And a T-shirt with the sleeves cut – that rugged Clint Eastwood look. The shower he had taken a few hours earlier would have to do. A quick brush of the teeth, some of which were original and some not, a little roll-on deodorant, and a baseball cap covering up what a comb refused to improve, made him somewhat presentable. Judging from how she was dressed the first time I met her, she'll probably come looking like a million dollars. Man, I don't need this right now.

Putting on the tennis shoe that he had just removed, Callahan begged for his brain to find his mind. He took it off again and slid it across the camper floor, looking for the boots that he intended to wear. He picked up one and struggled to get his foot into it. He searched for the other, then found it next to the bag of potatoes, exactly where Rufus had left it. Even if he hadn't, the dog was convenient to blame.

The night he met her sitting on the stone bench outside the debriefing room played over and over again in his mind. He tried to picture what she looked like. Several faces came to mind. Separate at first, then all mixed together. Who is Angela? And why is she coming all the way up here to see me?

Callahan stepped out of the back of his camper, onto the bumper, and one step down to the ground. A slow moving Camaro, silver or maybe gray, quietly turned into the campground on the first try. The car made its way through the small parking lot and parked immediately in front of his Ford truck with the brown and white camper. Callahan moved around the truck and curiously watched as the young lady inside the Chevy stepped from her automobile.

Her chestnut hair was pulled back into a ponytail, but expertly curled. A face that required no cosmetic attention was given just enough. Chocolate brown western boots peeked out from under the creased seams of well-fitting Wranglers. She wore a soft, ivory sweater with a light blue jacket over her shoulders, the arms knotted around her neck.

For a brief second, he found himself thinking something he wasn't capable of. Callahan was fighting his mind as his heart was resisting emotion. He couldn't go there, or anywhere close. He didn't dare to wake himself up from a dream that carried no responsibility and very little reality.

"Have any trouble finding us?" he asked. Callahan began to search for the reason for her visit.

"Not really, I've been here before." Angela dropped a hand to Rufus without lowering her eyes from Callahan.

"This is a nice secluded spot, isn't it?" he said.

"Is that why you chose to camp here?" Angela smiled, looking past him into the forest.

"Not initially. The first evening I drove up here, I had every intention of going up farther, but I checked my gas gauge and it showed about a quarter of a tank," Callahan answered, feeling more at ease. "If I went up any higher, I wouldn't have had enough gas to get to work the next day. So, I pulled in here."

"They don't care if you stay here? It says no camping," Angela said, glancing at the sign.

"The third night or so, they got curious and checked me out and seemed to think an additional badge could be an asset."

"So they pretty much leave you alone now, right?"

"They stop by every now and then. They're good people; they do a good job." Callahan smiled and looked down at his hands.

"You're almost laughing," Angela smiled. "You must have had a good thought."

"Sorry, I was just thinking about the name I gave this place." Callahan continued to study his hands. "It's kind of embarrassing."

"Oh, tell me. I've heard just about everything."

"I call it, 'womb with a view.'"

"That's not embarrassing; that's cute. And it's quite accurate," she said, looking up at the mountains that completely surrounded them. "I didn't notice all of this the first time I was here."

"Did you come up the first time to camp or picnic?"

"No, just for the drive with a friend. We pulled in, turned around and left. Your truck was here."

"You knew what my truck looked like before today?" Callahan was perplexed. He was already feeling comfortable with her, but at the same time very suspicious. "Tell me again, what is your job at TPD?"

"Communications."

"Really? Why haven't I heard you?"

"Obviously, we're on different frequencies."

"I often switch frequencies. Why haven't I heard you?" he repeated.

Angela walked by him. His eyes followed her as she went by, and then she turned to speak. "Maybe you have," Angela smiled.

"And didn't know it." She continued to smile.

She was so beautiful. And so familiar. "Good point."

Callahan moved towards her. She watched him as he walked and laughed at the way he looked at her.

Angela turned her back to him again and walked softly, but with purpose towards the woods. She and Rufus climbed among the rocks, through a trickle of water resembling a stream. The blue jacket had been discarded somewhere and his view of her Wranglers as she maneuvered up the rocks was impressive.

"Are you afraid of me or something?" she asked, looking back.

"How can I be afraid of you? I'm not even sure that you exist."

Callahan watched Angela as she laughed, and slid off of the boulder. Her attempt at being noticed had worked. She was part illusion and part fact. She was extremely attractive in person, but even more beautiful in his perceptions. He had never received her touch, smelled her skin, felt her breath, nor run his fingers through her flowing hair. Passion was her designer and desire was his dream, but neither, regardless of emotion, could become reality. He was sitting on a concrete picnic table with his arms folded as she began to walk slowly, seductively towards him, with the last rays of sunlight following her like a train on a wedding gown.

He studied her every step. Angela moved like images passing through a sleeping person's mind. His eyes were riveted upon her, not able to leave her stare. She represented everything that he desired, he thought.

"So," Angela sat at a picnic table and looked directly at him. "Why are you here?"

"I told you. This is a beautiful spot. It's peaceful and nobody bothers me here." Callahan began to scratch Rufus as a distraction.

"No, why are you really living here? Maybe it's not that you like the mountain so much; maybe it's that you are running from your problems in the city."

"What in the hell are you talking about?" Callahan's uneasiness grew as he sat on the truck bumper.

"Oh, c'mon Michael," her voice became softer, "everyone

knows that you are having trouble dealing with this."

"Dealing with what? I'm just fine." Callahan stood, shoving his hands deep into his pockets.

"Really, then why the camper? Why not a house in the city?" He stared at her. "Economics. If I live in my camper, I can afford to allow my children to stay in my house."

"Allow? That's mighty generous of you. You create a family and you allow them to stay in your house. How can you call it your house when you're not there? Because you pay for it? It's one thing to end a marriage, but to run and hide is an altogether different situation."

Angela rose from the table and walked right through his glare. "Do you know who you are? Do you realize what you are doing?"

Surprisingly, he felt no anger at what she was saying. Just relief. There was no control now. Just awareness. An awareness that she was as accurate in her perceptions as if she had walked into his very being, pulling out the ugly, and in the process, disturbing his myth. She had presented the evidence and it could not be refuted. She was making it his job to confront and accept or not to accept. The only thing left now was the acceptance and with that came an admission of weakness.

"The sun is going down," Angela said without looking up from Rufus. "Are you getting hungry? I know I am."

"I, ah . . . I don't have much to make a meal of. Sorry. I'm not used to having guests."

A brief honk from a vehicle's horn persuaded Callahan to look to the roadway. He saw the forest green truck indicating Jake was on his way off the mountain. He smiled as he watched Jake behind the wheel. If he hadn't known better he would have sworn that it was his dad driving.

CHAPTER EIGHTEEN

"FIRE UP YOUR GRILL," Angela ordered, not waiting for a response. "I invited myself for dinner, but not to worry," she said, noticing Callahan's dismay, "I brought the groceries."

Rufus and his master watched as she walked towards her car, not fully keeping up with the change in events. "I could sure use some help," she said as she glanced back over her shoulder with a smile.

In the trunk was an ice chest that Callahan removed as she carried a basket and one large candle.

"We have a lot to talk about — you and I, and that other guy running around inside your head. I hope you weren't planning on going anywhere soon."

The charcoal in the hibachi had turned sufficiently gray, causing the steaks to sizzle and the dog to drool. A white linen tablecloth was placed on the concrete picnic table to receive two place settings and a large round, vanilla scented candle, complete with a base. A salad, with lots of colorful, healthy greens, and a bowl of something with cheese on top was placed in the middle of the linen. Dinner rolls, in one of those baskets with red-checkered cloth, completed the menu. The result was a feast that felt completely familiar, but absolutely new.

"I'm not going to ask you why you did this," Callahan said as he filled his plate again. "Because I know why." He took one more bite and admired his ability to grill a steak. "Because you are an angel. You are always there for someone else when they, for some reason, can't be there for themselves."

"You are in pain, Mr. Callahan. And when someone is in need of the strength to heal, there must be someone there for him. And it's not easy to accept help, or to realize that you want help. But, the angels are out there. Everywhere. You just have to recognize them. And use them. Because angels don't push you or pull you, they just walk with you."

In a circular fire ring made from rock, Callahan began to assemble the makings for a small and intimate campfire, used to soothe and create a mood that the vigilant creatures of the neighborhood had learned to love. Small branches laid over even smaller twigs caught fire easily, keeping the fire simple and controllable. It did not depend on how much fuel was added, but instead how often, and for what reason. As he stared into the fire, his mind and his heart began a struggle. Old thoughts, nothing new, nothing constructive, were occupying his mind. It wasn't only him. Margaret was a mental wreck as well, maybe even more so. Why am I here was not a question, but instead, a statement, and a desire. It was never about who was right — logic and reasoning, or who was wrong — loneliness and despair. It was about strength and conviction.

He walked away from the fire and found a tree to lean on and support his thoughts. The sun had disappeared beyond the mountains to the west. The light of the candle and the dying glow of the charcoal became the only source of light. Ever so quietly, she came and stood an arm's length behind him. Angela wanted to place a hand on his shoulder, but she did not want to be a distraction.

"For the first time in recent memory, Angela, I can actually hear the birds and see them fly. I take time to watch the sun come up and the dew drip from the leaves. I can actually feel the smells, Angela, and touch the sounds. And these same senses that make me happy here, disgust me in my work. The filth and dirt of the streets, the sounds of violence, the odor of poverty, and the taste of fear, everywhere, cause doubt in myself and in my occupation. Vic criticized me for losing focus, when in reality I was probably achieving more than I ever knew existed. My job was my life, but in fact, it ruined a marriage and drew me from my home. I am not doubting my decision to leave Margaret. Not to sound like a martyr, but I believe she will someday be better off for that." He turned to look at Angela, moving closer to the fire as he felt the chill in the air.

"I see my children now, more than I did when I lived with them," he continued. "I'm not saying that I'm with them more. It's just that I see them more because, now, I take the time to look at them. I listen to them, not just hear them. I actually listen to them. I touch them, I smell their skin, and I wipe away their tears. They have a father now. I am where I belong. Vic told me that I was going to hurt someone and he was right. I hurt my kids; I hurt Margaret. I had failed earlier in my life, but my abilities in law enforcement allowed me to succeed. But, as I buried myself in my work . . . well, you're witnessing the rest."

"Are you saying that you don't want to be a policeman anymore?"

He did not answer, but his silence spoke volumes. Instead, he stared at her as a student to a teacher, in search of an answer.

"It's not that I don't want to be. I don't think that I can. I obviously need to make some adjustments."

Callahan noticed Angela hug her own body. "You're getting cold, aren't you? That jacket you brought is not going to be enough, is it?"

"It will do for now. To be perfectly honest, I didn't think you would want me to stay this long."

"Please, I want you to stay. You're good for me. You make me talk and you listen."

"Tell me about Sara. Tell me what she means to you."

"Sara?" he stepped away from the tree.

"Yes. Sara. How do you feel about her?"

"She's a friend, Angela." Callahan looked away. "A real close friend."

"Are you saying that for my benefit or yours?" Without him hearing or seeing her, Angela had moved away.

"What does that mean?"

"You know, the thing that guys do. When they're with a girl

they try to say things the girl wants to hear. Or at least, the things they think she wants to hear."

"I'm not playing any games," Callahan said, taking a deep breath. "And yes, I do feel something for her. But, I don't know what I feel or why I feel the way I do."

Angela said nothing.

He breathed in the night air deeply as the soft, crackling fire of numerous small, dead juniper branches and one large mesquite log created a brilliant visual echo throughout the canyon. The fire crackled, its dancing fingers changing colors in the blink of an eye. It created subtle reflections gently bouncing off of Angela's small, beautiful face. He couldn't help but stare at her beauty, without intent, but more what if. At times, as the fire glow changed its mind several times a second, he saw the past, releasing him from the present. Angela aroused something inside of him, but it wasn't desire or passion. It was the need of a friend.

Angela gently broke the silence, in a voice barely above a whisper. "Are you a religious person?" she asked, watching the fire perform a dance. "In a quiet way you seem to be."

"I don't believe in religions," Callahan responded, watching the same fire, but seeing different dancers.

"That's surprising," Angela said, looking at him very perplexed. "You give the appearance of being very spiritual."

"What's that got to do with religion?"

"Everything!"

"Like what?"

"You know, churches and beliefs, going to church on Sunday."

"So what you're saying is that, to have faith, and a belief in God, I have to be religious and go to church?"

"No, not necessarily. It's just the normal thing to do. You know, what everybody else does. Find a church, become part of a congregation."

"I know what you're saying, it's just that I don't subscribe to that form of a belief system. Being a part of the masses is not my idea of worship. Believing in God, having faith in God is. Like right here, look around. Can you envision a better church than this?" Callahan remarked.

"Were you brought up in a religious environment? Were your parents church goers?" Angela's questions created a silence, an abrupt stop in conversation. She felt the silence before she noticed it.

"Did I say something wrong?" Angela asked, feeling she had just gone somewhere she shouldn't have.

Callahan inhaled deeply. "No, not at all. My father was a Methodist minister."

"Really?" Angela exclaimed in surprise. "So you *were* religious."

He stared at her and paused, "I said my father was, Angela, not me. I saw the games he played. I saw what he wasn't; I saw and felt what he was. He taught love, but couldn't give it, unless it was on his terms. He preached family, but couldn't create the environment for one. I'm afraid that I have become my father, and that has always been my greatest fear."

"I'm sorry," she apologized.

"Don't be. It's not for pity. I need to get this out . . . but that could take until the 21st Century, if I live that long. Dad's faith was based solely on the Bible. But, as with teachings of the Bible, many questions of faith are unanswered."

"What do you mean?"

"Bad or unfortunate things happen to people with faith. And it's a real test. Those who believe, get through it, and go on. Get stronger, in fact."

"So, you don't believe in the Bible?" Angela asked, somewhat bewildered.

Callahan stood to stir the fire and looked off into the darkness above the mountains. "I believe in the Bible . . . for what it is, a collection of stories passed down through the centuries, translated several times and into several languages. They were passed down through the generations by word of mouth, not by the written word. And we know how reliable that is." He paused to adjust the embers and catch a breath. Angela watched him intently as the reflection of the fire bounced off of his somber face.

"Can you go on? Please?"

"After the crucifixion of Jesus there was a gap of 50 years. There was no written word about Jesus' life during that period.

Nothing about his birth, his teachings, or about his disciples. Nor was there anything on the Resurrection. The Bible as it exists today simply isn't a true record of what originally happened. It, in the original text, was on Papyrus scrolls. None of it exists today. Papyrus disintegrated quickly. It was made from a reed that grew by the Nile and was the only form of paper at the time.

"Jesus was and still is, the greatest teacher of all times, but fact is fact, and belief is, well, a belief. My belief is based on faith, not solely on the stories of the Bible. However, everything around us didn't accidentally happen. It was an act of God. Stories in the Bible try to depict how, and like I said, they're just stories passed on and passed down."

Callahan stared into the fire and took a breath. "Do I believe there should be churches and, as you put it, congregations? Absolutely!" He continued, "Many people find comfort in numbers. It just works for them. They believe in and study the teachings from the Bible. More power to them if it enriches their faith and makes them better persons. But it's the hypocrisy that I can't handle. I saw it firsthand. I see it everywhere! Dress up on Sunday, put five bucks in the collection plate, and make sure you're seen in church. To many of them, they have done their duty. Really? Is this what religion is all about? Not for me, it isn't. Sorry, that's the way I feel; but I won't argue a religion. No answers are produced from that debate. I bet you're sorry you asked, Angela."

"No, no, I'm not, in fact, I feel somewhat enlightened," Angela said smiling.

"Just remember, take it for what it's worth."

He wasn't aware until now, just how much he needed to talk. To talk to someone that would listen. And ask the right questions.

"Do you have something that I might wear?" Her eyes twinkled as she asked, anticipating his answer.

"Sure," Callahan blushed, "if you don't mind wearing my sweatpants."

"And a sweatshirt, a big bulky one. And socks that are way too large."

"Yeah, I can do that. I'll clear off the bed inside for you to sleep on later. I've got a big ol' lawn chair that I can sleep on out here."

"Do you have two big ol' lawn chairs?" she giggled. "I want to stay out here with you."

"Give me just a second," Callahan said moving into the camper. Amy's sleeping bag will work well, he thought, taking it from the bed above the cab. From under the long window bed, he took two heavy, wool Mexican blankets and placed them on her chair, on top of the sleeping bag.

While Angela changed clothes, Callahan stepped on the rear bumper and pulled the strap that held the aluminum framed chairs atop his camper. He placed them a few feet apart and put the sleeping bag on top, with the blanket folded neatly at the bottom.

"Crawl inside," he smiled. "This is one hell of a nest."

Callahan laid back into his chair, wishing this night would never end. "Can you feel the stars, Angela? Can you smell the wind?"

"Hmmm. Yes I can. And I can see your heart. You have a gift, Michael Callahan. A gift not to you, but instead, one that comes through you. You worry so much about becoming weak that you have forgotten how to remain strong. This life is not about what you are. It's about who you are, and what you can do for others. Someday you will see why you exist, perhaps in a very mysterious way. Perhaps not. That is your choice. I am very tired, Michael. My flame is about to go out."

"May I ask you one more question?" Callahan moved to the side of the chair, closer to her.

"You're going to ask who my friend is, aren't you? The one that came up here with me."

"Do you mind telling me?"

"Not at all." Angela smiled. "He's a friend of yours, too. Weaver. Weaver Bailey."

"The F.B.I. agent?"

"One in the same," Angela said. "We're like brother and sister."

Callahan tried to process what she said. Her and Weaver. They had driven up here before and didn't stop. He knew Weaver. And Weaver knew him. But he had no idea who Angela was.

"It's been awhile since I've seen him."

"I know." Angela yawned. "He told me about Dr. Downs.

How this guy had bought a child and was involved with a missing person. Amazing."

"Doctor? Weaver said that guy was a doctor? Where did he come up with that?"

Callahan didn't get an answer. He watched her as she pulled her legs close to her body and buried herself amongst the warmest of blankets. Her eyes were closed now, her breathing unheard.

The response of the smallest of wildlife to the pre-dawn light nudged Callahan awake as he lay buried beneath a couple of old, but warm blankets and a partially completed afghan. He very slowly turned his head towards Angela, to watch her sleep and to savor the sight, wishing that the previous evening had never ended.

But Angela was not there. The chair that she had fallen asleep in was gone. Callahan began tossing covers and calling her name. He startled Rufus. And Rufus barked, searching for the reason. Callahan ran to the front of his truck to find her car. It, too, was gone.

"How did I not hear her leave? And where were you?" Callahan asked of Rufus, as the dog cocked his head trying to understand.

He searched frantically for a note, anything that would indicate that her departure was temporary. He wanted to talk with her more. The lump in his throat was closely followed by a burning in his eyes. Callahan refused the tears. It was time to recapture his strength.

It is not the critic who counts.
Not the man who points out how the strong man stumbled or where the doer of deeds could have done better.
The credit belongs to the man who is actually in the arena, whose face is marred by dust and sweat and blood; who survives valiantly; errs and comes short again and again; who knows the great enthusiasms, the great devotions; who spends himself in a worthy cause.
Who, at best, knows in the end the triumph of high achievement, and who at worst, at least fails while daring greatly, so that his place shall never be with those timid souls...
who know neither victory nor defeat.

~Theodore Roosevelt

CHAPTER NINETEEN

DECEMBER 11,1978
1750 HOURS

CALLAHAN KNEW SOMETHING was different about this night. It wasn't anything he could talk about, because it wouldn't make any sense. Some feelings were just that, feelings.

"You haven't been off probation all that long, have you?" Callahan asked.

"No, it's not been quite a full year yet," Sara answered.

"Went fast, didn't it?"

"Looking back, yeah, it did. But sometimes it seemed to drag on forever."

"Because you didn't have the security of permanent status," Callahan nodded. "All rookies figure that the slightest mistake could get them fired. There's a lot to learn in the first year."

His window was open, just like it always was. The cool, almost cold December air rushed in, but he insisted that it stay open. He believed you couldn't hear what was going on outside with your window closed, and hearing was a big part of awareness.

"Can you believe it's almost Christmas?" Sara looked at the various lighted decorations along South 6th Avenue. "It's mid-December and it seems like these lights have been up for months."

Callahan chose not to answer. This was not his favorite time of year. To him, the holiday season represented pain. He saw it in the eyes of the under-privileged. Christmas morning would mean going without, just like every other day. It was hard for him to accept celebration when his work immersed him in suffering.

"Do you go to a lot of holiday parties?" Sara asked.

"Not really, but when I was married, we used to have a New Year's party at our house every year."

"A big one?"

"Yeah, kind of. Mostly cops, and I made everyone stay all night. They knew they had to check their car keys when they arrived. It was an unspoken rule."

"Sounds like a lot of fun."

"I remember the last one, two years ago," Callahan chuckled briefly. "The clock struck midnight, everyone kissed and hugged, then ran outside to the patio. They began to celebrate with those wind-up metal noise-makers that make that irritating '*rricck-rrick-rrrrick*' sound. Everyone but Vic's wife, Jenny. She chose her own form of celebrating by pulling a pistol from her purse, pointing it upward, and firing three shots.

"Somebody," Callahan continued, "hollered, 'holy shit,' and she fired three more, directly through my new patio roof. 'I don't remember that being here before,' she said. Those were the fun times, Sara."

1752 Hours

Barbara Wells unplugged her headset from the frequency and stood from her chair. "I'll be quick," she said. "That soda went right through me."

"No problem," the relief dispatcher responded, sitting in the chair in front of Frequency One.

Barb opened the door that separated the dispatchers from the desk aides and made her way from communications toward the restrooms. This meant going through the front desk area and across the lobby. She had a theory; if the lobby and front desk were busy, it would be a rough night on the frequency. Nothing was happening at the front desk and the lobby was vacant. Good sign.

"You look too good to be kept in a cage," Sgt. Rogers remarked as she passed by him standing at the elevator. "Let me take you away from all of this."

"In your dreams," she smiled, not looking his way.

1800 Hours

Barb was back in her position in front of the console. Nothing had happened in her absence. The south side frequency was calm, as was most of the city. She swiveled in her chair to watch the desk aides through the glass partition. The emergency telephones, normally busy, were silent.

Too silent. I hate times like this, she thought. The calm before the storm.

1802 Hours

"We have a priority coming in, Barb. Who do you have available?"

"Just about everybody," she answered, looking at the officer dispatch cards in front of her. "What is it?"

"10-31 . . . lots of screaming, sounds like a female being assaulted," her supervisor answered. "Where's Callahan?"

"He's free. Working a two man unit, or should I say a two 'person' unit."

"Is he in the area of the call?" Walker liked the confidence of having an officer like Callahan available. But he also felt guilty about always sending him to the most serious situations.

"Hang on."

"1-Baker-7," she said, keying her mike.

"Park and Irvington," Sara responded.

Callahan's thoughts were on Christmas presents, sit down dinners, and family get-togethers when Barb's voice broke the silence.

"They're close," Barb said to Walker.

"Give the call to them," Walker said, pulling another dispatch card from the track. "Send another unit with them. The situation is getting worse."

The desk aide was making frantic gestures through the glass.

The officers were needed immediately.

"Stand by, Baker-7 . . . 1-Adam-33."

"Ajo and I-19," came the response from Armando Rios, the officer behind the designator.

"10-84, 1-Baker-7 on priority call #318."

"1-Baker-7, copy priority call #318, a 10-31."

"Another damn family fight," Callahan said aloud.

". . .at 415 W. Washington. Caller states that a man is beating his wife at the apartment to the rear of 415 W. Washington. Weapons unknown."

He grabbed the mike. "Radio, where did this call originate? Is the desk still in contact with them?" Callahan had suddenly adopted a new seriousness.

"The original caller was in the front house at that location. She hung up with no further info. However, we are receiving a second call to that address for assistance."

The desk aide threw her hands up and shook her head, indicating "No."

"It seems the second caller has hung up, also," Barb advised.

Callahan acknowledged, the teacher in him continued, "It's a lot better if the desk can keep them on the line. It gives the officers more information to go on prior to arriving, especially about weapons," he clarified to Sara.

"Why is she sending three officers on this call?" Sara asked, "Isn't two enough?"

"All I can tell you is that I trust Barb's intuition. She goes by her gut feelings, just as we do. Something tells her this one is going to be more intense."

"Are you scared when you get a call like this? You know, possible violence or assaults in progress?" Sara asked, studying his face.

"Of course, I am," he answered without expression. "Does that surprise you?"

"Yeah. I didn't expect you to be so blunt about it."

"You were expecting John Wayne to say, 'Let's go get 'em, pilgrim,'" he said, imitating the actor's voice.

"Sort of," she laughed.

"I'm not afraid for my personal safety, but more an apprehension about not being able to perform, to not be able to do what's expected of me in a given situation. But you know, that's when training and experience kick in. And you calm yourself to be able to react, not overreact."

1803 Hours

The three officers' destination was situated in an old neighborhood, eclectic in housing structure and in the merging of generations. It was a very old area that had been predominately Mexican-American for a long time. Very small houses, clustered together on lots, approximately four to an acre. The landscaping, once meticulously maintained, was showing the signs of inattention. The houses were deteriorating with very few hints of renovation. The elderly, having nowhere to go, hung on to their roots. Their pride of ownership and heritage and the tidiness in their domains shined through. But, economics dictated the quality of individuals who had begun to inhabit the low rent housing. Violence, infrequent and not tolerated in the past, was now the norm. The gang-like behavior of the West Coast was starting to appear in the relative isolation of the quiet desert.

Like Sara, Manny Rios was a relatively new police officer, with tenure of just under two years. He and five other officers had comprised a previous training squad, so he and Callahan knew each other well. Rios was methodical, always in control. His appearance and job performance were impeccable. Victor would often refer to Rios as the "perfect cop."

To Callahan, however, perfection was nothing more than survival. In the next few moments, his theory would be put to the test. The situation that every officer trained for was about to occur. Without being talked about, this one single event preyed in the back of their minds like a tumor on the soul.

1804 Hours

Rios was less than thirty seconds away, traveling eastbound on Washington Street toward the designated address of 415, apartment to the rear. Callahan and Conners, equidistant in time away from the address were arriving from the east.

The headlights of each other's vehicles appeared and they immediately turned them off, not wanting to create yet another target in an unknown situation.

"Is that Rios?" Sara asked when she saw an approaching vehicle darken its headlights.

Callahan nodded.

Sara couldn't take her eyes off of her mentor as she watched his seriousness and apprehension, void of emotion, evolve into skill. What does he know that I'm not aware of? What is his experience telling him? The intensity of the javelin-like stare in his blue eyes could be felt in the dim ambient light of the police cruiser's interior. It frightened her. It made her focus. Speaking was not an option, listening and watching was a priority, an ingredient for survival.

No signs of anything out of the ordinary appeared on the street or in the neighborhood. The sounds of a normal December evening drifted into the open windows of the police unit as it stalked the street number like a cautious mountain lion.

"Do you think this was a prank call?" Sara asked.

Without a word, a quick, cold look from Callahan reprimanded her for talking. Calls such as this could speak volumes, or nothing at all. The arrival of police might be met with violence or silence and complete disregard, or somewhere in between. More than likely, police would be watched by one-eyed faces peering through slightly bent blinds or barely pushed aside drapes. Because of duty, the police strolled into the unknown, with training, experience, and God as their only companions. These were guidelines, not lifelines.

"I can't read the address on that house," Sara said as she strained to look across the street. "But, that has to be 415. Yeah, that's the house. Now I can see the numbers over by the porch."

"1-Baker-7, 10-23," Callahan advised the dispatcher. They stopped several yards short of the address. Simultaneously, 1-Adam-

33 pulled slowly to the curb from the opposite direction.

"I'm with Baker-7," Rios told the radio. They briefly sat in silence trying to hear or see anything that would provide them with prior information about the situation.

Callahan stepped from his vehicle, rolled up his window and locked the door. Sara did the same. In this neighborhood, as with many, entering an unlocked vehicle, especially a police car, for the purpose of stealing something was predictable.

Still no unusual sounds, nothing to indicate panic or distress. But they knew this lack of activity sometimes generated complacency — the killer of cops. If their guard went down, they went down. The officers crossed the street separately, not wanting to give a sniper the advantage of having all of his targets in a group. It seldom happened, but seldom was too often.

1805 Hours

A light went off in the residence in the front. The officers exchanged glances. "We're being watched by someone in the front house, behind the blind in the small window," Manny whispered.

"Two subjects," Sara quietly answered. "One just dropped below the other."

Callahan's lips showed a faint smile and a favorable glance at Sara. She acknowledged it with nothing more than a move of the eye.

The front house was a small structure, probably adobe covered in stucco, and over the years patched and painted several times. The roof was gabled and peaked to accommodate weather patterns that no longer existed, giving away the secret of the dwelling's age.

To the rear, at the end of a ninety-foot walkway was another house, even smaller than the main residence. The brown, stucco structure was no more than five hundred square feet. Current vernacular had given such dwellings the title of guesthouse, but it was very doubtful that this was the original intent. More than likely, this structure was created for one or two family members that required separate living quarters. Apparently, it was now rented out as an apartment. The only entrance that could be seen was on the right, at the end of the walkway.

Callahan believed that all officers investigating the scene of a crime made a two-part, glaring mistake — they never looked up and they never looked down. Approaching the apartment, his eyes followed the beam of his Kel-lite flashlight down onto the sidewalk.

"Hang on," he said softly, but sternly. "What in the hell is this?" He knelt to the end of his flashlight beam. Without moving the item, he inspected what appeared to be strands of hair. Light brown, almost blonde.

"This is human hair," he said quietly as he peered up at the apartment window, "and it's attached to skin from a scalp. These strands were pulled from someone's head." Callahan left the jagged skin fragment where it was found, hoping it would remain there, in its original position for evidence. The family fight call was now an assault.

1806 Hours

A figure dressed in dark clothing started walking toward them from the shadows between the two houses. It was a young woman, in her late teens or early twenties. She walked closer, not taking her eyes from the apartment. Callahan's flashlight found her hands and then her face.

"Do something. He's going to kill her this time," whispered the dark haired, frightened girl. She spoke quickly as her eyes darted into the dark surrounding them. She knew she was being watched. She was in the 'hood' and talking to 'the man'. She had better be right, because the police were always the last resort in handling problems.

"Who is he?"

"David. David Tapia. He'll kill her if you don't fucking do something," she said, raising her voice.

David Tapia was seventeen years old. His age still classified him as a juvenile. A very troubled juvenile. He had been in trouble many times for several different offenses. Early on, it was larceny, plain theft. Then his crimes evolved into assaults, burglary, and numerous drug charges. He needed help, but no one was there for him, no one to care for him. He was troubled and angry. After his parents separated, he was handed from relative to relative, ultimately forced into the well-traveled path of foster homes. No one could control him. His violent behavior became more prevalent as the child grew into the body of a man. His behavior became frightening. In the street, like water seeking its own level, he found a peer group to accept him as he was. Then he met a girl. A blonde named Lisa.

At fifteen years of age they became parents, by definition only. At seventeen years of age they were expecting their second child. The child was to arrive in less than four months, if she could survive his frequent beatings.

"Who's in there with him?"

"Lisa. His wife. I mean girlfriend, they're not married. I gotta go." She turned to leave.

"What does she look like?"

"Why?" she asked. Callahan grabbed her arm. "Hey, man, you're hurting me."

"Just answer me," he demanded.

"Okay, she's a white girl, kinda small with blonde hair."

She had given him the answer he feared.

Callahan saw toys in the yard. "Is there a child in the house with them?" he asked.

"No. He's up in the front house."

A bit of relief.

"Thank you. Now go out to the street, for your own safety," Callahan said as he pulled her arm in the direction he wanted her to go.

She took his advice and walked slowly toward the street, pausing briefly to look back over her shoulder. He caught her look and her concern.

"Does he do this often?"

"When he's fucked up," the girl answered and she walked away, more quickly than before. "Which is pretty much all the time."

The three officers were now less than thirty feet from the

apartment. There was a large window on the front side of the small house, just to the left of the walkway. The window was covered by a heavy drape. No one could be seen inside, no movement. It was the feeling that Callahan dreaded, like the ghostly calm before a tornado.

"Sara," Callahan directed, "go over by the window and try to find a crack to look through. But stay out of sight." She complied immediately. He and Manny stepped quickly to the single entrance of the apartment, flattening their backs against the wall on either side of the doorway.

"See anything?" Callahan whispered to Sara.

"Give me a second," she answered softly. "I'm having a hard time seeing what's inside. The light's real dim in there." Through a small slit in the drape, she could barely make out two figures, one large and one quite a bit smaller. The large figure moved slightly, allowing more light, more visibility. The large figure was a male, standing behind a slightly built female with his left arm around her neck. Sara saw something in his left hand but couldn't make out what it was. The woman started to struggle. He dropped his left arm from her neck, but quickly replaced it with his right. His left hand shoved the object into the waistband of his pants.

"Callahan," Sara ducked low, taking quick steps under the window. She slipped up behind him, gently touching his shoulder. "I saw the guy in there put something down the front of his pants. I couldn't tell what it was."

Callahan nodded.

1808 Hours

Callahan put the back of his right hand against the door and pushed. It didn't move.

They remained quiet and listened. Then a frightened female voice cried out, "They're here. Please don't hurt me. Please don't hurt the police. You're just afraid they're going to take you to Juvenile Hall again."

JUVENILE! The word crashed into Callahan's brain like lightning in an open field.

The door handle began to move. It was being pulled from the

inside, but the door wouldn't open. It was locked by a deadbolt.

"Leave me alone. I want to leave," the woman screamed.

"Get the fuck away from the door." A deeper voice demanded, in a whisper. And then scuffling sounds. The voice then spoke in hurried Spanish.

Callahan cocked his head to one side. "This is Officer Callahan, Tucson Police Department, please open the door."

No response.

The young woman's voice, farther away now, commanded, "Get away from the door. Please let them in."

Callahan tried the door once more, only this time he turned the knob and pushed. It wouldn't budge. It was locked. She pleaded again. "Please, please don't hurt anyone. Don't hurt me anymore. Don't hurt the police. If not for me, for Tony's sake."

"How bad are you hurt?" Callahan asked, unsnapping the holster guard over his revolver.

"Please, I'm . . ." she started to answer, but her voice became muffled.

"I'll kill you motherfuckers. Get the fuck outa here," a male voice screamed from behind the locked door. The voice was cruel and full of hate.

"Unlock the door," Callahan ordered. "Now!"

Callahan turned his head to look at Sara. It was a look she'd never seen before. His face was a recipe of determination. It was fear controlled by skill, mixed with the unknown. His eyes made an attempt to sooth her, but also pique her awareness. The normal ruddiness was gone from his cheeks, the pale skin made lighter by his darting, blue eyes. The male protecting the female was present, but in a brief second, he had whispered with his look; 'you are on your own.'

Rios' eyes darted between the two. What next? Could be read in his face. She breathed the cool air in deeply. Use it! Use my fear, she commanded herself. She was glad that she had asked Callahan that question just minutes ago.

"Get out pigs. Get the fuck out," the male voice bellowed. "I'll kill her if you don't leave."

"Officer, if you use a credit card," appealed the desperate

voice, "it will open the door. It's the gold one, not the top one, the gold one."

"Shut up, bitch." Something was thrown across the room as heavy footsteps moved away from the door.

Two locks on the door, one above and one below. One tarnished silver, one plated gold. Callahan did not carry a wallet. Nothing with identification that could link him to an address associated with his personal life. In every way, he wanted his family protected from the dark side of his job. He looked at Manny. Manny shook his head no, as did Sara. Callahan looked back at the lock. There must be another way. If he had to, he would tear the flimsy door from its hinges. But he realized that it had to be the last of his options. Violence begot violence. If he knocked the door down, there would be a momentary loss of control. Something they could ill-afford.

As his eyes passed from the door back to Manny, they stopped. And then they fixed on something in Manny's Sam Browne belt. A blue card. The police vehicle's gas card in a plastic pouch affixed to the vehicle's ignition key. Most officers inserted this key into the overlapping leather of their gun belt with the gas card dangling outside. The card was nothing more than a computer punched, hard plastic means of opening the secured gas pumps at the city service center. Maybe, just maybe. Depending on how strong the card was, it just might do the trick.

"Give me your gas card," Callahan directed at Rios. Quietly, he inserted it between the door latch and the door jam. The plastic buckled. He pulled it back and straightened it out. He turned it sideways, hoping it would be stronger. He forced the card between the door jam and the bolt. It moved slightly, just enough. The latch snapped open.

CHAPTER TWENTY

1810 Hours

THE DOOR SWUNG OPEN slightly providing a partial view of the apartment. Through the faint light, Callahan took a quick inventory of the room. He saw a green paisley print couch situated in the middle of the room, ten or so feet from the door. To the side of the large window, was a small table in the corner. Clothing and toys were strewn about the floor. An empty shopping cart was against the far wall. And a crib sat next to the far end of the couch.

"Officer, please help me."

"Shut up," David Tapia yelled, without taking his eyes off the door.

Callahan eased the door open wider. Four feet from the door opening was a large male, clad in a green, military fatigue jacket and jeans. He was a dark skinned man, with dark eyes and hair, probably in his late teens or early twenties. His eyes were on fire, his face tightly set — a mask of hate.

His arm was around the throat of a blonde girl, several inches shorter than him. Dried blood knotted her hair on the right side of her head. Callahan's eyes dropped to the red lettering on her white shirt. BABY, with an arrow pointing downward, covered her protruding abdomen. Callahan felt the lump grow in his throat.

"Come here," he said to Tapia, extending his hand forward. Somehow, he must get him away from the girl. "Let's talk about this."

Tapia's left hand dropped to his waistband. In a move choreographed by previous violent acts, he produced a large, eight-inch kitchen knife. He pressed the knife against her throat and she shrieked. The sharp edge of the knife broke her skin. Trickles of blood began to stain her neck, then her collar. The suspect had now become a criminal.

Callahan drew his revolver and pointed it directly at Tapia's head. Tapia stepped backwards, pulling Lisa with him. Rios quickly ran into the house behind Callahan. He moved to the left and positioned himself behind the couch. Tapia uttered something to him in Spanish and smiled.

"Shoot me, motherfucker. Go ahead and shoot me," he screamed at Callahan. With his hand under her jaw, he jerked Lisa upward, her feet barely touching the floor. "Shoot now, pig. How good are you, *pendejo?*"

Rios drew his weapon from the left side. Tapia held the knife in his left hand.

"Suelta la cuchilla . . . no seas tonto," Rios ordered him to drop the knife.

Tapia ignored him.

Lisa was desperate. With all of her strength she began to fight. His arm could not control her. In an instant, she pulled from his grip, but fell to the floor. She scrambled away on her hands and knees. She pressed her back against the wall, pulling her knees to her chest and wrapped her arms around her legs. She cried, pinching her eyes closed, and as if she were begging for the comfort of her mother, she rocked back and forth.

Callahan took a step, then another toward Tapia.

Talk to him, Callahan, Rios begged without speaking. Make him drop the knife.

"Come on, now. You don't have . . ."

Tapia's eyes gave away his assault as he slashed at Callahan. Instinctively, Callahan jumped backwards, the blade of the weapon came within inches of his chest. Lisa opened her eyes and screamed. Callahan backed away as Tapia lunged, slashing at him again.

"Please, please put the knife down. Please, they don't want to hurt you," Lisa begged. Her tears began to mix with her blood, turning the front of her shirt an awful pink.

Callahan repeated his earlier request, "Please put the knife down. You've done nothing that we can't work out. No one wants to harm you. Just do as we ask."

"Fuck you." It was Tapia's choice. Logic and common sense did not play a role in his thinking.

"*El tiene razon. Tenemos que hablar de esto,*" Rios begged Tapia to listen to Callahan, for the sake of his children. "*Piensa en tu hijo y el que tu esposa va tener.*"

Tapia began to laugh. He wasn't backing away anymore. He lunged at the officers; first Callahan, then Rios, daring them to fire. Suddenly, he began making overhand throwing motions toward Callahan. Quick, short motions at first. Then longer, until Callahan ducked, fearing that Tapia had actually thrown the knife.

Callahan waited for the pain. It did not come; the knife had not been thrown. Callahan was still moving backwards. He was at the doorway. His right elbow found the door casing and he stepped outside behind it. Because of training, or perhaps instinct, he transferred his service revolver to his left hand. The wall was now his protector.

Tapia turned his attention to Rios. "Drop the knife," Rios demanded from behind the couch.

Tapia lowered the knife, begging Rios to shoot him. Rios took a step back, but that was it. He could go back no farther. Tapia raised the knife overhead and slashed at Rios, placing a foot on the couch, ready to step over, he yelled, "*Tu eres uno de ellos. Tu vas a morir!* You are going to die!"

This time the officer returned the assault. Moving to his right, Rios fired. The inverted hollow point slug exploded from the .38 caliber Smith & Wesson producing a deafening noise and a fiery muzzle flash. The momentum from Tapia's last violent slash had twisted him to his right, away from the direct line of fire. But the bullet hit, striking the upper left side of Tapia's torso, sending him spinning violently to the floor.

"Oh my God, no . . . oh my God, you shot him," Lisa cried, covering her face.

The force of the slug had driven him backwards away from

the couch. Tapia was twisting, writhing on the floor. "Where . . . where am I hit?" he yelled. "Fuck! I'm hit, I know I'm hit."

His hands searched his body for wounds although he felt no pain. The slug had entered the front portion of the large muscle, just below the armpit, and exited. The bullet had hit, but it did not stop David Tapia. He raised his eyes as a wounded animal would. Suddenly, the sting of the wound found his brain. Now it was survival. And more anger.

Rios watched as Tapia spun away from him. Callahan moved into the doorway, his eyes also on Tapia. Rios holstered his weapon, stepping over the couch, expecting to subdue his wounded target.

"Don't!" Callahan shouted. It was too late.

In a violent burst, Tapia was on his feet. With a forearm to the chest, he drove Rios backwards onto the couch. Rios landed on his back with his feet directly above him. Rios' hand sought the weapon that he had holstered after he had fired. He frantically searched his holster, his belt, for his revolver. It was gone.

Tapia grabbed the knife from the floor and came at Rios. Tapia was coming at him from above. Rios tried to kick him away. Tapia raised his knife.

"Tu vas a morir," Tapia yelled, the sharp end of the blade starting downward.

Rios instinctively covered his head and face with both arms. *"Con Dios!"*

The large handgun discharged so loud, so cruel. A split-second flash of fire illuminated the darkened room. The explosion from its barrel was deafening. The slug tore into David Tapia's left chest. The power of the impact lifted him from his feet, sending him reeling out of control across the room and into the wall. The intended target crumbled and fell on his back. His body, fighting for life, began to contort in uncontrollable spasms.

"Please don't. Oh my God, what have you done?" screamed Lisa at the dying man. "You knew this would happen."

Tapia's knife dropped to the floor, spinning slowly around and around as the dying young man's eyes met Michael Callahan's. Both reflected pain, but for different reasons. One person's pain was to end abruptly. The other's would last indefinitely, perhaps eternally.

Callahan's bullet had found its mark. Instantly, he had become what he had detested for a lifetime. He had pulled the trigger to harm. He went to David Tapia's side as he lay on the floor in a vain struggle to remain in a life, that in health, he had rejected. Callahan knelt next to him. His hand searched for the wound. The blood from the attacker-turned-victim crawled between Callahan's fingers like silver after the final supper. The boy's body jerked. It stilled. And jerked again. Callahan looked at the young man's face, and into his eyes. But they were hollow, as if the soul had left.

Rios and Callahan stared at each other as they knelt next to the quiet body of David Tapia. The muted cries and sobs of Lisa echoed throughout the room.

Callahan stood and instinctively grabbed the hand-held radio attached to his gun-belt. Rios began talking to Tapia, telling him to hang on and not to give up.

"One-Baker-Seven, 10-99." Callahan spoke the code that made a radio frequency freeze and life briefly stand still.

The code for officer needs assistance broke into the police band airways like a cancer blow. "One subject down . . . 10-72, 10-59, 10-18 . . ." Callahan begged the radio for immediate response from fire rescue and an ambulance.

Police units, hearing the seldom-used code, scrambled to assist like a parent responding to a frightened cry from an injured child. They would respond Code Three until the first officers to arrive at the scene advised to continue or not.

Callahan rose to his feet, taking his last look at the seventeen-year-old boy dying from the violence that he had embraced throughout his short life. Callahan went to the girl, the pregnant battered woman, huddled against the wall of the room she could never live in again. He picked her up from the floor so quickly that she did not have time to resist. Carrying her in his arms, he took her outside and sat with her, searching for words of comfort and reason. No words were adequate.

He felt, more than heard her silent cries. She clung to him. He held her close. He wanted to tell her that everything was all right, but he couldn't. The silence was broken with the sounds of sirens. Many sirens from many directions. Callahan knew the eyes of the neighborhood were upon them, but he chose not to seek their source. Sara touched his shoulder and knelt next to them, sharing their moment of pain. He gently released his grip on Lisa, and for a fleeting moment, she denied his move to leave. Then she sobbed. Her body went limp, and without a look they shared the finality as he left and Sara became the consoler.

Sara turned and watched Callahan as he walked with purpose to the west side of the yard near a tall stand of hedges. She had witnessed the act of violence that every officer feared. She also witnessed its effects.

Sara held Lisa and could feel her pain; but she also felt and saw the effects of a street hardened child. Her features, even at her tender age, were showing subtle signs of neglect. Her life had been hard. It would remain to be seen how the hand of fate would direct her upcoming years. It could pull her from her bad-to-worsening life and free her to move on or push her further down into the murk of her present existence.

The sirens stopped; the officers came. And the paramedics. Eyes appeared in the oleanders. Shouts of, "the cops killed him, the cops killed him," echoed from the darkness. The surreal scene continued. Even the blur became blurred. The paramedics were instantly inside trying to keep alive the last faint beat of a futile heart. The first officers to arrive were scurrying to protect the scene of a yet-to-be documented unfortunate loss of life and the catastrophic changes in those left behind.

Callahan couldn't feel his feet touch the ground. He walked to a row of oleanders that skirted the property. Their height and density formed a natural barrier and offered solitude for his thoughts. In his own mind he needed justification for his actions and the design dictated to him by the Almighty. By the laws of the land, he was a defender and had in all likelihood, saved a life, or several. He was legally justified in the trigger pull, however, he needed the moral justification in his heart. The answer to the questions, "Why?" And, "Why me?"

Officer Michael Callahan gave the evidence to the jury with himself being the judge. The knife . . . he was, in fact, holding the female hostage . . . the attack with the knife . . . the female, his pregnant girlfriend, had been beaten . . . he was given every opportunity to drop the knife . . . he would not listen to or attempt to understand logic . . . another attack with the knife . . . he was shot . . . he came at Rios with the intent of killing him . . . shot again. He had reviewed the script.

It was not a matter of guilt or justification, but more a matter of acceptance for his actions — the acceptance of responsibility. In his heart, he knew he had exhausted all other means of apprehension. He had waited until the most final of seconds. Then he had to rely on God-given ability and intent. Once this was internally established, he could continue. It was, and he did.

"You pig, you bastard. You killed the father of my children. I hope you die." Reality had returned in the form of an outburst from the battered widow. As Callahan had expected, the blame had shifted. What she could no longer sling at David, she directed at him. So be it. Sara tried to calm her. Callahan stopped Sara with a wave of his hand as if to say, 'Let her be.' Sara backed off and Lisa's on-scene friends took control.

The smell of gunpowder still lingered in the air as the Tucson Fire Department Paramedics rushed the very still occupant of the gurney out of the apartment to the awaiting ambulance. The street was a virtual sea of red and blue flashing lights reflecting off the faces of onlookers trying to see tragedy in progress. The fireman, a longtime friend of the saddened officer, confirmed with a subtle side-to-side movement of his head that David Tapia had not survived.

Michael Callahan's eyes looked up into the sky and searched the cool night air for a friend. But he found no one. The only thing to be found was the unrelenting feeling of loneliness. He had failed. He had killed.

When you come to be sensibly touched,
The scales will fall from your eyes;
And by the penetrating eyes of love
You will discern that which your
Other eyes will never see.

~Francois Fenelon

CHAPTER TWENTY-ONE

"SARA. IT'S ME, CALLAHAN." I hope I'm not interrupting anything."

"No, not at all. This is a surprise. But, I'm glad you called." Sara did not want to appear too shocked.

"Thanks. I was wondering," Callahan said, stammering through the words, "if we could get together and talk."

"Sure. I've been worried about you. Are you all right?"

"I'm doing fine, I think." A deep breath was released by both parties. "The past couple of days have been a blur. My mind has kind of shut down."

Sara hugged her arms around herself, waiting for more words, but he remained silent.

"Is this, uh," Sara drew in a deep breath and hesitated, "about the shooting? Is that what you want to talk about?"

"No, it's not," he snapped. "I don't need to talk about it. It's over. I'm not going to keep rehashing it. That's it, it's done."

"I'm sorry, Michael," she said gently, "I just wanted you to know I'm here if you want to talk about it."

"I'm sorry too," his voice was calmer now, "I didn't mean to snap at you." They were silent for a moment then Callahan continued. "I just thought it might be okay just to get together. Ya know, away from work and relax a little." There was another long pause.

"When would you like to come over?" she asked, breaking the silence.

It had become awkward. He assumed she knew he meant now, tonight. Maybe he should back off. This was becoming a bad idea.

"Tonight? You want to get together tonight?" Sara rescued him.

"Ah, sure. If that's okay. I . . ."

"Do you know how to get here, or do you need directions?" Sara interrupted with a smile.

"I thought maybe we could meet somewhere, to talk." The thought of her house intimidated him.

"I can't just pick up and go. I have Abigail to consider." She closed her eyes in instant remorse as her last words came back to her. "I'm sorry," she said, catching her breath. "I didn't mean anything by what I just said."

Her words had hurt, but he knew they were spoken without intent. "I know. But it's my fault. I should have thought about Abigail. Uh, yeah, I do need directions. I don't spend much time in the city, you know." Callahan felt her smile as he heard her breathe.

Before he spoke again, she had loosened her hair from the elastic, letting it fall as she shook her head from side to side.

"Where are you now?"

He looked at his reflection in the window next to the pay phone and made a decision that gave him a much-needed twinge of excitement. Freshly laundered and hanging in the tiny closet of the camper was a blue, oxford dress shirt and light beige casual slacks. He never knew when an invite from Vic would come for dinner, so he kept clothes at the ready. He didn't own a pair of dress shoes, but his western boots, always highly shined, were also in the closet.

"East side, he responded."

"What brought you off the mountain?"

"Oh, I had a couple of errands to run." He lied.

"About five, then?"

"Five what?"

"O'clock. Five o'clock would be fine for me."

Stupid. I must have really sounded stupid. "Great. Now tell me where you live." He tried to recover.

"Sure." She smiled, feeling the excitement in his voice.

After giving him her address, Sara quietly placed the receiver down on the phone and stood for several seconds without removing her hand. Her mind began to race. "Oh, God. Now what?" she said aloud, but to no one.

Callahan fed Rufus at Randolph Park and the two took a walk by the ball fields and along the lake. As they did, he studied his motives. Am I going there because I'm lonely? He thought of his "Firemen's theory," if you rush in, you will be carried out. Self-preservation of the heart also entered into his equation, to guard against being hurt, to slow down and mistrust the feelings. He thought of the tragedy they had just shared, wondering if the incident had created a sad, but special bond. However, he could not ignore the stirring he felt inside or the energies that she was giving off. He liked her look and the way she looked at him. The thought of her, and the impending evening gave him a quicker step as he led Rufus back to the camper. He was glad that the evening was spontaneous, as it did not allow room for escape.

Showering quickly at the police station, he pulled his clothing from the cellophane, feeling like a senior on prom night. The excitement was altering his ever-present off-duty mood of personal conflict and self-imposed exile. Once dressed, he felt good, but clumsy. Was he making more of this than he should? What if I'm thinking of this as a date, and she, on the other hand, is viewing my visit as an intrusion?

She found herself looking into the mirror, staring at the person that was staring back. What am I ready for, she asked the reflection? Stop it! I'm reading far too much into this. She scolded her image as she furled her brow and pursed her lips. But, a smile broke out as she was thoroughly enjoying the moment.

From side to side, she turned her head to the audience of the mirror. Sara pinched her cheeks to bring a blush as she continued to smile, almost giggle. Look at me, she gushed. I'm treating his visit as if it were a date. "Oh, my God, what if he thinks it's a date?" she said aloud.

Quickly, she tugged her blouse over her head, discarding it in the direction of the hamper. In a reflex, she adjusted her bra and ran her fingers down the sides of her body. Nothing offended, so she went back to her friend, the mirror. "I don't care how he is dressed," she said aloud, not knowing that Abigail was close by. "I want him to see me as a girl instead of one of the officers."

"What did you say, Mom?"

"Nothing. I was just talking to myself." Now what? She slipped a white sweater over her head, then pulled a pair of denim pants over her hips. She assessed the hair that fell around her shoulders. I like this look, she said to herself with an evil smile.

Oh, my God! What's going on here? Am I attracted to him? She stepped back for a minute and sipped from her Coke, letting her thoughts wander. He is attractive. And his eyes are so blue! And sometimes when he looks at me with that half smile . . . stop this!

"Mom!" Abigail hollered from somewhere within the house. "I'm hungry. When are we going to eat?"

Dinner! I forgot about dinner! He'll be here at 5 and I never mentioned dinner. Maybe I should just let Abigail eat in the kitchen, and we'll sit in the living room and I'll eat when he leaves. What if he doesn't leave?

"Mommmm!"

"I heard you. We need to set another plate."

"For who? Gramma's not going to be here."

"Mr. Callahan. Remember the day at the grocery store? And he was at the Stark's house, also."

"Oh, yeah. He's going to eat here? Why? Doesn't he have a home and kids and stuff?" Abigail continued her questions into her mother's bedroom. "How come you're putting lipstick on to eat supper? Can I try some?"

"He lives alone. I just want to look nice for our guest. And no, you may not! Go set the table."

"He sure looks old enough to have a family. How come he doesn't?"

"He does. He has a girl, about your age. And a boy, a little bit younger. He just doesn't live with them."

"Does he miss them? What's for dinner?"

"'I'm sure he does," Sara answered, changing shades of

lipstick for the third time.

"Well, then he can eat with us tonight and be a part of our family." Abigail spun on her heels and left for the kitchen. "Can I have an apple?"

"Sure." Sara smiled as she heard her daughter's heart.

Should I get some flowers? Where would I get flowers? What in the hell am I talking about? This isn't a date! She thinks that I'm just coming over to talk. Get a grip!

Callahan checked his appearance again by turning the rearview mirror toward him as he drove. I sure wish that cowlick would lay down in the front of my hair. I wonder what I would look like in a mustache? Maybe not, the one I had before looked like a bad picket fence. Hey, it feels kind of good to dress up a little. He smiled.

The Sam Hughes neighborhood sat just to the east of the University of Arizona campus. The once elegant home had now quietly slipped into upper middle class. Tree lined streets, tall gabled houses that were unknown to most other sections of the city, presented a rich feeling of warmth. Arthur Martin, Sara's father, took great pride in his ownership of their beautiful house, until his death at the hands of an untimely cancer. Her mother, Anna, vowed to stay in the house, protecting it until the day she would leave this world. She asked Sara and Abigail to join her when Sara's marriage had failed.

Wine! That's it. I'll get some wine and a six-pack. I can't go there empty-handed. He had already pulled onto her street, but he drove past her house and onto another street at the intersection. Checking his watch, he saw he had ten minutes. Just enough time to get to the Circle K and back.

Sara saw the camper drive by as she stood in the kitchen next to the bay window. I hope he's not getting cold feet, she thought as she felt disappointment flood her body. Where is he going? Now she was nervous. She went to the front window, peering out from the side of the drapery.

In and out of the store in a hurry, he was back on the road to her house in eight minutes. Sara still watched from the window and turned her head to answer an Abigail question. Back to the window, and suddenly he was there. Quickly she ran back to the kitchen, as if it were a game of hide-and-seek.

"Abigail. Can you answer the doorbell, please?"

"It didn't ring, Mom."

"It will."

"*Bing-Dong!*"

How did she know that? Abigail asked herself, as she scurried to the door.

"Hi! Mom says that you always have your dog with you. Can I play with him?" Abigail asked as she moved to the step, searching for Rufus.

"Let's ask your Mom first. He's probably sleeping right now, anyway," Michael Callahan responded.

"I don't think he's sleeping. He looks like he's driving your truck and he's drooling on your dashboard."

"Abigail, who is it?" Sara asked from another part of the house, discreetly preserving her entrance.

"It's Mr. Callahan and his dog. Can I play with his dog?"

"If it's all right with Mr. Callahan."

"Let me get him," Callahan smiled. Rufus could not wait. He loved kids and this would be such a treat. "Go to the backyard. He'll follow you." And the love affair began.

Sara appeared around the corner, just as Callahan turned toward her. Neither spoke, neither could. He opened his mouth to speak, but caught himself.

"You were going to say something?" Sara asked, coyly.

"Wow!"

"What?" Sara blushed. She wanted to hear it again.

"May I set this somewhere? I'm about to drop the bag."

"Sure. Put it there on the counter. Let me turn the stereo down." Sara started for the living room.

"Don't turn it down on my behalf. I love that song." He had no idea who sang it, but for some reason, the words meant something, and they made him feel good.

Sara stopped and turned. "Really? Do you listen to music a lot?" Maybe it was the light, or maybe it was her mood, but for the first time, she actually saw him. She didn't see a uniform.

"It's very interesting," Callahan answered as he removed the drinks from the bag. "I've always listened to music, but for the first time in my life, I'm starting to listen to the words of the songs."

Sara felt an urge to walk to him and become close. Perhaps, it was because he was saying just the right things, or knowing the right things to say. She didn't care. But she knew, even if it was too brief, she was beginning to dance on rainbows, and her urge suddenly placed her by his side.

"When are you going to quit living in your camper? That has to be getting pretty old by now."

"Yeah, I've had about all of that I can handle for awhile. Last Tuesday I signed the papers for three acres out in the Tucson Mountain area," Callahan said, exhibiting a large smile. "I can't wait to get out there and get started."

"Is there a house on the property?" Sara saw his eyes glisten as the country boy in him shined through.

"Not yet. By the end of the year, I plan on having a manufactured home on the land, over to one side, so I can slowly but surely, build my dream home. You know, high ceilings, wood floors, and lots of windows to watch the moon and the stars. That's my goal, but life may have other plans."

Sara watched as he talked and she got a strange feeling that his thoughts sounded more like predictions than dreams. It was as if he knew more than he should about the future.

"But before that, I want to have the electricity in so I can park the camper out there. It's a beautiful piece of land," he continued. "I can't wait for you to see it."

"I would really enjoy that, Michael." She felt very close after hearing the words that he had chosen to speak, something that she desperately needed.

"But for now, would you like some wine?" Callahan asked without looking at her. He closed his eyes as he felt her emotion, fending off the feelings of desire. "Do you have a corkscrew?" he asked, not waiting for an answer.

"Yes, please," she responded, almost embarrassed by her tone. "It's in the drawer next to you. That wine looks wonderful."

"The finest vintage that the vast wine cellars of Circle K can offer. I spare no expense, my dear," he smiled, as he poured her just the right amount.

"Aren't you going to join me?"

"I'm going to have the aged Budweiser. Wine makes me do funny things," Callahan answered with a twinkle in his eye.

"Let's sit in the living room," Sara requested, warding off his leading remark. She smiled as she stared into her glass, knowing all too well the effects of its contents. Don't let this get out of hand, she told herself, feeling the blood in her face. But God, those eyes. Those soft, blue eyes.

She turned away and took a deep breath, questions filling her mind. Not about him, but about herself. It was as if she were choreographing her own emotions.

The screech of a screen door's hinges broke the silence, and Sara was glad for the distraction.

"Mom. Rufus and I are hungry. Can we have some ice cream? He's really looking pale," Abigail asked from the kitchen.

"We're going to eat soon," Sara answered, suppressing a laugh. "I think you can last a little while longer. Give Rufus a drink of water; that'll relieve his paleness."

"I don't know, Mom. Years ago, I heard that only ice cream would do the trick. I hope you're right, or you have some explaining to do."

Screech! Slam! Dog and child had exited as quickly as they had come.

"She's too much, Sara," Callahan said as they shared a laugh. "The apple doesn't fall far from the tree, does it?"

"And what is that supposed to mean?" Sara smiled, taking it as a compliment.

"Sara, I didn't mean to interrupt your dinner. I should have asked if you had eaten. Rufus and I can go and continue this later."

"Don't be silly! It's nothing fancy. Just some crockpot stew. Come on. You can warm the bread for me," Sara said as she rose from the couch and extended a hand. He took it and she felt something twitch inside, and it startled her. The feeling became more intense as he cradled her fingers inside his hand with a softness not expected.

Without another word, they came toward each other, and then together. He put his arms around her, drawing her close, as if it was the natural thing to do. They held each other tight, making it real.

They stayed that way for several moments, until the nervousness came. Stepping back, Sara's eyes brimmed with tears as she created an uneasy laugh. "I guess I should be sorry for that, but I'm not," she said quietly, stepping forward. Sara studied his face, detecting a cautiousness, almost resembling fear. She turned her face up to his as she parted her lips.

Screech! Slam!

"Mom!"

Sara pulled away. "Wash your hands, Abby. And come to the table." Abigail's voice had brought them back to reality, but it did not erase the moment of fantasy. Sara turned and walked toward the dining area, but this time with subtle bounces, resembling a dance.

Callahan smiled to himself as she left the room. She was spontaneous and passionate, and extremely sensual, the ingredients for excitement. Standing alone in the living room, he felt embarrassed as Abigail watched with bewilderment. She immediately left when he looked at her and smiled.

Abigail controlled the conversation, without punctuation, throughout the dinner. Sara and Michael quietly listened, but heard very little. Rufus was politely lying with his head tucked neatly against the patio door. A deep rumbling from the darkened sky caused his ears to become erect, but he did not stir.

The stew was a comfort food to Michael, bringing back memories of his country childhood and family meals. Sara had created a large, crisp salad, filled with greens and vegetables that he devoured much too quickly.

"Help yourself." Sara smiled at the somewhat embarrassed Michael. "I'm glad to see that you enjoy healthy food."

"Thank you," he replied as he filled his bowl again. "I've not been good about eating the right foods lately. This is a treat."

"You're always welcome here." And for the moment, Sara enjoyed what she saw; her child to her right, and a caring, loving man sitting across the table. No stress, no tension, or bitter words. She realized that this was just a temporary picture, but it had warmth, something she deserved and Abigail needed.

"You ate your dinner very well, Abby. Would you care for

some ice cream?" Sara had to change the subject that was beginning to occupy her mind. Her feelings were trying to run away, taking her to someplace she wasn't ready to go.

"Can Rufus have some too, Mommy?"

"Sure he can."

"Why are you guys looking at each other like that?" Abigail asked, looking from one to the other.

Sara blushed, not daring to look his way, nor able to respond to her daughter's last question.

Sara moved her chair back and walked the few steps to the counter, but paused briefly before she turned around. She could feel that he was watching her as she walked away. She wondered what he was seeing.

"Would you like some, too?"

He didn't answer at first, as his eyes followed her body up to her face. She was pretty, and starting to become beautiful. He noticed her move, and how she moved, which created a tingle, a twitch, the things men didn't allow themselves to say to others.

"I'm sorry, what did you ask me?" Michael felt his cheeks reddening as he shook his head back to reality.

"Ice cream?" Sara asked, watching him blush. She found pleasure in the fact that he had been watching her, and she didn't really care about his thoughts, just knowing that they were about her was enough.

"Ah, no thank you. I'll pass this time. I think I ate too much dinner."

After her bowl of desert, the tiring child yawned, stretched, and excused herself from the table.

"May Rufus come into my bedroom, Mr. Callahan?"

"Ask him if he wants to."

Abigail smiled and bent over to address Rufus. "Come with me, boy, so they can have grown up talk." Rufus obliged, as he got to his feet with some form of a body relay. He stretched, and then meandered down the hall, banging his head on the doorway.

Sara waited for a few moments, to allow time for the child to get to her room. "You seem uncomfortable here, Michael." She watched him as he searched for words, trying to imagine what he was feeling.

"Let me help you with the dishes," he offered, watching her rise from her chair.

"There aren't that many. I can do them later. Is being here making you uneasy?" Sara wanted the air to be cleared. If she had feelings about him, or for him, she wanted them to be honest, and with dialogue.

"No, I'm sorry. I just think too much sometimes, and stupid stuff bothers me." He sighed as he stood, forcing his hands into his rear pockets.

"What stuff? I'm sure it's not stupid. By the way, that word is not allowed in this house." She smiled.

He wanted to leave. She saw it in his face. "Is there something wrong?"

"No. I should go."

"Why?"

Callahan tried to answer with something intelligent, but the words wouldn't come. So, he did the next best thing. "Why not?"

Sara smiled instead of answering. She knew that her lack of response would get one from him. Girls do that, women do it even better.

"I was struggling with some feelings."

"Feelings?" she wanted to make sure that she wasn't reading something into his statement that wasn't there.

"Yes, feelings. But please don't make me explain. At least not now." He felt embarrassed by her examination of his choice of words. Damn, I should have never said anything, he growled to himself.

CHAPTER TWENTY-TWO

"IT LOOKS LIKE IT'S going to storm," Sara said, sensing his uneasiness. "Come with me while I start a fire."

She walked ahead, but instead of watching her body move gracefully across the room, this time his eyes glanced at the floor. His early thoughts began to perturb him, thinking that she would feel that he was taking advantage of the situation. He reluctantly followed her into a room of high ceilings, large upholstered chairs, and rich hardwood floors. But once inside, he visualized his dream. This is exactly what he wanted to build on his property. A handsome oil painting of a man and woman, presumably her parents, hung on a spacious wall by itself. Michael stopped to admire it and Sara joined him.

"My parents," she said with a soft smile. "Nice looking couple, don't you think?"

She did not wait for his reply as she continued, "This was done for their twenty-fifth anniversary, six years ago. They were so much in love. Dad has been gone two years now. He died a slow death from cancer."

"They still are."

"They still are what?" Sara asked, somewhat bewildered.

"In love. Just because your father passed away, doesn't mean that he left your mother. He went to his heaven, the one that he created while he was here in body, and now his soul waits for her to join him, in time. She can feel him, smell him, hear his foot steps, and sometimes, in her dreams, touch him."

Sara felt her tears, but did not bother to wipe them away. "I'm sorry that I made you sad," Michael said softly.

"You didn't make me sad, you gave me hope," Sara smiled as her head fell against his shoulder. He is so complicated, she thought, yet so simple. She had never met anyone like him.

Lightning cracked in the background as Michael insisted on building the fire. His hands deftly moved the logs into just the right positions, and soon the fire came to life with even, steady flames. He didn't notice her switch the room's lights off as she went to check on her daughter.

"I didn't hear you leave," he said, catching a glimpse of her against the doorframe when she returned.

"Abigail is asleep and Rufus is on the floor next to her bed," Sara said, as the shadows made by the fire danced across her face.

Michael was kneeling in front of the fireplace as he nervously poked at the logs. She took a quilt from the sofa and placed it next to him, in front of the fire. He held his breath. The thunder had provided a segue and relaxed the moment.

"You know your way around a fire, Michael. Do you like camping?"

"Very much. My kids enjoy it too. It's being outdoors and freedom. And fresh air."

"Are you a hunter?" she asked.

"Of people? That's our job."

"Come on, you know what I mean. Killing animals for sport."

"Oxymoronic."

"What is?"

"Killing and sport."

"That means you wouldn't kill an animal?" she asked, realizing it was an unfair question. "I'm sure you would if you needed food, right? After all, our meat in the stew came from a cow."

"Yes, but *I* didn't kill it and it wasn't for sport. I guess if it became a matter of survival. Even then, I'm not so sure I could harm an animal. But don't take what I'm saying to the extreme. I'm not a tree hugger. I have nothing against people who hunt animals — that's their thing. It's just not an endeavor I subscribe to or ever will."

"Do you think that some people would see you as, let's say, less macho?" Sara asked, smiling, already knowing the answer.

"Do I look like I give a shit if someone doesn't think of me as macho?" Callahan responded with a look of disgust.

"No," Sara laughed quietly, "I don't think you do."

"It looks like it's going to be a hell of a storm," Callahan observed as the rain crawled down the window glass. "I've always liked storms, even as a kid."

"Me too," Sara remarked, as she sat cross-legged on the floor. "I was going to kiss you, you know," she stated, changing gears.

He sat quietly at first, not looking for words, necessarily, but savoring the precious time. Their eyes met just as the lightning flashed again.

"You mean in front of the picture of your parents?" he asked, framing the moment.

"Yes."

"Because of what I said?" Michael asked, trying to remember his exact words.

"In a way. The feelings behind your words told me who you are, what you represent." She suddenly felt flushed as the heat rose in her neck and breasts. Quickly she turned away, not wanting him to notice. She shuffled the quilt, looking for anything to busy her hands. "You say just the right things. You have a gift, Michael."

"It's nice of you to say that, Sara, but I don't even know if I know how to talk to a woman. It's hard for me to explain," he said, poking aimlessly at the fire. "I guess listening is a big part of knowing what to say. To be perfectly honest, I never took the time to hear what my wife had to say, let alone ask her how she felt."

"It sounds as if you've done a lot of thinking lately," Sara said. Her hand found his, and their eyes lingered for an exaggerated moment.

He smiled, leaning toward her. He let both of his hands glide up her arms, moving his face close to hers. Her eyes followed him, and then closed. He first kissed her forehead, her cheek, and then her partially separated lips. She felt a shortness of breath as his hands caressed her shoulders and then moved down her back. She moved her hand to his face, brushing it softly. He released his kiss as his body came closer to her. She kissed him back, tenderly.

She paused, resting her head on his shoulder. She loved his smell, so fresh, so clean. He gently tilted her head up to him and kissed her again. Sara ran her hand over the muscles beneath his shirt while his lips caressed her neck. She wanted to take his hand and lead it to her breast, but she didn't. Not now. His hand found the curve of her back, the tightness of her thigh. He felt her flinch and move closer, inviting him with short, soft breaths.

Lights suddenly bounced through the drapes as a car pulled into the driveway.

"That's mom," Sara said sweetly. "Her timing has always been incredible."

Without speaking, he pulled away, kissing her forehead. Rufus' head appeared through the doorway, wondering if he should be concerned about the automobile noise in the driveway.

"To be continued," Michael said, sheepishly. "I guess our security systems kicked in at the same time."

"Whew. It's getting nasty out there," Mrs. Martin said, closing the front door against the wind. Instantly, she caught the mood of the room, her eyes darting first to Michael and then to her daughter. "I hope I didn't interrupt anything."

"Not at all," Michael said, moving to greet her. "I was hoping you would come home so I could meet you."

Mrs. Martin smiled. She knew he had lied. But, he did it well.

Fire is the test of gold; adversity of strong men.

~Seneca

CHAPTER TWENTY-THREE

JUNE, 1979

"WHAT DO YOU THINK the temperature is right now?" Callahan asked. He was sitting on the front of the hood of his squad car watching emergency lights spiral up the side of 'A' Mountain.

"Hell, I don't know, about a 100 or so," Alex answered.

"A hundred and eight. Man, this is Africa hot," Callahan proclaimed. "And it'll be dark in a half hour. Isn't it supposed to be cooler when the sun goes down?"

"It's summer in the desert. What do you expect?" Alex followed Callahan's eyes and saw the flashing lights of what now appeared to be a paramedic on the mountain.

Sentinel Peak sat innocently enough overlooking the ever-growing city of Tucson. At only 2,987 feet, it hardly qualified as a peak, let alone a mountain. In the center of it was a large cement 'A.' History has it that University of Arizona students placed this 'A' there after their second ever football victory. Since then, Sentinel Peak has been affectionately labeled with the obvious name of 'A' Mountain.

History taught us about a Papago Indian village at the foot of Sentinel Peak, just across the valley from present day Tucson. The Indians referred to this village, or pueblito, as *Styook-zone*. This hill was still known to the Papagos as styook, meaning black, deriving its name from the weather-stained volcanic rock with which it was covered. The word zone meant foot or base. Styook-zone simply meant the village at the base of the black hill. Styook-zone could have become Took-zone and then possibly, Tuc-son, but then who really knows for sure?

'A' Mountain's popularity as a viewpoint and a landmark more than made up for its lack of stature. Through the centuries it had overlooked all sorts of bloodshed and violence, none the least bit acceptable. What stories it must have known about the mountains that surrounded the multi-storied, man-made canyon walls of the desert city.

Callahan and Montoya were clearing a call of a silent alarm at the Pueblo Vista Park's recreation center. The alarm, as was so often the case, was tripped for some unknown reason. But, each and every one must be investigated.

"Wonder what that's all about?" Montoya asked, as they continued to watch red and blue lights twirling against the mountainside.

"Don't know," Callahan answered as he stood from his car, "but if they need us, they'll call." Just as the words rolled off his tongue, the radio came alive.

"Any unit that can clear, 10-25. A 10-72 unit needs assistance on 'A' Mountain."

Callahan did not hesitate, speaking immediately into his hand held radio. "1-Adam-7 . . . go ahead, we can clear."

"The original call to fire," the dispatcher advised, "was of a man down on the side of the mountain, below the road. Paramedics found the subject, and also found him to be extremely combative."

"I'm en route; 1-Adam-35 can 84 me." Callahan was in his unit in an instant as Montoya began to run the considerable distance across the park to his vehicle.

"10-4," the voice responded from the radio with a sense of urgency. "Fire wants us to expedite. The paramedics are being assaulted."

Callahan clicked the microphone twice in response, not taking the time to talk. With a flick of the wrist, he engaged the emergency lights and slammed the accelerator to the floor, causing the tire-spinning Dodge to slide sideways as it left the gravel lot. The scream from the siren instantly made his pulse rise and a new focus begin. Taking different streets and changing directions four times would bring him full circle to the only access up 'A' Mountain.

"Is Patrol Two available?" Callahan hollered into the microphone above the siren's scream.

"Negative . . . it's down for fuel."

"Twenty-one the heliport and get it up."

"In progress."

He soon lost sight of the paramedic unit as he curled around the base of the granite filled mountain.

"1-Adam-35, en route to 'A' Mountain," Montoya advised, about two and a half to three minutes behind Callahan.

Callahan's police unit slid perilously close to the edge of the paved road as it powered up to the top. He now had sight of the idling medical vehicle, but no one was around. He drove around it before he stopped. Still no one. I can't wait for Alex, he thought.

Stepping from his car, he stopped to listen. He heard a voice yell, "Get off me!" He ran to the road's edge, just below the right leg of the enormous 'A' and looked down. Approximately twenty yards over the side, he saw a sight that briefly paralyzed him. A shirtless subject was screaming incoherent words and repeatedly striking a fireman lying on his back. Lying precariously on his side among the rock and cactus, a few feet away, was the second paramedic.

"Freeze! Police!" Callahan demanded, but the assault did not stop. The road did not have a guardrail. Off the roadway wasn't a sheer a drop-off, but close enough. Callahan looked down at the jagged rock, mixed with scraggly desert vegetation, broken glass, and hard litter that made the drop-off treacherous and the footing unsure. For the most part, it was an uninterrupted descent, except for an occasional small plateau, one of which contained the two paramedics and their assailant.

The violent man was Martin Escobar. He was young in years, but well known by the authorities. At 23, his arrest record was extensive. His first arrest was at the age of thirteen. Nine more as a juvenile, ranging from burglary, to attempted rape, to auto theft. From his eighteenth birthday until four months ago, he had been incarcerated in the Arizona State Prison for drug possession and assault. Again he had assaulted and was in possession of drugs, this time internally. His drug of choice was PCP, also known as Angel Dust.

"Get away from him!" Callahan shouted again.

The assailant was a man possessed. He was not physically large, but that didn't matter. The drugs gave him his strength. It would take more than one person to contain him, but Callahan was alone in his pursuit and he could not allow the beating to continue. He bent over and found a rock the size of a baseball. He threw it, striking the assailant in the side, below his right shoulder. With a shout, Escobar stood, straddling the paramedic beneath him. Callahan threw another rock. This time he missed, but he had gotten Escobar's attention. The fireman scrambled away from the madman, leaving the situation to the armed officer.

"Now, get down. Put your hands where I can see them." It was worth a try.

Escobar shouted back in 'Spanglish,' a language mixing English and Spanish. He wiped at his eyes with his bloodied knuckles. His chest heaved as he breathed heavily through his mouth. He turned and looked down the slope, entertaining thoughts of escape. He took a step and grunted in pain. His right shoe was missing, only the bloody remnants of a sock remained.

Callahan stepped from the roadway and took two steps down, kicking rocks aside to assure his footing. Escobar crouched down, not taking his eyes off Callahan. The fingers of his right hand searched the ground until they found a rock to throw. Callahan's hand went to his revolver.

"Shoot the son-of-a-bitch," screamed a voice from the side. Callahan knew shooting him at this point was not an option, although he considered it.

"Drop the rock," Callahan ordered.

Escobar heard the command and began to laugh as he clawed at the flesh on his own chest. He stood upright and slowly moved backwards, in short, unsteady steps. Callahan repeated his order, taking two more steps down the side. Escobar's hands began to frantically search the waistband of his pants. Callahan stopped. Bending at the knees, he used his left hand to brace himself, to keep from falling.

Four feet down and to the left of Escobar, Callahan's eyes found what he feared. Protruding from among the rocks and debris was the handle of a revolver. This was more than likely the object of Escobar's search.

Escobar followed Callahan's stare to the area to his left. He also saw the weapon and tried to step toward it. Stumbling, he uttered words that could not be understood. He was now just inches from the handgun. There wasn't time to walk. Callahan let his body go into a slide, hitting Escobar before he could grab the gun. Escobar was on his knees, reaching for the handgun that was now several feet away, but still visible. Callahan reached for Escobar, but slipped and fell on his back. Escobar was so close that Callahan could hear his labored breathing and feel the stare from his insane eyes.

Escobar grabbed another rock and dove at the officer. Callahan's boot caught him just below the eye and he felt the cheekbone give as it splintered. The blow drove Escobar backwards, onto his back. He tried to get up, but Callahan was quicker to his feet. He hit Escobar with his fist behind the left ear and the savage went down. Instantly, Callahan was on him, rolling him over, placing both knees to Escobar's spine. Drawing the handcuffs from the pouch on his gun belt, he pulled the struggling Escobar's arms behind his back, one at a time.

With another burst of violent energy, Escobar jerked his arms from Callahan's grasp. The cuffs flew from Callahan's hand and off to the side. Callahan hit him in the face again and again. Escobar went limp, spitting blood, fighting to stay conscious.

Up above, nearing the road, a fireman staggered to his feet, exhausted from fighting the terrain and his injuries. He immediately turned and dropped to his knees, extending his hand to his partner. The assault had closed his left eye and dislocated a shoulder.

"Are you going to make it?" he asked his partner.

"Think so," answered the other as his hands found stable rocks to pull himself up. "What was that asshole's problem?" he asked, gasping for a breath.

"Is another unit up there yet?" Callahan yelled from below.
"Not yet."

Escobar was trying to pull away. Callahan jerked him to his feet as he struggled to maintain a foothold on the hideous landscape; it was like dancing on ice. He had to get him to the top. Trying to control him here was too treacherous and he must get him farther from the handgun that was somewhere among the rocks. He pulled Escobar's right arm behind his back and slowly forced him up the side. By placing a shoulder in the small of his captive's back, he could use his own body weight as leverage to force him to the top. He knew if his prisoner were to gain only a partial measure of his consciousness, it could mean disaster. On the uneven ground, the person with no fears would possess the advantage. That would be Escobar.

The sun had dropped below the mountain and seeing was difficult in the shadows. The trip up had to be quick. Using all the strength he could muster from his legs, the officer pushed and half carried the 160-pound man up the unforgiving slope. They were less than ten feet from the roadway and the footing was getting more difficult. Callahan was starting to slip. It was becoming apparent that he had made an unfortunate error in judgment. He should not have tried to bring Escobar up the side without help.

Escobar was conscious enough to know that he was in danger of falling backwards. Leaning forward, he pawed at the ground in front of him, trying to pull himself up. With his effort we might make it, Callahan prayed. A fireman was on his stomach, leaning over the side from the road, trying to grab the shirtless prisoner. He was reaching for his hair, the only grip he could get.

"Keep shoving him up," the paramedic urged. "You're almost here."

Callahan couldn't see. His head was buried in Escobar's back.

But then came the sounds of an approaching automobile, tires sliding in the loose gravel. The bright colors of the flashing lights created an impromptu kaleidoscope to the drug-induced, crazed man. The confusion that the visual events caused added to his internal turmoil.

Alex Montoya, Callahan's backup, had arrived, unwittingly,

at the wrong time. The lights and the voices of the firemen and newly arrived police officer triggered Escobar's violent behavior once more. Callahan's eyes caught sight of Montoya running toward him. Two feet to go, just a few seconds more. It wasn't to be. Martin Escobar came to life, avoiding the out-stretched hand of the fireman. His strength suddenly came with a scream and an intense and sustained burst of energy. Callahan felt Escobar's violence before he heard it. Callahan's knees and feet were in agony as they searched futilely for more leverage to force his prisoner to the top.

Montoya dove to the ground in front of Escobar, grabbing at him. His fingernails dug into Escobar's flesh, on his arm, just below the shoulder. It wasn't enough. His grip was weak. Escobar jerked away as Montoya's fingers tore through Escobar's skin.

Callahan felt his captive's unnatural strength gain a frightening advantage. Escobar's feet began resisting the slope, thrashing and pushing against the rock, trying to remove his ever-present aggressor from his back.

"Down, down, put your face down," Montoya demanded as he tried to force the head of Callahan's prisoner to the ground. Escobar was yelling back unintelligible noises.

"Dammit, down!" Callahan commanded, to no avail. His two hundred pounds pushing against one hundred-sixty had lost the advantage. The drug in the man inspired him to endure pain and persevere. His only thought was not to be captured. At any price.

The fragile foothold was giving way; the trip up the slope had stopped. His grip on his prisoner was gone. So was his balance, as reality instantly replaced fear. Escobar, realizing that he was free of the officer's grasp, pivoted to the left, lost his footing and landed on his right shoulder. Callahan tried to recover, but couldn't.

"Grab my hand!" Montoya was on his knees, extending a hand. Callahan tried, but missed. Trying to recover his balance, he had inadvertently pushed away from the ground he was trying to stand on. He was airborne, headfirst and backwards, movement too quick even for a prayer.

Callahan's body bounced, his shoulders hit the jagged lava rock first, causing his head to snap backwards. But he felt nothing. Mortar shells from a previously experienced war burst into his brain.

Story-like sentences entered his mind like a phonograph record played at too slow of a speed. It was as if the present had been read to him before in a violent form of deja vu.

Escobar was not far behind, falling awkwardly like a large rag doll.

As Callahan tumbled down the side of the mountain, the black rock and broken glass shards ripped through his uniform. He had no control of his flailing body. Only the survival instinct kept his face from the terrain. Abruptly, he came to rest on a brief interruption of the jagged lava slope. His mind was moving, but for a few seconds his body wasn't responding. He tried to sit up. It was a struggle as his mind searched for his prisoner.

And then the darkness came. Escobar, tumbling like an out of control boulder, landed squarely on the top of Callahan's head. Escobar had found yet another victim. The impact forced Callahan to violently jerk to his left, falling face-first into the dirt and rocks. There was no feeling within his body or his brain. Just exactly how long he was unconscious would never be known for certain but the result of the encounter would last a lifetime.

The night became still. Movements around him refused to make sounds. A police officer and a fireman that he recognized from somewhere before, pulled an injured man from the ground and dragged him up the slope to a sea of swirling, flashing lights.

A second bare-chested man, identical to the one being dragged, hovered a few feet above Callahan. He came closer and closer, smiling with hollow eyes. "You're going to die," an angry, harsh voice whispered in an echo. Callahan stared wordlessly at the vague shadow looming over him like an avenging giant. He searched for his own words, but the combination of shock and pain had stolen them. Callahan tried to force the image away, but he could not move his torso. His hands flailed above him, grabbing at air. He felt the image gather his legs together like pieces of firewood. Callahan tried to kick, but his legs were held down.

"No," Callahan cried and grabbed at his legs. At the sound of his voice, the image vanished. Callahan tried to sit up, but his pain would not permit it. His breathing was labored and heavy. Anxiety and fear gripped his brain.

The events of the evening raced through his mind like a TV rerun. "I had him up there, on the road. Something happened . . . . I don't know . . . something happened." Callahan knew it was real, but the details were sketchy and draped in a fog. As his violent dream started to become more clear, he could feel the anger rise inside him. That bastard assaulted the firemen, and now me.

"I'm going to kill that son-of-a-bitch," he yelled as he attempted to stand up. Callahan felt rigid, unstable as his mind swirled, disoriented. Any attempt at control was futile as he fell backwards onto the rock, sliding even farther down the hill. He cried out in pain as the current fall created new cuts and more injury. The wounded paramedics were over the side again, this time to care for a fallen comrade. Callahan's eyes saw their faces and they too, showed the painful evidence of their occupation.

CHAPTER TWENTY-FOUR

THE DARKNESS suddenly turned into daylight. The brilliance confused the injured officer as the paramedics pulled him to the safety of the paved roadway. Trying to clear the cobwebs from his fuzzy mind, he stared upwards as the firemen placed him on his back in the road. Why is that light so bright?

Callahan closed his eyes. His mind was spinning. Reality was slowly and silently seeping back into his brain, but confusion remained. Throughout his life he had thrived on competition, with his toughest competitor being himself. But now the opposition was the unknown. His bewilderment was his enemy.

Lying on his back in the roadway, he felt his left arm begin to draw up to him like the claw of a dying bird. He watched as it began to pull inward, without control. It could not possibly belong to him. He wanted it off of him. He grabbed it with his right hand and pulled it straight. A stabbing pain shot through his elbow, causing him to cry out, but the arm relaxed and the pain subsided.

Callahan's head was starting to clear, accompanied by more pain. His entire body began to throb. He tried to raise his head to a sound above, the distinct 'whap, whap, whap' of the rotating blades of the police helicopter. Its presence was welcome, but also disturbing. He opened and closed his eyes rapidly, attempting to comprehend what was happening. Why was the helicopter here?

His head felt heavy, he couldn't lift it from this angle. He tried to roll over, on his left side, but his elbow would not permit it. Callahan rolled on his right side, put his arm down, and forced himself into a sitting position. His head was not as heavy this way, but he was dizzy. Nausea came and he swallowed hard. He remained dizzy, but not as bad. His thoughts became a subtle rush, filled with circumstances surrounding the recent events. Along with the recollections, came panic and anxiety . . . but also strength. He was now on his knees, fighting to get up.

"Lay back down," came the order, "you're hurt."

"Not that bad," he said. "Help me up. Where's the asshole that caused all of this?"

"The other officers have him. He's not going anywhere. They have the situation under control."

Control!

With a burst of testosterone, he pulled himself upright, fighting off dizziness in the process. The left arm was starting to function. His pain was now numbness, not as debilitating as it had been before. He could function, and his fear was starting to subside. Cuts, scrapes and bruises he could live with, but being unable to control himself and his surroundings was a situation he could not bear. Without realizing it, he was seeing a glimpse of his future.

Escobar was lying face down on the cracked asphalt of the road's shoulder. The drugs in his body were losing their effect. He did not give the appearance of the menacing animal of before. His energies were depleted. Even if he wanted to move, it was not an option. Montoya's knee in the middle of Escobar's back, riveted his chest to the surface of the road.

A wave of anger and hate overwhelmed Callahan. Within him, a struggle began between common sense and an urge for vengeance. He wanted to inflict pain on the evil man, but his soul rejected the idea, much like the hunting of a defenseless animal. Instead, he knelt to look into the captured man's eyes and found him smiling. "Who is this punk?" Callahan demanded.

The labor of his walk was transparent to others, but not to him. However, his physical appearance was not as well hidden. No one had ever seen him so beaten, so vulnerable. The once proud officer stood before the others as a beaten victim in a fight for survival. Dried and fresh blood were visible on his exposed skin, as well as the shredded cloth of his once white police uniform shirt.

Unaware of the extent of his injuries, Callahan struggled to keep his balance, as he looked down toward his waist. In total disbelief, he found that his gun belt was missing. He grabbed at his waist. Shit, where in the hell is my belt? Where is it? How could I have lost it? As he looked down, the dizziness came back. He did not realize that the movement of his neck was further traumatizing his exposed spinal cord. The dizziness was again producing nausea. He looked up, and the dizziness and nausea subsided.

Callahan's sense of awareness came back to him like the arousal from an alarm clock. He began walking to the side of the roadway where his fall had taken place. Every step was an effort, his legs and his mind fighting to function together.

"Sit down, goddamn it." The paramedics stopped him again, but this time their mood was not so congenial. "You're not doing yourself, or anybody else any favors with your macho bullshit. You're hurt. Use your head."

"But my weapon, my revolver is gone," Callahan said, his rigid fingers searching his waistband.

"We'll find your weapon. Now, sit your ass down," Alex ordered, leading Callahan to the front of his patrol car and leaning him against the hood.

"We've located your prisoner's vehicle," an officer waved from a few yards away. "It's parked around the curve. The registration in the glove box indicates that it belongs to Roberto Escobar."

"Escobar?" Alex said, questioning himself. "What kind of car is it?" he asked the officer.

"It's a '72 Ford."

"I know that name and that car. There was a 10-82 out on that vehicle earlier tonight," Alex said, leaving Callahan's side. "Show me the car."

The helicopter had brought the light, and with it plenty of attention. For miles around, the public down below the mountain had seen the flashing lights and the circling helicopter. And as people do in search of a catastrophe, they jumped in their automobiles and headed up the road to where the lights of urgency were beckoning.

Additional units were dispatched to stop the traffic flow, but about a half dozen vehicles with curious citizens had already arrived before the road could be blocked. As they approached the scene, only one side of the equation was visible. They witnessed a shirtless man, a minority, lying face down with his hands and arms bound behind him. Add the fact that two police officers were holding him that way, and the cries of police brutality and other unkind, verbal offerings could almost be expected.

The dark blue Ford pulled alongside Callahan's police unit. He squinted, trying to see the occupants, but couldn't. The driver turned off the headlights and immediately two men in sport coats, khaki pants, and dress shirts open at the collar stepped from the car.

"What in the hell happened to you, Callahan?" Detective Wells asked, his eyes showing his concern. "Are you all right?"

"Yeah, I'm fine." Callahan tried to focus, turning to watch the second detective approach. "What brings you guys up here?"

"That piece of shit that's laying on the road over there."

"Really." Callahan smiled. "Did I miss something? You guys are still in Homicide, right? I didn't think anybody died here."

"Not here, somewhere else. Earlier this evening," Wells answered, placing a hand on Callahan's shoulder. "A little after six, officers responded to an 'assault in progress' down on South Liberty. When they got there, they found a man severely beaten and unconscious. The asshole that did it was gone and the only one at the residence was the wife, who spoke only Spanish. The paramedics arrived and immediately put the guy on life support. The two officers at the scene did not speak Spanish, and by the time we could locate a bilingual officer to respond, the victim and his wife were en route to St. Mary's Hospital."

Callahan listened closely, studying Wells' face.

"George and I were called to the hospital when they determined the seriousness of the victim's injuries. I don't think in all my years, I've ever seen anybody beaten that badly. George is fluent in Spanish, so we were able to talk to the wife. She said that her husband, Roberto Escobar, was upset with their son about his drug use and told him to get out of the house. The son, Martin, went crazy and started beating his father with anything he could get his hands on. Apparently, Martin left when his father lost consciousness."

"And he showed up here," Callahan said.

"Roberto Escobar didn't make it," Wells continued. "He died of massive head injuries before they could get him to surgery. What kind of asshole would beat his own father to death?"

"You're out of uniform," a paramedic scolded with a smile as he handed Callahan his Sam Browne uniform belt, "and your shirt's ripped. Man, you need to take care of yourself a little better. We have an image to protect, you know."

Callahan stared at the two pieces that were once a gun belt. His .38 caliber Smith and Wesson revolver had remained intact, secured in its holster. The slide down the sharp and jagged slope had slashed his thick leather gun belt in half. It was found sitting on a foundation of lethal fragments of broken bottles and shattered lava rock.

"One little dive off a short little mountain, and all I get from you guys is shit. You're just jealous because you don't know how to make the job fun." Even in pain, humor became the diffuser of gut-wrenching seriousness. Obviously only a mask, it served its purpose. It settled the nerves and lowered the blood pressure.

Under the uniform shirt, next to the bare chest and beating heart was a bulletproof vest. It was made of a special lightweight material that could stop, or at least slow down, a projectile fired from a weapon. The testing of the vest by the manufacturer did not, by any stretch of the imagination, include placing it on a two hundred pound man and sending him head first and upside down through a bed of multi-century, hardened lava rock. However, it had been tested now, and it passed . . . barely. Thank God the vest had done its job. It had protected the protector. But there were other areas of the body, just as vital, that nothing but fate and good fortune could protect. Or in this case, couldn't protect.

Basically, all of his faculties had returned. Taking inventory, he found nothing more than a torn up uniform and scratched up skin. He had been through worse, and more than likely, would be again. Re-group and go on. That was the nature of the beast.

The helicopter crew left as quickly as they had appeared. Immediately, the artificial daylight turned into night. The constant, pounding noise of the rotor blades faded, leaving behind a deafening silence. Callahan sat in a daze, watching the emergency vehicles leave the impromptu mayhem. A call of a "man down" resulted, ironically, in many men down.

He drove himself down the short, winding road from the small mountain, heading to the nearby police station. In spite of the numerous wounds, he felt surprisingly well. A little neck discomfort, but he had no pain of any great significance. The lesson taught by his own vulnerability was his most obvious wound, a wound that must heal quickly or its effects could linger forever.

The parking area behind the downtown police headquarters was usually cluttered with police vehicles and personnel. This particular night, there was very little activity. It seemed a quiet epilogue to the evening's events. Rows of unassigned marked patrol units sat motionless in silent readiness, waiting to respond to tragedies and calls for help.

Inside the department, the usual hustle and bustle was apparent everywhere. Officers were completing their debriefings and others were just arriving to begin their shifts that would take them through the dawn of the next day. The couches and chairs of the public lobby were littered with people, victims and witnesses of the numerous criminal episodes from the evening. There were no smiles, only the hushed voices of the frightened and bewildered.

Strings noticed Callahan walking slowly across the lobby. "You look like hell," Strings said, slapping the dirt from Callahan's shoulder. "You've got blood all over you. Hope it's not yours. Are you all right?"

"Yeah, I'm okay," Callahan answered, surveying his wounds. "I just feel like I've been shot at and missed and shit at and hit."

Strings chuckled. "The Sarge here just told me that you beat the hell out of some homicide suspect that was assaulting a couple paramedics. You probably look a lot better than the other guy."

"Regardless, you better fill out a Workman's Compensation form," the on-duty First Sergeant broke in. "I know you're saying you're all right now, but you just never know."

Nothing in life is to be feared.
It is only to be understood.

~Madame Curie

CHAPTER TWENTY-FIVE

NOVEMBER, FIVE MONTHS LATER . . .

"WOULD YOU LIKE SOMETHING to drink, Sir?" The passenger did not answer, unaware that the flight attendant was beside him. "Sir?"

"Oh, I'm sorry. I didn't realize that you were talking to me."

"Would you like a beverage?" she asked with a polite smile.

"Yes, thank you. An iced tea, please," he answered, staring out the window, wondering about the source of his anxiety.

Lieutenant Ben Thompson had been in Virginia for the past three weeks at the F.B.I Academy in Quantico for advanced supervisor training. Paid for by the City, periodically the Department would send upper level supervisors there for what was considered state of the art skill improvements. While there, day-to-day operations of his hometown police department were not a concern. Just a few casual remarks from his wife during daily phone conversations kept him in touch with Tucson. So he knew nothing major had happened, nothing of real significance. But something nagged at his subconscious, telling him that all was not right.

His wife, Cassie, picked him up at the airport, but gave no indication of a problem, personal or professional. But, the annoying fear persisted. They arrived home within fifteen minutes. Kelly, their nine year old daughter, had stayed at the neighbors' while dad was being picked up. She ran home immediately when she saw their car and all was well as they hugged in the driveway.

"I need to go downtown," and Cassie knew "downtown" always meant 270 S. Stone. She never put up an argument when he went to work at unscheduled times because she knew it was part of his progression within the department. She also knew a huge part of his success was his intuition.

"I'll be back before Kelly's bedtime."

She just smiled as he kissed her cheek, knowing his mistress would garner all of his attention. And her competition was his badge.

"Welcome back, Lieutenant," the First Sergeant stated as he looked up from his paperwork. "How was it back East?"

"Quantico was very interesting, well worth the trip. But, damn it was cold. I'm glad to be back in the desert and the heat." A couple of officers, not used to seeing him in civilian attire, nodded as they walked by. An officer at the front desk was listening to a citizen complaining about how unfair parking tickets were while a second officer typed something with one hand and sipped coffee with the other. Nothing seemed to be out of place, he thought to himself, except "the feeling."

"I thought you were going to quit smoking while I was gone," Lt. Thompson said as he waved a hand in front of his face to clear the smoke. "That shit is going to kill you someday, Arnold."

"Yeah, that's what Vic said before he left for the mountains," the Sergeant said as he winced and snuffed his cigarette out in the ashtray.

"Anything happen while I was gone?" he asked while going through the mail in his office.

"No, not really. Just the same old crimes and criminals," Sergeant Lester Arnold answered as he put his hand to the back of his neck to massage out some stiffness while checking the clock on the wall. "It's been a long shift already and it just started."

"Are you sure that nothing has happened that I should be aware of, Les?" Ben was unsuccessfully trying to shake his uneasiness.

"Yeah, as far as I know. But, I'm like a mushroom, Lieutenant.

They feed me bullshit and keep me in the dark."

"I'll go nose around and see what I've missed," Thompson said, as he smiled and walked away.

His present assignment was as a Force Commander, one of eight in the Uniform Division. His hours would vary, but more often than not, he found himself supervising the evening and night shifts, mostly by choice. Checking the schedule, he found his name penciled in on the midnight to 0800 shift, a bit of news that would surely delight his wife.

Uniform shift briefings were held in the lower level of the police building, and as usual, he took the stairs instead of the elevator. He loved exercise and never passed up the chance to walk instead of ride. He checked his watch and it was a bit after seven o'clock. The briefing room was empty as was pretty much all of the downstairs. He hit the door bar and went into a small, dimly lit break room of six round tables and various vending machines. Two young, female civilian employees looked up briefly when the door opened, before returning to their conversation. He opened a second door, this one requiring an issued key to enter. A short hallway took him to an open debriefing room that seemed almost eerie with its absence of people.

Might as well check my locker since I'm down here, he mumbled to himself as he backtracked slightly down the hall and into the men's facility room. He immediately heard the clanking of weights coming from the small, but adequate exercise room nearby.

Officer Curtis Mulley appeared in the doorway with a towel over his head, having just completed his daily workout. Eighteen years he had spent on the department, with all eighteen in uniform. Pound for pound, Mulley was arguably the best street cop that Tucson ever had. But, somewhere early in his career he had pissed someone off in the hierarchy of the department, and it had stuck, foregoing any chance of promotion.

"Hey, Ben," Curtis said as he walked by the Lieutenant. "How was the F.B.I. Academy?"

"Good. How have you been? Haven't seen you in a while."

"Well. I'm doing fine," the bulldog looking officer responded. "Have you seen Thumper?" he asked knowing that they shared a very good friend in Michael Callahan.

"No. Ever since he started working T.A.C. a few months ago we've found it hard to get together. Have you talked to him recently?"

Mulley took the towel from his head and pulled it slowly across his face, taking time to wipe the perspiration off before he spoke. "You haven't heard, have you?"

"Heard what?" Thompson asked as his guts grabbed his vocal cords.

"Thumper is in the hospital, TMC. He's paralyzed. He can't walk." The strong officer wanted to cry, but his life wouldn't allow it.

"What? When did this happen?" He had no idea what emotion to feel. Anger, because he wasn't told? Disbelief? Fear?

"From what I was told, it was an old injury from last June that finally caught up to him. Somebody said that it was that fall off of 'A' Mountain. I don't know much. Sorry." Curtis walked off, not being very good at times like this.

Thompson stared into the mirrored wall of the workout room without seeing an image. His thoughts were elsewhere as his mind could not visualize an injured Michael Callahan. How could this happen to a man so strong? And then the Lieutenant's anger began to swell. "Why in the hell wasn't I told of this?" he yelled aloud as he ran from the room and up the stairs.

"Arnold!" Lieutenant Thompson said loudly as he pushed the door open to the lobby. The Sergeant was standing with his back to the door and turned quickly upon hearing his name. "Why in the hell didn't you tell me about Callahan?"

"I wasn't sure what was going on with him. You know, his condition," the First Sergeant stammered.

"What in the hell do you mean that you're not sure? Jesus Christ, Arnold. We have an injured officer, and you don't know his status?" Thompson was furious.

"All I know is that he went to Tucson Medical Center late Tuesday evening, and they kept him for observation."

"Tuesday? I have an officer tell me about this in the fucking locker room. Are you telling me that he knows more than the goddamn First Sergeant? How did he get to the hospital, Les? Can you at least tell me that?"

Sergeant Arnold could only stare back at the Lieutenant.

"I can, Lieutenant." The words came from Barbara Wells as she stepped from the communications room. She was standing quietly to the side, listening to their conversation and waiting to add what she knew.

The officers stood in silence as she walked towards them. "Tuesday we received a call from the Forest Service. A ranger had found Callahan lying on the floor of his camper, parked in Bear Canyon. Evidently, he had suffered some type of seizure and was unable to move."

"How did they know to go to his truck?" the Lieutenant asked.

"The ranger station had received a call from someone stating that they were worried that they had not heard from him and it was an emergency number he had given them. He usually called them every day, without fail. Except that day."

"Who was the caller, Barb?" the Lieutenant questioned as he shook his head.

"His daughter, Amy."

"Oh, God." Thompson stated as he grabbed his keys from the desk. "I'll be at the hospital if anyone needs me."

He hated sitting in chairs. Always had. A counter, a table, anything that would allow his feet to dangle above the floor was his preference. Other than athletic shoes, and sandals occasionally, western boots were his choice, polished to perfection.

Callahan's eyes opened and he immediately sensed another presence within the room. Turning his head slightly, he found a figure perched on the counter top in the corner with his feet several inches above the floor. The tall man with his arms folded across his chest jerked, as intermittent sleep caused him to contact the wall. I wonder how long he's been here?

A nurse that talked much too fast and moved even quicker entered the room and found something in a drawer that was needed elsewhere. "What does your friend have against chairs? It must be uncomfortable sitting on the counter. Sorry if I disturbed you. Bye!"

Lt. Thompson shook his head in the dim light, erasing airplane flights and pending exhaustion. Squinting through his glasses, he found Callahan watching him.

"How long have you been here?" Callahan asked as Thompson moved forward to stand.

"I was going to ask you the same thing," he answered back with a yawn.

"Oh, I don't know, three or four days, maybe."

"What happened, Thump?" Ben asked, as his face was now awake and stern. "I wasn't aware that you were having health problems. Of course, we haven't seen a hell of a lot of each other lately, either."

"Whatever happened is scary, Ben. It was strange, real strange."

"Did it hit you all of a sudden?"

"It seemed that way. But lately, I've had a lot of time to think about it and I guess there were quite a few warning signs. First, there was pain across my shoulders then down my arm. My hand would start shaking and my arm would go numb. Then the headaches began."

"Did you tell anybody about what was happening to you? Surely, someone could look at you and tell that . . ."

"The Industrial Commission Doctors said it was soft tissue damage and that it would heal in time," Callahan interrupted. "I believed them at first and was trying to ignore it, but the pain became too much. At first, I would stumble. Then I began to fall. Some days were worse than others. And now, my lower body won't move. Is this the way I'm going to live out my life?" The Lieutenant could only answer with silence.

"And they tell me that surgery is my only hope. Hell, they're going to operate and they don't even know what's wrong with my spine."

"So that's your biggest fear?"

"What? Being confined to a wheelchair?"

"No," Thompson said, pushing himself from the cabinet. "The unknown. That's what's kicking your ass. If you knew exactly what your injury was, you would know what to fight. So, change your attitude, Callahan. You've never backed down from anything in your life. Don't start now. You have a lot of friends who are pulling for you. You also have a lot of people that depend upon you."

"You're right, Ben. That's kind of what Angela tried to tell me." Callahan stared at Thompson. "Have you talked to her?"

"Who?"

"Angela. She works in communications."

"Don't know her. Must be new."

"No. Not really. I met her at the station quite awhile ago."

"That's interesting. I thought I knew everyone in commo." Thompson walked to the front of Callahan's bed.

Michael stared at the ceiling. "She talked about voices, as if voices were her life. She let me talk. No, she made me talk. About life and religion, and my parents. She took my strength, and then she gave it back to me. I saw my daughter in her, as a grown up woman. She brought back memories of time I spent with my mother when I was a child."

"Sounds like a special person."

"Yeah," Callahan smiled. "Sometimes I think she knows more about me than I do."

"That's scary in itself," Lt. Thompson laughed. "I've got to get out of here. I'll see you tomorrow," he said, slapping Callahan's foot.

"By the way," Callahan said. "Angela is a good friend of Weaver Bailey, our old F.B.I. buddy."

Thompson stopped. "That's quite the coincidence."

"He came up the mountain with her to see me. She said they were like brother and sister."

"When was this?" Thompson asked, turning toward the bed.

"I don't know exactly," Callahan said, searching his memory. "Couple of weeks ago, maybe. My mind's kind of shaky on time."

"Did you actually talk to Bailey?"

"No, that's the funny part. He told her that it would be too dangerous for us to be seen together. He said he was working some special case. She didn't ask anymore questions and they left without getting out of the car."

"Are you sure it was Bailey she mentioned?" Thompson asked.

"Yeah. Why?"

"No, nothing to worry about. I'll be around tomorrow. Get some rest." This is strange, real strange, Thompson thought to himself as he scratched at his two-day old beard.

CHAPTER TWENTY-SIX

SOMETHING THAT ROLLED down the hall, then stopped, and then rolled again made a squeak. WD40 would probably take care of the problem he thought, but he was glad it wasn't fixed. In the deafening stillness anything that moved, regardless of its annoyance, pleased him. It could be someone dispensing medications or a housekeeping cart. Whatever it was didn't matter, because it served as a distraction from his fears.

It was November 21st, almost five months to the day since the incident on 'Λ' Mountain. Michael Callahan had been dealing with constant neck and back pain and numbness in his withering left arm since that day in June. The Industrial Commission doctors were adamant that his injuries only affected the soft tissue and it would just take time to heal. They could not have been more wrong.

A nurse appeared in quiet efficiency at Michael's bedside. She was thirty something, with lovely, auburn hair, and large, emerald eyes that sparkled above olive skin.

"Mr. Callahan, my name is Julia Millor, and I will be your nurse in the evening hours." Something about his look overwhelmed her just for a second as she paused to smile. "I understand that you are a police officer," she continued, "and that your injuries were suffered while you were on duty. Is that correct?"

"Yes, I am, or was. I'm not real sure what I am at the present." His face was starting to lose the softness of youth, taking on an edge created by stress.

Julia smiled as her mind searched for words, but none came. However, a distinct feeling of helplessness caused her to briefly close her eyes. She would not allow herself to look at him, eye to eye. Her hands began to tremble slightly and she made them into fists and shoved them into the pockets of her smock.

"Are you my regular nurse or a relief?" Michael asked.

"I'll be your regular nurse," Julia answered. "I've been off for three days."

"Just never know what to expect when you come back, do you?" he smiled.

"Kind of like your job."

"Yeah. I suppose so."

"I see you have your own security," Julia said, glancing at Sara and Alex in uniform.

"Not hardly. They're waiting for me to die. He wants my watch and she wants my dog. Or the other way around."

"That's not true," Alex rebutted. "His watch is cheap and the dog is a pain in the ass. It's the truck and camper we want."

"See what I mean? They're nothing but vultures," Callahan grinned.

"Well, I guess they'll have to wait a long time, won't they?" Julia smiled and patted his knee as she walked from his bedside.

"Have you been in 803?" Julia asked the others at the nurse's station. "We should feel safe with all of the cops around."

"That's Thumper's room," Dr. Mathias answered with his back to the conversation.

"Who?" Julia asked. "The chart indicates that a Michael Callahan occupies that room."

"Yeah. Thumper."

"Thumper. That's an interesting name," Julia grinned. "Do you know how he received his injuries?"

"He was making an arrest up on 'A' Mountain and something went wrong. Evidently, he went off the side and he suffered severe trauma to his cervical spine."

"Did you know him before he was admitted?" Julia asked, intrigued by her new patient.

Dr. Richard Mathias smiled and chuckled as he turned toward

her. "Not exactly. We had seen each other in the ER, but never spoke. But then one evening, I was driving to the airport and was late, of course. The speed limit on Campbell is around forty-five and I was doing, oh, about sixty-five or so." The doctor folded his arms across his chest and stared into the distance. "And sure enough, the red lights came on right behind me. Like I said, I was running late and being stopped would not have helped the situation. This cop comes up to the window and asks for my driver's license. I look up at the officer with the 'Thumper' nametag and say, rather arrogantly, 'What's the matter? Don't you have your quota, today?'"

"The cop says without changing expressions, 'Actually I do. Now I'm working on the trip to Hawaii. Now, may I see your driver's license, please?' I handed it to him, and without a word, he checked it, smiled, then gave it back to me. He got in his car, made a U-turn, and left." The nurses laughed at his story, but became instantly silent as the doctor tossed his clipboard onto the counter and walked away.

"I'll be in 803," Julia said to the nurse behind the desk. She had to learn more about Officer Callahan. Entering his room, she walked to his bed and began to rearrange his bed coverings and fluff his pillows, obviously trying to conceal her agenda. It didn't work.

"What's up, Julia?" Callahan asked, sensing her nervousness.

Julia looked at Sara, who nodded and smiled approvingly.

Julia sat in the chair next to his bed and began to apply lotion to his arms. "Would it be too painful to tell me how you'ended up here? The doctor said you were injured in June and it's now November."

Callahan began to briefly relate to her the situation involving his divorce and his choice to stay in the camper away from the city. He told her about the incident on 'A' Mountain, and how his injuries were not considered serious. Then he described the five months of symptoms. Intermittent pain. Loss of memory. Unable to make decisions. And then the day he was found unconscious.

"I was sitting in a lawn chair, watching the sun rise over the mountains. My left hand had been tingling for several weeks, but it suddenly became numb. I tried to lift it, but it wouldn't move. I tried again and it moved, but a sharp pain hit my neck, just below the back of my head. It was like I had been hit with a 2 by 4. I started to black out. Somehow, I got up and pulled myself into the camper and found the bed."

Julia stood and moved to the other side of the bed. She swallowed hard, fighting back tears.

"Pains started to shoot down my arms and my legs. The lightning shocks kept hitting my body, again and again. I tried to take myself somewhere else in my mind so I wouldn't feel the pain. It didn't work. I started to black out again. I was confused, afraid to close my eyes. Then I must have lost consciousness because when I woke up it was dark, and Rufus was licking me. I tried to move, but I couldn't.

"I guess I was unconscious when I came here because when I woke up I found myself hooked to machines and tubes up my nose. I felt no pain. Just beeps from my heart machine, telling me that I was alive. People were in my room and I tried to look around but the pain returned, but not as intense. Doctors were talking softly, mentioning 'paralysis' and 'loss of movement.' A Deputy Sheriff was there, saying that he had secured my truck and that my dog was safe. And then he was gone. But strangers appeared at my side, all smiling, saying that everything would be all right. They made me sick." Callahan quit speaking and the room was uncomfortably silent for close to a minute. Julia and Sara stared at each other with identical, expressionless faces. No words could explain their feelings.

Julia stood and excused herself. Slowly, she walked down the hallway. She thought about the similarities between the man she just met and her husband at home.

She entered an empty patient room seeking temporary refuge and resurgence of her strength. She crossed the darkness of the room to the window and stared off into the lights of the surrounding city. The few moments that she had spent with the injured police officer had triggered a terrible memory from her past. Three years ago this coming December she had made the decision to take a break from her marriage and her career. Without an itinerary, she set out in her automobile for parts unknown with no forwarding address. Five days later, her husband, a lineman for the local power company, was severely burned in an electrical accident, nearly costing him his life. It wasn't until she arrived back in Tucson that she learned of the incident and that the injuries to his eyes had resulted in permanent blindness. Even though she had been with him ever since, the fact that she was not there when he needed her most had created a haunting guilt.

After several deep breaths, she took control of her emotions and quietly left the room to focus on her profession.

Alex slouched in his chair, writing something in a small spiral pad. He appeared uninterested as Sara stood by Michael's bed making small talk as she gently massaged his arms. She whispered something that was obviously intimate into his ear because Callahan smiled with a hint of a blush. While placing several light kisses on his forehead, she whispered good night. Waving goodnight to Alex, she left his bedside and disappeared from the room.

Michael followed her footsteps with a frown. "This whole ordeal is taking a toll on her, Alex. Please, convince her that she doesn't have to be here constantly. It's wearing her out. She has a daughter and her job to contend with."

"And you, Callahan. She also has you. She knows her limits. Don't break her spirit by making her feel unwanted," Alex said sternly. "My people have a phrase for someone special like Sara. Corazon de melon, the heart of the melon. It's a term of endearment to describe someone that's kind, caring, and gentle. You know, kind of angelic."

"Corazon de melon," Michael whispered. "That's beautiful, Alex."

Melons. And blackberries growing wild next to the hidden lake in the Sycamore woods. "Your words just brought my childhood back to me. That was strange."

"Really, what was it like growing up in the country?"

"There is no better way to spend your youth, Alex. It was fresh air and water, green grass and fishing, and swimming in the strip mine ponds. I grew my first tomatoes when I was eight, perhaps nine. The soil was so rich and fertile. It was the color of mahogany and it smelled sweet. My Grandfather once told me that if you were to stick your thumb into the ground and hold it there, you could actually grow a whole new hand."

"Did you ever try it?" Alex asked as he smiled.

"Yeah, actually I did. But, my arm got tired and I had to

quit."

God, it's good to see him laugh, Alex thought.

"I dug a garden by hand, about 4 feet by 10 feet, I guess," Callahan continued. "I planted green beans, some kind of squash, and tomatoes, of course. All from seed. And man, I didn't think that first tomato would ever turn red." He began to laugh aloud at his recollection. "Morning, noon, and night I would check my vines, keeping track of the fruit as it started to change color. And then there was one that was more mature than the others. I let it get redder and redder, protecting it with my life. And when it was just right, I got the saltshaker and ate the whole cotton pickin' thing, right there in the garden. I can still taste the juices as they squished out of my mouth and down my chest. To this day, it's the best tomato I've ever had."

Alex found the edge of his chair, as he wanted to hear more about the country he had never seen. "Tell me more, Callahan. What was it like in Indiana?"

"Colors, Alex, lots of color, especially in the fall of the year, greens, oranges, reds, yellows, and every shade in between. Mushrooms would grow wild for the picking. And everything that grew wild produced a fragrance that would be embedded in your memory forever. Just like the twinkle of lightning bugs, and the deep throated conversation of bullfrogs off somewhere in the distance. Gravel roads that went everywhere, and as a kid, I traveled every one of them."

Callahan's eyes were shining and his voice was higher than usual, with the words coming much quicker. "People didn't lock their doors. There was no need to. Everyone trusted everyone else. Can you believe that? Especially seeing what we see everyday? And I didn't have indoor plumbing until I went into the Air Force. We just lived a very simple, uncomplicated life, Alex."

Callahan's thoughts of yesterday ended abruptly as Julia, followed by Dr. Raines, entered the room. Alex stood to go and grimaced as he observed reality suddenly change the expression on the face of his mentor.

"You're all right, Alex. Hang tight. You don't have to leave," Callahan requested as he forced a smile. "Right now, I need all of the support I can get. Right, Doc?"

A hint of a smile crossed the neurosurgeon's lips, but nothing more.

"Dr. Raines, what is actually wrong with my spine?" Callahan asked, desperately seeking some answers. He needed an indicator. He was in an occupation that survived on reading body language and subtle physical clues, however, the doctor remained stoic.

Callahan watched as the specialist proceeded through the information on his chart. Raines wasn't exactly sure what was wrong with Callahan's neck and that fact annoyed him. He had a pretty good guess, but that wasn't adequate.

"To tell you the truth, Michael," the doctor responded with a sigh, "we probably won't know until we actually perform the surgery."

"Do you have an educated guess?" He desperately looked for any hope to grasp. "I need something to process, something to focus on."

"All right. Let's look at your injury," Dr. Raines said as he sat on the edge of the officer's bed. "It was a compression blow. The impact was full force on the top of your head. Something had to give, and that something was vertebrae. To what degree, we don't know. You have quite a bit of swelling and probably bruising around C4 and C5. The X-rays, even at different angles, can't tell us everything. And then there's the spinal cord. To what extent it's damaged, we don't know. Hopefully, the tests that we will run can give us some insight, but I really don't think there is any way that we can avoid surgery. So, prepare yourself for that fact."

"When this is over, will I be able to walk?"

"I think so. But, you know as well as I do that there are no guarantees. You will be going through quite a few tests before we schedule surgery, so bear with us. We just have to believe."

And with a tap to the foot of the injured officer, the doctor started to leave, but paused. "Remember, you are going to have good days and some bad ones. We will try to alleviate as much pain as we can."

"I can handle the pain, Dr. Raines. My struggle is the unknown."

"That's my struggle too, Michael," the doctor stated as he

pulled his fingers through his hair. "Mine, too." Still studying the chart, Dr. Raines walked swiftly from the room.

"Are you sleeping?" The soft voice of the night shift custodian drifted into #803. He did not have a job related reason for entering the room, but he wanted to meet the patient. He had observed several police officers visit the occupant of the bed, talking and laughing softly with him. The hospital employee had always had a dream. A dream of wearing a badge on his chest. He realized early in life that this would not be possible, but he never lost his passion for law enforcement.

"No, I'm awake," Callahan answered, welcoming the words. "Come on in."

"I was wondering," he asked while standing in the doorway, not wanting to be an intrusion, "if I may come and sit with you during my break."

"Sure you can. I would appreciate some company. It can get pretty lonely in here when you can't sleep." Callahan did not know the man's name, nor had he ever seen his face, but instead, recognized him from his gait. In the nights before, he had listened to the same voice greet other staff members as he moved up and down the corridor. This person would first plant one foot, then ask the tardy one to catch up. Callahan had pictured left foot forward, with the right leg dragging behind in labor and he smiled as the man's entrance proved him accurate.

"Bring your chair over here, Sir, next to the bed," Callahan requested in a soft demand as the gentleman began to sit across the room. "We can talk easier if you are closer."

The custodian took delight in Callahan's respectful reference to him and he immediately complied by pulling the nearest chair to the bedside. His charcoal colored pants and shirt were neatly pressed and creased and his work boots shined to a luster. His weight was a little more than most charts allowed on his five foot, eight inch frame, but it was hardly noticeable.

"How long is your break?" Michael asked, observing the 'Ronnie' nametag sewn neatly onto his uniform shirt.

"Fifteen minutes," Ronnie answered, not taking his eyes off

of the man in the bed. "But, I can take longer if I don't take my other break later on." He had turned forty just last Tuesday, but age meant nothing to him. A birth defect had kept him from his lifelong dream and he had learned early to accept his fate.

"You're a police officer, aren't you?" he blurted out with a smile.

"Yes, I am."

"Are you a patrol officer, Sir?" Ronnie asked, moving to the front edge of his seat.

"No, I am presently assigned to T.A.C. That means that I . . ."

Ronnie interrupted with his left hand held in front of him like a school crossing guard. "I'm sorry to interrupt, but I know what T.A.C. is. It's undercover work, but you handle all kinds of situations. Right?"

"You got it," Callahan answered with a grin.

"What's your designator, if you don't mind me asking? I can't recognize your voice."

"I am TAC 12."

"*You are TAC 12!* That means that you used to be 1-Adam-7, right? Man, this is great meeting you." Ronnie just realized that he was talking louder than he should be and lowered to almost a whisper. "I volunteer to work the midnight shift so I can listen to my police scanner during the busiest hours." Ronnie then stood from his chair, checking his watch as he rose.

"I'm going back to work now so I can save my other break to come back later, if that's all right with you?"

"Sure it is, Ronnie. Just walk in. You don't have to ask permission. And I didn't introduce myself. My name is…"

"Please," Ronnie interjected, "you are 1-Adam-7. That's all I need to know." Ronnie began to walk toward the door, but this time, maybe a bit more quickly than usual.

He returned later, but found Callahan sleeping peacefully. The fact that he could not talk to his new friend did not matter. He sat in his chair, next to the bed, making notes for future conversations. He remembered calls that "1-Adam-7" had been on and wanted him to relate the details. He didn't know what was wrong with Callahan, but in overhearing the numerous conversations, he knew his friend was in need of everyone's prayers.

Not till we are lost,
in other words,
not till we have lost the world,
do we begin to find ourselves.

~Thoreau

CHAPTER TWENTY-SEVEN

EVERY NIGHT THE CUSTODIAN would make his appearance in Room 803. They would talk mostly about police work and sports, but it never really mattered what the subject was. What they both needed was a friend, a friend with no qualifications designed by status. The tests were taking their toll on Callahan's stamina. Quite often, he would fall asleep during conversations. This didn't bother Ronnie. The next time, he would just pick up where they had left off.

"Is it hard to hear when you drive with the siren on?" Ronnie's eyes sparkled at the thought.

"Yeah, it is. You have to turn the radio way up to hear it."

"Does the siren make you nervous? You know, all excited?"

"Not as much as the drivers of the cars in front of me." Callahan laughed.

"Have you ever wrecked a police car?" Ronnie was never without questions. He just wished that he could remember all of them.

"Yeah, twice." Callahan grinned.

"What happened? Did you get hurt?"

"The first accident happened when a lady was driving too fast in the rain and ran into the side of me. Tore the livin' hell out of the squad car, took the whole front end off. I got banged up a little bit, but the seatbelt saved me."

"Did she get in a lot of trouble for crashing into a police car?" As usual, Ronnie hung on Callahan's every word.

"She got a citation and her insurance paid for the car, I'm sure. She was a very nice lady. It was just one of those things. That's why they call them accidents."

"How about the second one? What happened then? Did somebody run into you again?"

"I was afraid you were going to ask that." Callahan blushed. "Somebody ran into me, alright. But, this time it was my fault."

"Really?" Ronnie's facial expression changed.

"Yeah, Ronnie, I screwed up. I was driving down by the University and I thought I heard someone holler at me, and without thinking, I swung around to make a u-turn and, *crunch.* I had forgotten about the car behind me."

"Did you get in trouble?" Ronnie had moved to the edge of his seat.

"Well, I got a ticket and a written reprimand from the chief."

"You got a ticket? Policemen don't get tickets." Ronnie was astonished.

"Oh, yes we do. Just like everybody else when they screw up."

"I'll be darned. Just one more question, then I have to go, okay?"

"Sure."

"You don't have to answer this," Ronnie prefaced, "but, it's something I need to know." He studied his fingers as they massaged his palms.

"What is it, Ronnie? I'll tell you if I can't answer your question."

"What's it like," Ronnie asked as he cleared his throat, "to shoot someone and watch him die?" The words were out before he could take them back.

The words momentarily took Michael's breath from him. The question stunned him. He realized that he had never been asked that before. His eyes found the ceiling as an uneasiness stirred inside. Ronnie's blunt inquiry had taken him by surprise. What gives him the right to ask that question? He's just a wanna be. He wants to live his dream vicariously through my experiences, Callahan thought as his anger grew.

"Why did you ask that, Ronnie?" he asked with a glare. Just two, maybe three nights earlier Michael had relived the entire incident in a dream. Every detail had come back to him, the house, the knife, the firing of the weapons. It was all so vivid.

"You're mad at me, aren't you?"

"Just answer the question. Why do you need to know?"

It was then that Michael realized the question he had just asked Ronnie was meant for himself. His dream had accounted for the data, but not the emotion. In its own way, his reluctance to have dialogue about the homicide was a form of survival. Keep it hidden, for God only knew that he might have to do it again.

The custodian tucked his thumbs into his fingers making fists of insecurity. "I don't know. It's police stuff. Things I want to feel. Sorry. I just don't have the words to say it right."

Police stuff, just like on television and in the movies. People don't have a goddamn clue what it's like to be a cop. Callahan felt a tightness in his stomach as he mused. You just pin the badge on and go shoot someone. They can't begin to understand that with one pull on the trigger, lives, many lives, change forever. If there wasn't violence on TV cop shows, nobody would watch. Sick bastards. His anger had urged him to speak, but he resisted, knowing it would mean relinquishing control, the same control he had retained since the shooting.

A long minute passed and Ronnie became annoyed with himself. He rubbed his forehead with both hands in an odd way as if he were in pain. "Why do I say stupid things?" he said, as he bit the inside of his lip and rose from the chair. "I think I should probably go. Sorry I upset you."

Callahan did not see Ronnie leave nor did he hear his footsteps, but he soon felt alone in the hollow room. He didn't like the feeling. At one time, he used to be his own best friend, but not anymore. He had let himself down on that mountain by making an error in judgment, destroying his myth of immortality. Now a man with harmless motives had asked the question he was afraid to answer. He wanted to call out for Ronnie and when he came, laugh out loud and create some fabrication about how he was just teasing him. But he couldn't because he knew it would be a lie. Maybe it was time to go back and dig it out, he thought. Maybe it was time to make peace with the past.

The corridors were unusually quiet as he glanced at the clock showing half past three. "That's exactly what's going on here," Michael exclaimed out loud.

"Are you talking to yourself again?" Sara smiled, peering around the corner. "What have they been giving you tonight?"

"No, listen to me. A few days ago I dreamed we were back at the house on Washington Street. And then tonight, Ronnie asked me, God bless him, what it was like to shoot someone and watch them die."

"Oh, Jesus. Why would he ask such a question?" Sara shook her head in disgust.

"He's just curious. He doesn't understand," Michael responded in Ronnie's defense. "I was angry too, when he first asked it. But I got to thinking. The dream, now this." Michael paused as his eyes toured the room.

"Go on," Sara replied as she stroked his leg. They had talked many times about the incident itself, but never about the emotions surrounding the shooting.

"I have to release that pain." His voice was strong and the words concise. "For the past few months, I've been engulfed in feelings of why me? But I've just realized that I can't work on improving my own health until I come to terms with all of the pain and anger that I've suppressed. Whenever my mind would take me back to the shooting I would think of how many other similar incidents that I had been involved in without taking it to that fatal level. And it started my first night back to work after the shooting. Remember?"

He took a deep breath, staring into Sara's eyes. "Scribbled on the blackboard in the briefing room were the words, 'The in-service training for tonight will teach Callahan how to bring a prisoner back alive.' The words stung me. It was meant to be funny. It was their way of using humor to break the tension. I've done it many times myself." He felt strong as he talked, feeling the relief. "But this time it was personal. I smiled while the others laughed, but I wanted to cry."

They both sat in silence as they digested the words. They

heard the familiar walk in the hallway, one foot, a slight drag, then the other, but slower than usual. It was as if the walk had lost its purpose. Sara glanced at Callahan out of the corner of her eye. His stare didn't change. Sara felt the pain in Ronnie's walk, as did Michael.

"Will you ask Ronnie to step in here for a second?" he requested. Sara said nothing, looking away as she fought her own demons. She should have been the one to get Callahan to talk about his pain. Not some stranger.

"Please," he asked.

Sara turned and slowly left the room. The walk in the corridor stopped abruptly. Not many words were spoken, but were enough to persuade the custodian to come with her into the room.

Ronnie did not look at Callahan when he entered the room.

"I'll answer your question, Ronnie. Please have a seat," Michael said. "I'm sorry if I was rude before."

"It's not my break time."

"Don't worry. I'll tell them it was my fault. I'll tell them that I needed to talk to someone special."

"I'm sorry, Sir, but I can't let that happen," he said emphatically. "I have a job to do. It wouldn't be fair to my employer if I sat down and talked to you now. But I will come back when my shift is over. Okay?" And he began to walk away.

Pausing, he looked over his shoulder to Sara. "You'll still be here, won't you, Officer Conners?" She smiled and Ronnie left.

Sara and Michael stared at each other in silence. The man they had stereotyped as simple had presented a brilliance. The common man with the common thoughts had embarrassed them with his honesty.

"We're in his beat now, Callahan," Sara said, removing her boots. "And he showed us exactly who is in control."

Nobody cared for a hospital room like Ronnie Ashford. The other custodians were not jealous of him, just perplexed as to how he could do such a thorough job in such a limited time. If they cared enough to watch, they would surely have been intimidated by his efficient and meticulous work ethic. Two of his peers had approached him one morning after his shift, confronting him with the statement, "By doing what you do, it's making us look bad." In the brief meeting, he informed them, "I am doing the job that I was hired to do, to the best of my ability. If you're looking bad, it's because of your work, not mine." That was the end of the conversation.

This particular late night would be no different. He had two rooms on which to work his magic before his final break. He would not compromise his work ethic, in spite of his anticipation to hear Callahan's account of the shooting. That didn't keep him from wondering why the officer had reconsidered.

Sara looked at her watch. It was coming up on seven o'clock. She was curious to see if Ronnie would actually come back.

"Are you going to describe the shooting to him, Michael?"

He didn't hear her. He had retrieved the events of the shooting in his mind.

"I didn't hear my weapon fire."

"What?" Sara asked.

"It's strange how the mind works and what it controls." Something inside was pushing him to go on. "When I pulled the trigger that night, I never heard the bullet discharge." Callahan was slowly choosing his words. "I saw the flash. But I heard nothing. Isn't that amazing?"

Sara chose not to answer. Her mind followed him back to that evening in December, almost a year ago.

"He looked up at me as he went down, Sara. I can still see David Tapia's eyes. Every time my mind goes back to that house, I see his eyes. It was as if his soul were asking, 'Why? Why did it have to come to this?' But, there was no hate in them, no pain, no fear. I remember looking down at my hand, my right hand, and it was empty. For a brief second, I was stunned, bewildered. Then I realized that my weapon was in my left hand and I wondered why. It wasn't until later that I realized that I had switched hands for my own protection. Was it God's will or training that made me do that?"

She smiled as she watched the moonlight's brilliance filter through the vertical blinds, casting mysterious shadows throughout the room. And then a shadow of a different sort, next to the doorway, caught her eye. The subtle light from the hallway created a distorted silhouette as it merged with the light of the moon. Sara squinted as her eyes saw the outline of a person standing quietly, obviously intending to remain unnoticed. Sara moved slowly from her chair, as if to stretch, and cocked her head to catch the eyes of the custodian. She placed her right index finger softly to her lips and Ronnie understood. Bracing himself against the hidden wall, he remained still.

"And then I heard her screams," Callahan uttered softly, "but my eyes were on Tapia as he went down, twisting and jerking. She screamed again and I watched her fall against the wall, her hands first covering her mouth, then her eyes. She began to pound her thighs with her fists, shrieking, 'No! No! No!' over and over again." Callahan's voice had become stronger, but then he paused as his thumb and forefinger massaged his temples.

"I had never felt so useless in my life. I wanted to help, but I couldn't. I went to where he was and knelt on my knees next to him." Callahan took a deep breath as his wide eyes focused on Sara, standing away from his bed. "Somehow, my left hand was on his chest and it felt warm and damp. I rolled my hand over and the color of his blood shocked me as it ran through my fingers. 'Don't go, please don't go,' I pleaded. But, I knew he had already gone."

Ronnie stood still, his back to the room. He wanted to tell Callahan that he was sorry for wanting to know. To tell him that it was a stupid thing to do. He took a deep breath as he turned and took the few steps into the room. Sara acknowledged his presence with a faint smile, and it was then that Ronnie realized that there was no longer a need to apologize.

"I felt sick as I fought back the vomit," Callahan continued. "His girlfriend started to sob and I turned and watched her trying to decide if all of this was real. Then I looked at the blood on my hand, my left hand." Callahan stopped talking and stared at his left hand, palm up with the fingers spread and watched the crimson color reappear. "I tried to scrub it off on my pants. Harder and harder I tried. I felt alone. I looked at you, and then at Manny. It was as if you both were asking, 'What next? What do we do now?' But strangely enough, the expressions on your faces gave me strength. I felt in control. I pulled the radio from my belt, and began to speak, so calmly, that it even surprised me. I called for help. I told the radio that someone had been shot. I remember hearing an echo. An echo of my own voice, and I wondered why. Manny was suddenly beside me, trying his best to bring life back into the man who had almost killed him; the man I had shot. I remember closing my eyes and praying to God to let this be a dream, a nightmare. Then I heard the sounds from outside, people yelling, then sirens. I looked back at Manny and he lowered his eyes to the floor."

Callahan continued, "I went to the blonde girl in the corner against the wall. She was curled into a ball, like a rag doll. I put my hand out to her, but I stopped. I didn't know what to do. I didn't know if I should touch her, but I knew she needed someone. Someone to hold her, and comfort her. My hand went forward and I touched her shoulder. She looked up at me. I can still see her face. I will never forget the panic in her eyes. I placed my arms around her and I could feel her body tremble. Shake. I lifted her from the floor and she buried her head into my chest. I had no idea what to say to her. How to comfort her. I still don't. And I never will."

The tears flowed down Sara's cheeks as his recollection had also produced her own set of memories. She shuddered at the sights and sounds from the past. She recalled the smell of gunpowder as her thoughts of that horrible night climbed back into her brain. She closed her eyes, not wanting to imagine what it must have been like to actually pull the trigger and live with the guilt of taking a human life.

The hospital room fell silent, leaving each person with their own visual of that night. They stared at nothing, no one wanting to break the silence.

Callahan slowly turned his gaze to Ronnie. "You see, cops, like firemen, don't get paid for what they do; they get paid for what they might have to do."

"I'm sorry you had to do that," Ronnie said through tears, turning to leave. "I didn't know."

"No one does," Callahan said, shaking off the memory. "Until it happens to them. The unfortunate."

"Ronnie," Callahan said, as the custodian walked toward the

door.

"Yes, sir?" he stopped.

"You have helped Sara and I more than you will ever know. Thank you."

"FRIENDS OF YOURS?" Dr. Raines asked, nodding at the four off-duty police officers having an impromptu party in the corner of the hospital room.

"Not anymore," Callahan snickered.

"Well, I've got some news for you," the doctor said, moving to his bedside. "All of the test results are back. We know that you have crushed cervical vertebrae, but nothing more. The condition of your spinal cord is unknown."

"And that means what?" Callahan swallowed hard.

"Surgery. As I said before, it's inevitable."

"When?"

"Tomorrow morning."

"Tomorrow?" Callahan's heart began to race.

"We can't afford to wait. Your respiration is starting to suffer and we need to know what's going on in there," Dr. Raines said as he touched the neck of his patient.

The room became silent. The friendly chatter quit, their eyes darting between Callahan and the physician.

"Here, let me show you. Would you hand me that napkin, please?" Dr. Raines asked of the closest person. "Thank you. This is going to be rather crude since I'm not much of an artist, but you'll get the idea."

Bringing the napkin to the serving table next to the bed, he began to illustrate. "Suppose this is your spine and these are your vertebrae." He drew two straight, vertical lines. Between the lines, he made four shapes resembling distorted hourglasses with small spaces between them. "Now if these are crushed, and I suspect that they are, they'll be removed." Dr. Raines crushed the hourglass figures with violent scribbles of the pen. And in between the first two vertical lines he created two more, but close together. "It's then we'll find out the condition of your spinal cord. That's the tricky part." Raines' hand found his own neck for a brief massage.

"Then I'll make an incision in your hip and remove bone to

replace the crushed vertebrae. Follow me?"

"You've got to be kiddin' me, Doc," Callahan said, staring in amazement at the diagram. "You honestly think this will work?" "I know so. You just have to believe. But I need your help. You ready?"

"You're the man."

"See you in the morning," he squeezed Callahan's arm and nodded. "Good night gentlemen," he said to the group. One of the officers walked toward the door with him. Dr. Raines hesitated, turning to the officer. "Be around tomorrow. That's when he'll really need you."

CHAPTER TWENTY-EIGHT

TUESDAY
6:56 AM

"WHAT DID DR. RAINES say to you last night?" Julia asked, wide-eyed. "I saw that you're scheduled for surgery today. This morning. I couldn't believe it."

"He drew me a picture."

"A picture," she said confused. "Of what?"

"My surgery. See?" Callahan held up the napkin, continuing to study it.

"Raines doesn't waste any time," Julia said. "Did he mention why he scheduled you so soon?"

"He said my respiration was beginning to suffer." Then Callahan smiled. "But I told him I always get short of breath when Nurse Julia bends over my bed."

"Tell me you didn't say that," she blushed.

Two more nurses entered the room. One with a razor. "Time to get you prepped. You'll be going for a ride pretty soon, Mr. Callahan."

"What's the razor for?" he asked wryly.

"To shave your neck and chest for surgery."

"You can put it in your pocket."

"Why?" the nurse asked.

"Nothing here," Callahan answered, unbuttoning his shirt. "Grass doesn't grow on a playground."

"Oh, Geez." Then laughter.

"But, before you go, I need a favor."

"Sure," the nurse responded, still laughing. "What do you need?"

"Hand me a pen."

And on the napkin, he began to print: P-L-E-A-S . . . .

"You're okay. Everything is going to be fine," Julia said as she tried to soothe the bedridden officer. Her comfort was needed and it was immediately felt. "Let the sedative work its magic." She looked into the soft blue eyes that begged for strength and she prayed for justice. How could someone who offered his life to serve and protect become so unprotected?

The drug was taking its effect. Callahan became passive and his muscle spasms ceased. "Are they going to operate on me soon?" Michael's eyelids were heavy.

"Yes, it won't be long now," Julia said as she felt a tear well up in her eye. She turned away, feeling a wave of anxiety.

"How are you doing?" Someone from somewhere had just asked the question. Opening his eyes he expected to see his mother, but she was not there. Just the remnants of her voice lingered in his sedated brain.

"What time is it?" he asked, trying to force his eyes open.

"Almost time to go," Julia answered as she bathed his lips with ice chips. "Your surgery is scheduled for 11:00. That pre-op shot seems to have relaxed you."

"I don't know about relaxing me, but it sure has me floating. I detest drugs, ever since I saw what it did to my buddies when I was in Vietnam. Man, this stuff has me on a flight I don't remember buying a ticket for," he said as his eyes fought to stay open.

"Don't fight it . . . just let yourself rest," Julia responded softly while patting his hand. "They'll be coming for you soon." She felt him squeeze her hand as tears slid down his cheeks and dropped quietly to the pillow.

Julia watched him for a few more moments as he slept. She prayed for God to do his will through the hands of a gifted surgeon.

The door to the room opened abruptly. The same two surgery nurses appeared, smiling, pushing and pulling the transport gurney to Callahan's bedside. His eyes opened immediately and he became conscious of his surroundings. Sara entered behind them, trying to hide the fear on her face. Julia's call to her about the urgency of the surgery woke her from a sleep of just two hours. He smiled when he saw her, giving her relief. She smiled back, knowing Michael Callahan had found his enemy. And he was ready to fight.

"Mr. Callahan, I'm Dr. Mikkelson, your anesthesiologist. I'm going to ask you a few questions and then we can get started. Okay?"

"Yes, sir, but first I need to ask a favor."

Callahan was made ready in the pre-op room and wheeled through the swinging doors into the large, impressive operating room. He wasn't ready for what he was about to see. Gowns, caps, and facemasks greeted him in a frightening display as he rolled by. It was happening much too quickly, like a movie that you wished you could pause. Gadgets and gauges were positioned around a bed that sat in wait for him. Trays of immaculate instruments lay on several rolling tables like soldiers waiting for a command. A tray of stainless steel chisels of various sizes lay next to a mallet, better described as an ordinary hammer. On a separate table was an electronic box that resembled a microwave oven.

"What is that?" he asked.

"A microwave," someone answered. He was sorry he asked.

"Okay, pretend that you're under. I hear Dr. Raines coming," Dr. Mikkelson ordered.

The doctor entered, hands held upright in front of him to remain sterile. "Okay everybody, let's go. Are you ready, Mik?"

Dr. Mikkelson smiled and stood, pulling Callahan's untied gown from his chest to reveal a note, on a napkin.

"What in the hell is this?" Dr. Raines asked bending to observe his diagram from the previous evening, and the words printed below: "PLEASE READ CAREFULLY."

Callahan smiled. "I didn't want you to forget your game plan, Doc."

Eyes smiled behind masks.

"You're crazy, you know that?" Raines laughed, shaking his

head. "Now, let's get to work. Give him his cocktail."

"What's the microwave for?" Callahan asked.

"Popcorn. Go to sleep."

Not far away, in a house on David Street, a woman stared out the kitchen window as she prayed for the life of a soldier. Many times in the past, she had stood in the same position as she watched her husband leave, not knowing when, or if, he would return. For years she had fought the fear of the phone call or the police car pulling into the driveway with an unsmiling officer regrettably delivering bad news.

Margaret felt very different in this fight. Time and circumstance had distanced her from his day-to-day life, but not her heart. As the tears came, she begged to God to spare the life of the father of her children.

"Mommy, why are you crying?" Amy hugged her mother's waist. Margaret wiped away her tears with the back of her hand. "Is Daddy gonna be okay?"

"He'll be just fine."

"Why are they operating on him?"

Margaret turned and leaned forward, pulling Amy close. She pressed her cheek against Amy's and drew in a deep breath. "To make him better. When he got hurt, a part of his neck was damaged and now the doctor has to fix it."

"Will it hurt him?"

"Maybe a little, but your father is a very strong man."

Margaret's faith began to put her at ease. She knew everything would be all right. It just had to be!

8:15 PM

The taste of Sodium Pentothol was in his every breath. The rancid tang of the drug was just as hideous as the smell. He felt better before when the drug was sedative instead of punitive.

"My mouth is so dry," he tried to say aloud, but managed only a gruff whisper. The recovery room nurse came to his side.

"Let me give you some ice chips. They'll help." Brushing ice softly across his lips, she would let one occasionally fall refreshingly into his mouth.

Callahan smiled, and drifted back to his memories.

"DAD," TOMMY SAID as Michael walked out the door to work, "can we build a bird feed thing? Our birds don't eat good."

"What birds?" Michael asked as he bent down to kiss his five year old good night.

"All the birds that live in our trees."

"Yup, we can do that."

"Can we do it now?" Tommy asked as his eyes widened.

"Not now, I have to go to work."

"When then?" The boy's shoulders slumped, pleading for some quality time.

"Sunday, let's do it Sunday. We'll go to the store and get the stuff and make one, okay?"

"You're not going to school or something else?" Tommy grinned.

"Nope, just you and me."

"And doughnuts?"

"And doughnuts," his dad answered with a smile.

Callahan vividly remembered shopping for the materials and creating a feeder of wood and plastic. It took most of the day. He didn't care, but they knew the birds would.

Once completed and strategically hung from a branch in the large mesquite tree, it was time for a beverage and admiration. It was a magnificent creation, as 'V' shaped plastic sides funneled the birdseed to the bottom where round railings provided a perch for the starving little creatures.

"Where's the birds?" Tommy asked while sucking lemonade through a straw.

"They'll be here soon," Dad said, drinking a beer.

And they were. One found it, all soon knew it, including one big pigeon. When he landed on the railing, all of the small birds flew away. The pigeon's weight caused the feeder to tip slightly, littering the grass below with seed.

"I need to get that pigeon out of there," Callahan reached for a stone to throw.

"Why?"

"Because he's big and he's scaring the other birds away."

"Dad."

"What?" Callahan said as he cocked his arm to throw.

"He doesn't know he's big," Tommy observed. "He just thinks he's a bird, just like all of the rest."

Callahan dropped his arm and looked at his child and then at the rock.

"Whatcha lookin' at, Dad?" Tommy said, staring up at his father.

"You, son. You amaze me."

"You 'maze me, too, Dad. You sure know how to do a lotta things."

"And, I sure learn a lot from you, Tommy. All I have to do is listen."

SARA WAS ALONE now in the surgical waiting room. She was beginning her tenth hour, changing chairs only once. She tried to guess how many people had come and gone during the day. It would have to be close to a hundred. Some happy. Some not so happy. One family was taken to the chapel, and she could only guess. Her appearance was beginning to show the stress. Several strands of hair had eased their way out of her hairclip, falling straight around her face of worn out make-up and reddened eyes.

She heard footsteps coming down the hall, but not from the direction of the operating room. The steps became louder and then the uniform appeared. It was Alex. Sara stood when she saw him.

"Any news?" he asked, taking her hand.

"No, and I'm getting scared. Why is it taking so long, Alex?" He put his arms around her, giving her the comfort she desperately needed. "Do you think something went wrong? Do they think that he doesn't have anyone here for him?"

"C'mon, now," Alex said. "We've got to think positive."

"Sorry, I was alone all day and my mind came up with all kinds of situations."

"I'm off duty now, but I can't leave," Julia said, leaning over

the counter at the nurse's station in a separate wing of the hospital.
"Callahan?"
"Yeah," she answered, massaging her own neck. "Callahan.

If anybody is looking for me, I'll be up in the surgical lobby with Sara."

8:38 PM

The surgical nurse watched as he fought. Twitches and spasms occupied his face. His ability to function meant everything. Callahan's eyes opened again, but he saw nothing, at least not in this environment. Again they closed . . . reluctantly.

9:16 PM

The door opened from surgery with the sound intensified by the empty lobby. Dr. Raines saw Alex's uniform and walked briskly toward them. "Does Michael have family here?"
"We are, sir," Alex answered.
The doctor smiled and nodded. "He did well, especially considering the length of the surgery. We experienced a few problems, but nothing we couldn't handle. It was pretty much what I thought. Crushed vertebrae. The good news is the spinal cord is intact, but it's bruised and swollen."
Sara looked at Alex, then back at the doctor.
"How successful we were, only time will tell. He's in recovery now and will be for a while. I don't think he'll have to go to ICU. We'll know more in an hour or so."
Dr. Raines touched Sara's shoulder. He left, walking much slower, smiling at Julia coming down the hall.

10:07 PM

Suddenly, his eyes opened fully and abruptly . . . not partially, nor halfway. Wide open. Opening like the eyes of a doll that has just been placed upright. He was alone as it was scripted to be. Even with the after-effects of strong anesthetic, his anticipation of regaining physical well being made his mind instantly alert and awake. His preoccupation with a life that ambulatory people took for granted took precedence over his current situation. Nothing in the present meant as much as what could be in the future.

Time meant nothing now. It was like a movie set, a play to be played, a story where the good guy won. He found himself looking into the eyes of the demon. He looked at the clock more for help than for reference. Time did not register in a brain that was occupied with the performance of a simple movement. He touched his lips with his tongue and his eyes tried to focus. Almost immediately they complied. He could see, but nothing he was seeing made sense. What was real, what was surreal, what was unreal? Could he return to the health he had before the injury? Questions he could not answer.

10:41 PM

Without a fight, Callahan's mind slid back into the comfort of a drug-induced sleep that relieved the intensity of the physical pain, but also accepted random illusions from the past. His prayer was to awaken and find that the episode on 'A' Mountain was, in fact, a dream, a nightmare. He prayed that his injuries were fabricated in his own mind. He craved the strength to fight the fight of his life.

"Michael, it's all right. It's going to be okay." She smiled. "Give it a little time. You're just coming out of a long surgery and a lot of anesthetic."

Callahan tried to listen, wanting to believe her. His heart beat faster, trying to touch her. She was just out of reach.

"Calm yourself. I'm here for you," Angela said softly, as her gentle fingers moved through his hair, bringing relief to his anxiety-ridden mind. She walked softly from the room, allowing him a moment to gather strength and to fight off fear.

His head moved slightly to allow his eyes to trace her steps. As she left, he thought to himself, to believe in God you must see the angels.

"Please, don't go," he requested. But she was gone.

11:10 PM

The anesthetic was leaving Callahan's body through his respiratory system, making him taste the memory of the surgery. He had no idea what day it was, nor did he care. His brain began to shuffle thoughts, his mind started to clear. The numbing drug was replaced with anxiety. His future seemed intimidating.

Consciousness suddenly made him aware that he was back in Room 803 and he was not alone. He wondered how long they had been there as time began to matter. The two women were asleep in their chairs. Sara was lying back with the unfinished afghan serving its purpose before its time. Julia's head was cast to one side, perched precariously in her hand, as her arm was anchored on the chair. Neither appeared comfortable, but it wasn't about that. They were there for him. He must return the favor.

WEDNESDAY
12:20 AM

The sounds of the brightly lit corridor filtered into his darkened room like an unwanted sales call. Nothing was making sense and thinking was becoming a chore. Every sense was becoming an intrusion. The sounds were sharp; his taste was bitter, and his sight was blurred and restricted. His eyes closed. The sound he made trying to clear his throat woke both Julia and Sara, but neither moved. They watched his fingers dance in the air, trying to find the source of his pain. Tears filled Sara's eyes and trickled down her cheeks. Both of his arms moved upward, reaching for something that wasn't there.

Julia placed her forefinger to her lips and mouthed to Sara, "I'll be right back."

Sara nodded.

"Page Dr. Raines," Julia ordered the nurse behind the counter. "Just tell him that Callahan is not fully awake, but he moved his arms and fingers."

CHAPTER TWENTY-NINE

"COME HERE," Callahan requested without opening his eyes.

Sara moved closer to hold his hand. Callahan tried to respond with a touch of his own. He could not. The fingers refused his command.

"Angela?" he uttered. Sara took a breath before she answered. "No, it's me. Sara."

"Sara?" Callahan opened his eyes. Her voice startled him. Now awake, he tried to move his fingers, but they would not comply. He could not move, but then again he didn't expect to. He felt his pulse quicken as fear-induced adrenaline was released within his body. He took a breath, trying to relax, but could not. Pain resisted his ability to swallow. Don't expect too much, too soon. It was drilled into him, but what was too soon? In his mind, he continued to fight for control of his destiny.

The anesthetic again closed his eyes, but it could not steal his smile. The drug pulled him back, refusing awareness, delaying life. He drifted off to a dream that brought his children and his dog. Again, in his subconscious, he raised his hand and sought to find his companion's ear to scratch.

"I talked to Dr. Raines," Julia advised in a whisper.

"And?"

"He is encouraged, but reminded me that upper extremity movement was to be expected. The next few hours are critical."

"So, he's at least back to where he was before the surgery?" Sara asked.

"Apparently so," Julia answered. "Now that he's sleeping again, why don't we go grab a drink, stretch our legs a bit while we can?"

"Did you see him move his head? His fingers jerking on his right hand?" Sara asked, ignoring Julia's suggestion. "What does that mean? Did the surgery work? Is he going to . . ."

"Yes," Julia interrupted, "I did see his head move, and that is a good sign. But I think it would be premature to speculate on anything else. Like Raines said, we have to be patient. Come on, I'll walk with you."

They both were showing the effects of their vigil as they slipped into the corridor. Sleep deprivation and on and off again tears had reddened their eyes and blurred their vision. A brief respite from the room would do them good.

Michael opened his eyes when he heard them leave. He heard what they had said. They said that he had moved. He heard Sara say that his head had moved and his fingers had jerked. It wasn't good enough. He had to know if he could move. Just move, anything. He tried moving his finger. Nothing. His right arm, nothing again. Tears began to fill his eyes and he became upset with himself for crying. Quit pitying yourself. Without thinking, he wiped his face with his hand, starting low on his cheek, then upward to his eyes.

His arm had moved! Michael tried to speak, but could not, not even to himself. Reality had replaced the illusion. He slowly turned his head to the left, his eyes watching the screen flashing numbers, 93hr... 97hr... 96hr. Above the numbers were lines, darting and jumping, making beeps as they crawled across the screen and out of sight, only to start again. Stay calm. No, become calmer. Don't let my heart rate get out of hand. He lifted both arms, one at a time. Julia was right. I'm back where I was before the surgery.

"Do you love him, Sara?" Julia asked as they approached the open, sliding, electronic door.

"I do," Sara answered as they encountered the cold of the early morning. "But I don't know if I know how." She was glad she hadn't changed out of her uniform, as her heavy jacket made the bite of the air bearable. Once outside, she stood still, forcing her hands deeply into her pockets causing her shoulders to shrug, indicative of her response.

"Meaning?"

"I'm not sure what he wants, in his life or in a woman," Sara answered as she stared at the ground. "Especially after listening to him talk about Angela."

"This is new to me. Who is Angela?"

"I don't know, Julia. Under the anesthesia he kept referring to her. Something about her working in communications," Sara pulled her collar closer. "And visiting him on the mountain. Before now, I've never heard him or anybody else speak of an Angela."

"Someone from his past, perhaps?" Julia was searching for something to help. "You know, like a good friend?"

"How good a friend is my concern." She was scared and torn. "I'm just being stupid. He's fighting for his life and I'm worried about an unknown relationship. I'm such a dumb ass."

"Come on, let's walk a bit."

Callahan watched the monitor display its numbers, 84hr… 86hr...83hr…and back to 84hr...84hr…84hr. That's more like it, he thought. He brought his hands together across his chest, making a steeple and then a spider on a mirror. He turned his head farther to the left and felt a pull, no, more like a sting at the right side of his neck. His right hand moved up to his jaw, and just below it he felt something raised, a bandage. Raines follows directions well, Callahan smiled, thinking of the napkin.

"How are you doing?" the voice of the male nurse startled him.

"Sip of water," Callahan whispered.

"Sure thing," the nurse responded, placing a straw to Callahan's lips. "Anything else?"

"Could you," Callahan paused, painfully clearing his throat, "move the heavy blanket off of my legs?"

"You bet. I think you have two on here," the nurse said, moving to his side. "Yep. One's thicker than the other. What if I leave the thin one on for now? Let's not let your legs get cold."

Callahan nodded and the nurse with the 'Kenneth' nametag smiled as he left. In less than ten seconds, the nurse returned. "You said the blanket felt heavy. Could you feel the weight on your legs?"

"Just a few minutes alone, okay?" Callahan smiled, staring at his feet.

"Here," the nurse said, placing the emergency call button on Callahan's chest. "Let us know if you need anything."

"Would you raise my head?" he swallowed.

"I'm not sure how much I should raise your bed," the nurse cringed. "That's up to your doctor."

"Just a bit?"

"Okay." He touched the control lightly, moving the angle of Callahan's head a few degrees. "How's that?"

Callahan made a circle with his left thumb and forefinger, forming the okay sign. He could now see his feet, toes pointing upward under the cotton throw.

The remaining anesthesia was still in control, causing his eyes to close and his efforts to be put on hold, one more time.

"I want to ask him about her, but I know now is not the time."

"You're right," Julia offered, "and so is he, Sara. Look, I know what you're going through. I'm in a similar situation with my husband."

"I'm sorry, I guess I'm just frustrated," Sara said, ashamed. "You've told me what you've gone through and I'm being selfish."

"Don't be sorry. There is no room for pity. It hasn't been easy for me, but it's a part of life. You know, good with the bad and all of that crap. The bottom line is survival. Not just survival as a person, but survival as a man. Michael hasn't been a whole man for some time. Maybe, he can be again. My husband never will be again. Does that mean I love him any less?" Julia took a deep breath, looking up at the stars.

"Sara, you have to remember that it's his fight and he's handling it his own way. Maybe, he's afraid to love you because he will never be able to fulfill your needs. Perhaps in his dreams he is whole again. A man with desires and capabilities. You have to respect that, Sara, even if they are just dreams."

Julia and Sara walked slowly down the sidewalk and to the bridge that went over a culvert, separating the hospital from nearby doctor's offices. They stopped at the exact same time, looking at each other, hearing sounds, the soft sounds of beautiful music. Music that was not usual in a hospital parking lot, especially in the middle of the night. They continued to walk toward the combination of tones and rhythm. But as they came closer to the parking lot, the music did not become louder.

"That's not coming from a radio or a tape player, Julia," Sara said, squinting into the parking lot, filled with fluorescent lighting.

"It looks like . . . ," Julia stopped herself. "As if you can actually see music," she laughed. "I mean it sounds like it's coming from that truck over there. The reddish colored one with the dog standing up in the bed of it."

"Strings!" Sara called. "And he has Rufus with him. And John."

Rufus saw her first and barked with happy feet, deciding if he should bound from the truck. His discipline told him to remain. Strings nodded and smiled, as did John. John Francis, the appliance salesman. The happy John Francis.

The face of the man called 'Strings' lovingly floated above his guitar, not unlike looks given to a lover that lie softly below him. His fingers moved with practiced precision over the frets of the Spanish guitar. He stared at the music his fingers created, allowing his soul to judge their merit.

Julia stood in awe. Sara moved closer, as did Rufus. "I wish Michael could hear this," she said.

"He can," John smiled.

Strings nodded, playing just a little bit louder, not that he had to.

Julia stopped at the nurse's station while Sara continued to the room. Callahan was sleeping when she arrived. Sara kissed his cheek and gently caressed his ear. Sometime in the past, he had told her that his mother would lay his head in her lap while in church and fold his ears, very gently, until he went to sleep. Sara tried to offer the same comfort. Ever so softly, her lips found his, not as a kiss, but more as a union. She placed a chair next to his bed and leaned forward, resting her head next to his. She could stay like this forever, she thought.

WEDNESDAY
5:05 AM

Callahan tried to understand the words that were being said to him, but they ran together in a muffled echo. He could see Sara's face. She was standing over him in the midst of a fog. Her lips were moving, but the sounds were not making sense. He closed his eyes and when they reopened, she was gone, and so was the fog. His head remained slightly raised. He remembered his movements from earlier, recapping the events in his mind.

From the hall, he heard the welcome sound of Ronnie's signature walk. And then it stopped. Callahan opened his mouth and tried to call for him, but it was too painful. Instead he smiled and listened as the walk resumed, one foot planted, waiting for the other to catch up. It was the left foot first, Callahan recalled, and then the right.

Left first. Stop. Drag the right one to catch up. Left, stop, drag. Left, stop, drag. Left. Callahan first saw, then felt his left big toe. Stop. It did. Drag. This time he felt the right big toe and then saw it. Walk, Ronnie, walk. Left, right, left, right. The other toes reluctantly began to join in. Keep going, Ronnie.

The monitor beside him began to beep, drawing his attention, and most likely the attention of others. 105hr ... 112hr ... 117 hr ... the numbers scrolled across the monitor face.

Ronnie's walk stopped. Another began, coming hurriedly in his direction. Then another.

"What's going on in here?" Julia asked, her eyes darting between Callahan and the heart monitor. 118hr ... 120hr ... 122 hr.

"I guess I was," he swallowed painfully, "walking too fast."

Julia suddenly froze. Her gaze was fixed on the blanket that was shrouding his legs. Her face changed as a seriousness created energy. Without realizing she was doing it, Julia made a back and forth, vibrating movement with her hand as she discreetly nodded toward his leg. Without warning, tears began to gather in her eyes, as an involuntary twitching of his thigh could be seen, causing the blanket to move, ever so slightly.

"What's up?" Kenneth asked, staring at Julia.

Michael's left knee suddenly jerked, answering his question.

"Julia! What's happening?" Callahan asked, disregarding the pain in his throat. His bewilderment would not permit tears.

"Muscle spasms, Michael. Your leg is having spasms, involuntarily. Yes . . . yes, it's a good sign, but we still have to wait and see. Try and calm yourself. We need to get your heart rate down." Thank God I'm not wired to that thing, she thought.

Michael smiled, and then laughed, a real laugh, as he made his big toe move. Two, three, and then all of them. Not much, but they moved. He saw the quadriceps muscle on the thighs twitch as the brain sent the electric current to them. His right knee moved upward. Michael tried the same with the left leg, this time with a different response. The knee came up slightly and then flopped to the side, causing Callahan a grunt of pain.

"Slow down, Michael. C'mon now. Don't get ahead of yourself. It's going to take time."

"I feel a sharp pain in my hip." His hand moved to just below his waistline.

"It's an incision, Michael. That's were Dr. Raines got the bone to repair your neck." Julia smiled.

"But I can feel it, Julia. Pain has never felt so good. Sit me up. Can you do that?"

"I can't and I won't. Let Raines make those decisions. Just *calm* down. I understand your excitement, but let's be reasonable." Julia wiped his tears and kissed his forehead. "You're back, Michael. You are back. Better than ever."

Michael Callahan heard a voice from the hall. Then another. Voices he knew and sounds he loved. Sara's ears also caught the intrusion as her head abruptly turned toward the scene that she had so carefully choreographed.

"Son, you can't bring that dog in here," a nurse ordered as

she scurried around the counter of the medical staff station. "In fact, you aren't supposed to be in here. You're not old enough. This is a hospital!"

"It's okay, Nurse." Victor Stark smiled. "I'll take responsibility."

With each leg being forced into its own agenda, the ninety-pound German shepard's paws were not suited for the slick surface of the polished linoleum floor. As he was pulled through the corridor, Tommy was beginning to resemble a tail on a kite. Rufus was on a mission and his nose was his navigator. The usually erect posture of his pointed, furry ears was not in evidence as they lay back on his head as if he was running into the wind. The scent of his master was getting stronger and nothing else mattered.

People pinned themselves against the walls and watched as the impassioned animal's feet found the footing that allowed him to separate himself from his unsuspecting handler. Rufus was free and Room #803 contained his prize.

Rufus had found the room and parts of his sliding body entered before the others. He could not contain himself or his emotions as a well-timed leap placed him squarely on his master's bed. But then, a puzzled frown rippled up his furry forehead. Suddenly, his energies began to quiet. Rufus sat back and peered at his friend, knowing that weakness had a scent. He smelled the odors of the hospital as they hung precariously around his coach and provider. Slowly, Rufus lowered his head to his paws. The animal felt his master's pain, but also knew that for him to heal, he must reacquire his magic.

As their eyes searched for clues of well being, Amy and Tommy cautiously approached their father's bed. They didn't know what to expect even after many calls of "I'm all right," or messages to them that "your Dad is doing just fine." The children were not prepared for what they saw, but were well prepared for what they felt. The once two hundred pound man now carried less than one-forty, his body wrapped loosely in his skin. Tommy reached for his father's arm, making sure that he found an area covered by cloth. Amy fought her bottom lip as a million "how comes" ran through her mind. And then they saw the strength, and the power of a smile.

DURING THE FOLLOWING WEEK, Callahan's body became surprisingly efficient. Every waking moment found him moving and strengthening. He could raise himself from a chair, and with the aid of a walker, move around the room and to the hallway. Every day he would go farther, gaining more mobility with each attempt.

It was just past noon when he started his walk toward the door, counting every step as a reference. He heard voices coming from outside the room. The quiet tones of conversation used when two parties wish to conceal their words. Callahan stopped and remained silent.

". . . I've done some research," Vic was saying. "There is no Angela. She does not exist. It appears that he has fabricated her in his mind."

"Oh, my God. How do you know that?" Sara said in a whisper.

"I tried to find her in Communications. There is no Angela working there or in any other section of the police department."

"How about the place where she volunteered? You know, over by Mama's Kitchen."

"No such building. I even asked Chester if he knew of such a building. He thinks I'm crazy."

"But Michael said Jake received a call from Angela saying she was coming up to see him. Did you talk to Jake? Did you look him up?"

"That's another thing. There is no Jake, Sara. Never has been." Vic turned, forcing his hands into his pockets. "Lt. Thompson and I drove up to the Mt. Lemmon Ranger Station and talked to the supervisor. No one has ever heard of him. Not now, not ever."

"But he believes that Angela and Jake are real. His descriptions are so detailed." Sara looked confused, staring into Vic's eyes. "I'm not doubting you, Vic. It's just that . . . I'm having a hard time understanding what's going on here. Do you think that they may exist in some other way? By another name, perhaps?"

"I have no way of knowing that Sara," Vic answered, pulling his hands through his hair. "They were his dreams, used for his purpose."

Sara took a deep breath and closed her eyes. She felt a relief, but also confusion. What is it he needs?

"There is one more thing, Sara," Vic said. "He mentioned that the F.B.I. Agent, Weaver Bailey, was with Angela when she made that first visit to Bear Canyon."

"So?" Sara stared at Vic.

"Weaver Bailey disappeared. Gone without a trace."

"When?"

"Within hours of when Thumper told Lt. Thompson about Angela's visit."

TO SAY MICHAEL CALLAHAN'S LIFE had changed forever would be an understatement. He could walk, unaided, before he left the hospital, with everyone calling it a miracle. He looked at it differently. His purpose for living was not fulfilled. And now he must rely on his dreams in another way, thinking of the future, not relying on the past. Two months after surgery, he was to have another, this time on his left arm to repair the crushed ulna nerve.

And then in Dr. Raines' office he was told the news. Because of the magnitude of his injuries, there would be too much risk involved to allow him to return to duty in the near future. Michael Callahan's days as a police officer were in limbo. Fate would have to make the final decision.

And the words of Victor Stark played silently in his mind, "Someday what you know and your ability to care will be your life. In the meantime, start your own healing process to end your own brand of grief. You're good at what you do; be great at what you want to be."

As she lay next to him, her rhythmic breathing created a sensuality that must be watched as well as felt to appreciate. Her soul knew he was taking time to savor the soft richness of her very being. She subconsciously turned to him, with eyes closed and a faint hint of a smile on her full moist lips. He stared at her. No aspect of her face was not dear to him.

"How is your neck?" Were her first words before her eyes could focus. Her fingers gently found the small curls of hair on the back of his head, creating a feeling of tenderness and passion. Her eyes twinkled awake; her lips partially opened. His hand found its way slowly across the suppleness of her breast and onto the smooth contours of the small of her back. A hand that could make a basketball seem small could also make a wounded bird feel at peace in its gentle confines. The power in his caress showed its strength in its tenderness.

"What are you going to do now, Michael?"

"I don't know, Angela. Like they say, once a cop, always a cop."

Something we were withholding made us weak,
until we found it was ourselves.

~Robert Frost

Thornton Edwards
author

I am now medically retired from the Tucson Police Department and live in Arizona, twenty miles south of Tucson in the retirement community of Green Valley. No, I'm not retired, just the contrary. I don't think I have ever worked so hard in my life. My new wife, Victoria, and I work with the aging and their numerous physical limitations. My experiences in my own life can now be passed on to those in need.

If you were to ask me (and it's been asked many times before) if my life turned out for the best, I would have to say, "Yes, my broken neck wasn't so bad after all." In fact, many of my clients are thankful for the inspiration it provides them in their own struggles to get their lives back.

For more information about the author and his writing, check out his web site:
        www.thorntonedwards.com

Thornton Enterprises

Quick Order Form

Postal orders: Thornton Enterprises, Thornton Edwards, 190 W. Continental Road, Suite 220-235A, Green Valley, Arizona 85614

email orders: thorntonent@cox.net

DANCING WITH ICE   Qty. _____ @ $18.95 ea.= _____

Name: _____

Address: _____

City: _____ State: _____ Zip: _____

Telephone: (   ) _____-_____

email address: _____

Sales tax: Please add 7.5% to all orders shipped to an Arizona address

Shipping by priority mail:
U.S.: $3.00 for the 1st book and $2.00 for each additional book ordered.
International: $8.00 for each book and $5.00 for each additional book (estimate).

For charge orders visit our website: www.thorntonedwards.com

Quick Order Form

Postal orders: Thornton Enterprises, Thornton Edwards, 190 W. Continental Road, Suite 220-235A, Green Valley, Arizona 85614

email orders: thorntonent@cox.net

DANCING WITH ICE   Qty. _____ @ $18.95 ea.=_____

Name: _____

Address: _____

City: _____ State:_____ Zip: _____

Telephone: (   ) _____-_____

email address: _____

Sales tax: Please add 7.5% to all orders shipped to an Arizona address

Shipping by priority mail:
U.S.: $3.00 for the 1st book and $2.00 for each additional book ordered.
International: $8.00 for each book and $5.00 for each additional book (estimate).

For charge orders visit our website: www.thorntonedwards.com

NOTES

NOTES

NOTES

NOTES